Now, Richard Harris has written

HONOR BOUND

... a novel that will keep you on the edge
of your chair.

Also by Richard Harris
Published by Ballantine Books

DECISION

ENEMIES

HONOR BOUND

RICHARD HARRIS

BALLANTINE BOOKS • NEW YORK

Library of Congress Catalog Card Number: 81-23213

ISBN 0-345-30671-6

This edition published by arrangement with
St. Martin's Press/Marek

Manufactured in the United States of America

First Ballantine Books Edition: September 1983

There is nothing serious in mortality. Solomon in all his glory was Solomon with the elements of the contemptible lurking in every fold of his robes and in every corner of his palace.

—WILKIE COLLINS

CHAPTER

1

Looking one more time at the plain pine coffin before it was lowered into the precise grave, Hasher turned and walked off, quickly but unsteadily, as if he might lurch and fall.

Margaret caught up to him and took his arm. "At least it's over," she said quietly. "They can't hurt him anymore."

He stopped and pulled free of her hand and stared at her indifferently. Only the two of them were there, except for the undertaker and his men, who stood apart at a discreet distance. After all that had happened, none of the old man's friends could have been counted on to come, so Hasher hadn't ordered a funeral service.

"Now you can go on with your own life," Margaret said.

"That's over too," he said.

Abruptly he left her and hurried, with the same awkward gait, across the damp grass that was littered with soggy yellow autumn leaves, and through the small unkempt grounds. It had rained most of the night before and now the sky was perfectly gray, without a cloud or a glimmer of sunlight.

"Thomas!" she called, her voice startling in the silent morning.

He knew that his departure was too melodramatic—here he was, nearly forty and acting like a schoolboy—but he had to get away. He couldn't watch the rest.

"Thomas!"

Hasher walked on without pausing to the narrow road across the cemetery from where the hearse and the black "family" car were parked. They could take her to town by the main road and he would walk the mile along the nearly unused back road. He needed the time, the privacy.

"Peace," he said aloud and grimaced at the sound and, more, the irony of the word. There was no peace; there would be no peace.

He wasn't sure that it had been right to bring the old man here. There were too many memories, too much regret, too deep a pain. But the old man had left no word about where or how he was to be finally disposed of. And of course Vivian hadn't cared; she wouldn't even take Hasher's calls. So he had made the decision himself, for his own personal and sentimental reasons. It was a place he would want to visit, a place where he felt comfortable —an old neglected country graveyard rich in sadness, a depository of gentle grief. When Margaret had asked him why he had chosen this spot, he said only that Mary, the old man's first wife, lay there, now beside her husband.

Hasher scarcely remembered her; it had been nearly thirty years since she died, in the car accident with his parents, when he was ten. The old man had spoken of her only once to him—two years ago, on an autumn day much like this one. They had been fishing for yellow perch, the old man in an ancient corduroy suit and Irish wool hat, his long solemn face taut with pain as he stared at the spot where his line broke the dark water. Suddenly he had looked up and twisted around to stare at the dock in front of his log cabin, halfway down the pine-fringed lake. Then he had shaken his head and smiled at himself, saying, "I thought I heard Mary—calling me for dinner. I'm getting old." He had just turned seventy.

There hadn't been any flowers, Hasher realized suddenly, then dismissed the cliché thought. Funeral services, eulogies, prayers, hymns, tears, flowers—they were for the living. He smiled at the further cliché. Still, he was uncomfortable because nothing had been done, nothing even said about whom they were burying. He would get some flowers for the grave—a few dozen crisp white daisies. The old man had loved them. Stiffly reserved, shy, old-fashioned, and rigorously decent, he had allowed himself only a few bits of softness—tending his fine garden by the cabin at the lake, taking his strange photographs of the dread and magic streets of New York, fishing out on the lake at dusk when he came here from the city, as he had more and more often in the past couple of years, to mend his hurts.

Hasher relaxed a little as he moved into the woods, half-leaved and still, and his walk became slower and more natural. He knew that Margaret had watched him until he disappeared into the trees and wondered if her eyes had made him nervous. It seemed difficult to believe—now that the old man was gone and she was the only person on earth he loved—but he knew it was true. He must leave her. Only he could do what had to be done, alone.

Turning a bend in the road, he saw the lake down the hill below—black and forbidding. There were only two cottages on its shore, his and the old man's, facing each other from opposite ends, but from here he could see neither place. Maybe he should stay for a few days, to remember. He frowned—as if he could forget. He left the road and started down a path through the woods toward his cottage. He would stay over at his cottage and go to the cabin too. Being there would deepen and fix his hatred and resolve.

It was colder, and damper, inside the cottage than it was outdoors. Shivering in his raincoat, Hasher lit the gas heater and turned it up nearly to maximum. Then he put a taper to the log fire he had laid before leaving last time. When was that—two weeks, three weeks ago? he wondered, pausing for so long that the taper scorched his fingers. He swore and threw it into the fireplace and ran cold water on the burn. When the pain eased, he took an Irish fisherman's sweater out of the closet and hung it over the back of a straight chair facing the fire, to get the damp out of it. Then he poured half a glass of straight Scotch, without ice, and stood before the fire to warm his chilled body.

Hasher had no idea how long he had been sitting in the big rumpled easy chair facing the fire—an hour, perhaps two—but he knew when a car door slammed that Margaret had come for him. The outside door to the kitchen opened and closed and he heard her footsteps, then silence.

"I was going to walk back to the village," he said, not turning. "But I came here instead. I figured you'd know where I was. Sorry."

"Are you ready to go back to the city?"

She moved close to the fire and he looked up at her and shrugged.

"You want to stay here?" she asked.

Hasher looked at her again, this time in surprise, then wondered why he had been surprised. She always knew, or nearly always. "I guess so," he said. "Do you want a drink?"

Without answering, Margaret walked out to the kitchen and he heard the gurgling splash of liquid being poured. "What about the Sillitoe case?" she asked from the kitchen.

"You take it over."

"He won't like that."

"He doesn't like anything."

"Only a full partner, not an associate, will do for him," Margaret said and came into the room. She sat in the other big chair, set at an angle to his and also facing the fireplace.

"Call Judge Birrin, tell him I'm sick. He'll understand. Everybody understands."

"No, they don't," Margaret said, staring into her glass. "No one understands. They all think it's true."

Hasher got up abruptly. "Do they?" He faced her, as if she were on the witness stand.

"They do." She sipped her whisky.

They were silent for a long time, until she said, "It's the system, isn't it?"

Hasher waited impatiently even as he dreaded what was to come.

"You finally see that it's all wrong, that it's always been wrong," she said. "Nothing is what it seems."

Stunned, he could only nod and wish that she would stop. This wasn't the time for such talk; they should be trivial now or recall fondly some stories about the old man. But after what had happened, that was impossible, Hasher knew. Neither idle talk nor anecdotes could help now.

He sensed a tremor passing through Margaret and looked at her. She was watching him. He hated that. Although she shared his life and had a right to study him, to think about him, to wonder about him, still he hated such moments. They denied him his own right: to be left alone.

"What?" he asked irritably.

Margaret looked at him in silence, then shook her head. "Nothing."

Hasher tried to calm himself. Anger was roiling in him and he knew that in a minute he would take it out on her with a shout or an insult. "Not saying it is worse than saying it," he told her and finished his drink.

Again she waited, again watching him. He got up abruptly and went to make another drink. When he sat down, she said softly. "All right, Thomas. I'm frightened."

He looked across at her in surprise. "Of what?"

She hesitated before saying, "Of you."

"That's absurd," he said, even though he had expected exactly those words. She knew him too well. He didn't like that either.

"Deep inside you, in some dark place, is a kind of fury," she went on, her voice trembling slightly. "It frightens me."

He stared into the flames.

"I don't know what caused it . . . maybe the loss of your parents—"

Hasher silenced her with a curt gesture. "You're afraid of me?"

She looked startled. "I hadn't thought of that but I guess I am—sometimes."

"Like now?"

She nodded.

He wanted to scream at her to stop but that would only prove her point. "Don't I have reason to be furious?" he asked calmly.

"Because of what they did to him?"

"What else?" He was barely able to control himself. Their closeness had turned into a guessing game.

"Oh, Thomas, you don't understand—"

"Don't understand what?" Hasher shouted, his fists clenched on his knees. "I understand all right!"

Margaret shook her head regretfully. "No, you don't. It's only a game."

"What is?"

"Everything. They played dirty and they won."

Hasher looked at her in weary exasperation. "The next thing I know you'll be saying that good guys end up last."

"Don't they?"

"No!" He glared at her, unable to go on.

She watched him, then smiled fondly, hesitantly, and said, "I love you."

Hasher sat back and let his breath out in a noisy sigh. "Because I'm a fool?"

"Because you're innocent."

"Like him?"

Margaret thought for a moment and nodded. "I suppose so. He didn't know either."

"He did at the end."

She looked surprised and waited.

"A couple of months ago we were sitting one day out on the porch of his cabin when he said to me, 'You have to figure out life from the one per cent you're sure of. That's about all we ever really know. The rest is lies.' "

"And yet he spent his whole life in a lie."

Hasher turned on her. "You mean you believed all along what they said about him?"

"No, no, not that," Margaret said quickly. "I only meant that he believed the law was an instrument for justice and fairness and decency. They showed him it can just as easily be used for evil. More easily in fact." She paused for a few moments before adding, "You didn't know that either, did you?"

Hasher smiled sourly. "I do now." He got up and poked the fire, as if to change the subject.

By the time Hasher was twelve, the old man had planted in him the beginnings of what were to become his deep respect and love for the law. He was a quiet thoughtful boy and he listened intently as the old man told him stories about the great landmark cases of the common law in England and later in its adapted form in the United States—cases that had transformed feudal autocracy into Western democracy. To young Hasher, the heroic advocates and the great jurists were more stirring figures than all the Alexanders and Caesars and Napoleons; and the momentous court contests made the most ferocious battles and sweeping conquests of history seem pale shadows by comparison.

"The glory of America is that it is a nation of laws, not men," the old man often said to him in those days. And later, when young Hasher was able to understand better, he was told that the law was an "art form" that demanded the utmost in creative intelligence from anyone who wanted to be more than a legal craftsman. To see "the living law" in action, they visited the New York State Court of Appeals in Albany to hear oral arguments by some of the finest lawyers in the state. They attended trials at the Federal District Court and listened to oral arguments before the Federal Court of Appeals for the Second Circuit, at Foley Square in downtown Manhattan. And finally they went to Washington to watch the debate over the great landmark case of Miranda v. Arizona before the Supreme Court. When Chief Justice Earl Warren entered the august chamber to take his place at the center of the nine justices, young Hasher knew that the highest honor his country could bestow upon a man was to put him in that chair.

But later what Hasher remembered most vividly was a simple scene in a hectic lowly courtroom—in the Supreme Court, County and State of New York—where they went one day to watch a custody case involving one of the old man's clients, who was being represented in this matter by a matrimonial lawyer he had retained. The client was a pretty dark-haired woman in her mid-thirties—in this case the defendant—and she seemed almost certain to lose. The issue at trial was whether she was an unfit mother because her ten-year-old son had come into her bedroom early one morning and found a man she had been dating for several months sleeping, naked, beside her. The boy had been shocked and upset, he had told his father, who had divorced his mother three years before to marry another woman, and the father had sued for custody.

The time was the rambunctious 60s, when all rules seemed about to be cast aside, but there were still legal precedents and traditions and, most of all, there was the judge, an elderly man, an Italian, and a Catholic. The woman couldn't have drawn a worse combination, Hasher realized. The judge listened sleepily to the testimony and he questioned the woman himself sternly—especially about her claim that ordinarily her lover spent nights at her apartment only when the boy was at his father's but that on rare occasions the man slept there during the week and got up to leave early, before her son awoke.

The trial lasted nearly a full day and at the end the judge delivered his verdict without retiring for deliberation. If he gave the father custody, he said, the son would inevitably conclude that his mother had committed some terrible act, which would not only estrange him from her but might grievously affect his own sexual development. Her act, the judge went on, was perhaps indiscreet but hardly unusual. "She is not a nun, she is a healthy normal woman and that is how she has behaved," he said. "If she is happy, her son will be happy. And to be happy she must have a normal life." He then rebuked the husband for unnecessarily creating discord, for using his son as a weapon against his ex-wife, and for wasting the court's time. After ordering the man to explain to his son that he, and not the boy's mother, had been wrong, the judge dismissed the suit with costs.

Thrilled by this display of humane simplicity and common sense, Hasher turned to the old man beside him to express his delight. "Of course I'm pleased for our client," the old man said. "But it wasn't very good law."

Now the memory of that day was a bitter one to Hasher and he gave a soft grunt of dismay at the thought of it.

"What?" Margaret asked. She knew that sound and what it meant: Hasher had recalled something unpleasant.

"Nothing," he answered and poked the fire. Yet it was everything. As he knew at last, the old claim that ours is a nation of laws, not men, was the most preposterous sham of all. The elderly judge had been the law in the custody case and the vicious judge in the old man's case had been the law too. Judges were the law and it was only what they said it was. Hasher put a couple of logs on the fire and slumped down into his chair.

"Do you remember how he always said he was 'a man of the law'?" Margaret asked.

He nodded glumly.

"He never knew there is no such thing as *the law*," she went on. "If there were, there couldn't be any split decisions by the Supreme Court."

Hasher knew she was right but he wished she would stop. He wanted silence, he wanted privacy—there was so much to figure out.

As if sensing his thoughts, she didn't speak again for several minutes, then said, "Isn't that too much wood on the fire? It'll take an hour to burn down. We ought to be leaving."

"I think I'll stay for a day or two," he said, not looking

at her. "I've got a lot to sort out. If I'm in town, they'll call and want me to come in to the firm. After the way they treated him, I'm afraid of what I might do or say."

Margaret went to the kitchen and he heard her open the refrigerator and some cupboard doors. She came back and said, "Let's go to the village and get some supplies for a couple of days. You promise—that's all?"

He had no idea whether that would be long enough but he nodded. They had been together for nearly five years now and Hasher looked at her longingly, fearing that their time was almost over. She returned his solemn gaze mockingly and asked, "Don't you think we ought to get married?"

"Sure," Hasher said, "But who'd have us?"

It was an old joke between them but they always laughed at it and did now. Then they went to the bedroom.

After putting Margaret on the train for New York, Hasher drove back to his cottage, put away the groceries and liquor, and hauled the frail canoe from under the screened porch overlooking the lake. It took him twenty minutes to find the paddle and he cursed, nearly screaming in frustration, because he had to get there, search the place, and be back before dark.

The log cabin was colder even than his cottage had been when he got there after the funeral. Hasher stood in the large living room trying to relax, to loosen his taut stomach muscles and stop his shaking. He put the palm of one hand to his forehead; his hand was cold but his head was hot. The exertion of paddling the length of the lake, he told himself, but he knew that it was actually his fear. His friend had died here, alone, in the agony of madness that drives men to murder themselves.

The telephone rang like a scream.

Hasher stared at it in terror. A wrong number, he said to himself, but when it kept on ringing and ringing and ringing, he knew that it was Vivian.

He walked to the table in the corner and lifted the receiver and put it to his ear without speaking.

"Thomas?"

He slowly took the receiver away from his ear to hang up but the insistence in her voice—*"Thomas!"*—caught him. "Hello, Vivian," he said.

"I knew you'd be there sooner or later," she said, her tone amused. "You couldn't keep away, could you? How was the funeral?"

She had known then. And still she had done nothing. He imagined her now, seated on the plum-colored sofa in the luxurious apartment that Lucius Slocum had bought for her. She was tall and slender, with narrow hips and full breasts, and had unusually small and delicate hands and feet for a woman her size. He could see her fine hand holding the phone, her thick chestnut hair loose to her shoulders, her great brown eyes and full lips. Bianca lips, he often thought when he saw them. Her lovely face would be all innocence now, he was sure, except for the slight smile of contempt. She would be amused by Hasher's presence at the cabin and she would enjoy his pain. He had asked himself a hundred times how she had come to be like that and had finally convinced himself during the old man's trial that all he would ever know about her he already knew: She was like that.

"Are you there, Thomas?" Her voice seemed to be full of suppressed laughter.

"Yes."

"What are you doing in my house?" she demanded, in the same unruffled tone.

Hasher hesitated, then said, "I gather you haven't seen the will."

"Will?" she said and laughed outright—a lovely laugh full of warmth and joy.

Who was it who had described Vivian Slocum's laughter as an aria? he wondered, astounded again at the depth of her malice and the success of her deception.

"I've seen the purported will," Vivian went on. "One

final fraud perpetrated by a deranged old man who was driven by the exposure of his vicious life to end it."

Breathless with outrage, still Hasher had to admire the coolness of this venomous creature who could deliver a line like that, who could calmly commit the worst, and most convincing, perjury on the witness stand he had ever heard, who could laugh at him and try to seduce him at the same time.

"Of course I shall contest the will," she added flatly. "I am assured it won't stand up in court."

"Haven't you taken enough from him?" Hasher asked wearily.

"Quite enough—from him. But not from you. He left you that property while deranged by his obsession for having vengeance on me."

My God, Hasher thought, stunned by the way she always turned the truth into a lie and a lie into the truth. He often wondered if she had come to believe all her lies; if she did, she was the one who was insane. The old man had told him two years before, prior to her divorce suit, that he would leave Hasher the lake property so that his own place wouldn't be spoiled for him by developers. Vivian had taken nearly everything else the old man had —more than $600,000 under court order at the end of the trial—and now she was after the modest bequest he had made to his oldest and closest friend.

"I might consider selling it to you—*if* you don't try to uphold the will," Vivian said lightly. He didn't reply and she went on after a pause, "There's no reason why we can't be friends, Thomas—better friends than ever." There was the seductive hint again; she never spoke to him without that slipping through.

"Forget it." He wondered what the place was worth. Forty thousand maybe. An old four-room log cabin and half a reedy muck-bottomed lake. Probably not that much. "Is there anything else?"

"Only one thing. As soon as I hang up, I'm going to call Sheriff Worthy and tell him that someone called me to say they saw a man near the cabin. Get off my property." The line went dead.

Hasher hung up and switched on two lights so that his presence wouldn't seem surreptitious. He hurried into the study and turned on the brass student lamp with its green glass shade on top of the antique chestnut desk.

He recoiled suddenly, wondering if this was where it had happened. Collecting himself, he quickly opened all the drawers in the paneled desk. Empty. He smiled. The old man had loved fine furniture but had loathed clutter. "A symbol of a disorderly mind," he'd once explained to Hasher.

He turned to the wall at his left—covered from floor to ceiling and the length of the room with bookshelves. The books, ragged and stained with mildew, were old, the books of Lucius Slocum's childhood and youth and early manhood. He had never been able to get rid of them. "Most of my mind is there," he had said to Hasher as he waved a hand at the thousand volumes.

"Clutter?" Hasher had asked with a smile.

"Of course, of course," the old man had said genially. "But the clutter of words, not things."

Now Hasher saw at the bottom shelf near the desk what he had come for: a stack of legal papers in manila folders. On top was the last file, dated two weeks before and labeled "Slocum vs. Slocum—Final Disposition." Hasher opened it and found on top the decision of the New York Court of Appeals, which declined to review the earlier decision of the Appellate Division, which in turn had declined to upset the verdict in the divorce action of Vivian Slocum agianst Lucius Slocum.

When the trial neared its end, Hasher had gone to the District Attorney, who smiled nastily when he was told that he *had* to prosecute Vivian Slocum for committing perjury and Marvin Rail, her lawyer, for suborning perjury. The D.A. waved at the piles of papers on his desk and on nearby tables and shouted, "I've got tens of thousands of muggings, burglaries, armed robberies, narcotics sales, rapes, murders—and you want me to prosecute a spouse and her lawyer for lying in a divorce case? Jesus Christ, man, when haven't such people lied?"

"Our entire legal system is meaningless if people can go into court and lie under oath without fear of punishment," Hasher said.

"Okay, so it's meaningless," the D.A. said wearily. "Now I've got work to do."

"Three months in jail for her and disbarment for him," Hasher persisted. "That would stop the others overnight."

The District Attorney ignored him. In his business lying was a way of life—on both sides of the bar of justice.

Now Hasher went to the kitchen and selected a large paper sack and a larger plastic shopping bag from a cupboard and went back to the study. As he finished packing the stack of documents, he noticed an old-fashioned record book with an imitation-leather red binding on the shelf directly above where the legal papers had been. The book was stuck between a red volume of *The Scarlet Letter* and a red volume of *Moby Dick* and was hardly noticeable.

He slipped it out of its place and opened it. On the first page, in Lucius Slocum's precise handwriting, was the word "Diary" and below it his name. Quickly leafing through the first few pages, Hasher saw an account of the case of Slocum vs. Slocum—the legal strategy and tactics employed by the other side, counter-strategy and tactics, precedents for given steps, analyses of the judge's rulings, and possibilities for appellate review.

Pausing, Hasher listened intently. He hadn't long, he knew, for surely Vivian had carried out her threat to call the Sheriff. Hasher put the record book in with the legal papers and carried the bag through the cabin and out to the dock and his canoe. He stowed the bag in one end and concealed it with a sheet of canvas that he used to cover the craft.

Theft pure and simple, he told himself as he went back into the cabin. Until the will was probated, the property belonged to the State of New York. The old man would have been furious. One—most of all a senior partner of Slocum, Whitby & Barker—didn't do such things. But

Hasher felt elated; he hadn't stolen anything since he was a boy and he knew this was a beginning. Now the law meant nothing.

Back in the living room, he stopped before a block of framed photographs of Lucius Slocum and members of the Boys Group. For almost two decades, the old man had taken in homeless wayward boys; he found homes for them, sent them to school, got them odd jobs, gave them money, and spent nearly every summer weekend with them. Hasher stared at the old man in one of the last pictures taken of him, and the sight of the dignified erect old gentleman with thick white hair and the kindly smile almost brought tears. Hasher hadn't wept yet and he wouldn't now, he assured himself as he turned to look at two other photos—of himself as a young infantry officer in Vietnam. He scowled at this further evidence of his innocence—the gung-ho patriot ready to die for a flag.

Something caught his attention and he turned back to the photographs of the Boys Group and saw the single picture of Lyndon Johnson James—slender, handsome, smiling, the only black face in the photographs. Hasher felt a surge of rage as he saw the scene that had been driven into his memory by shock, like a spike. It had tormented him since it happened, weeks before, near the end of the old man's divorce trial. By accident, Hasher had been there, although the old man hadn't wanted him to be, because Hasher had to get his partner's signature on some legal papers. Hasher had waited at the rear of the room, watching his old friend's back, stiffly erect, as Lyndon Johnson James sat in the witness chair and pointed a long wavering brown finger at Lucius Slocum and cried, "He made me a fag! He did it—*him!*" Then the boy broke down weeping and when at last he recovered, he shook his head and said, "Now there's nothing I can do to stop—nothing, nothing, nothing!" He wept again.

Hasher had turned to look at Vivian Slocum and saw that she was watching her husband. Her face was composed, noncommittal, but her eyes were dancing; she had vowed to ruin her husband and now she was doing it.

Hasher looked around the living room for something to smash the photograph of the boy. Nothing less would still his pounding heart. He reached down for the poker beside the fireplace and at that moment heard the kitchen door open. He straightened up and turned. Sheriff Worthy appeared in the doorway with his gun in his hand. He saw who it was and slipped the revolver into its holster.

"Hell, Bill," Hasher said. "I've been waiting for you."

"Vivian Slocum called me," Worthy said, looking embarrassed. "Said she'd got a call about someone messing around here."

"Yeah, I know," Hasher said. He described his phone conversation with Vivian, including her threat.

"She's going to fight the will?" Worthy asked.

"Apparently."

"Whether she does or doesn't, whether this place is yours or hers, you really shouldn't be here, should you?"

"I guess not," Hasher replied. "Not legally at least."

"What else is at stake here, except the law?"

Hasher smiled. "I sort of expected you at the funeral, Bill."

"Did you?" He was on the defensive now, as Hasher had hoped he would be. "Newspaper said it was private." Worthy paused, then added, "It's an election year, you know that. All the news from the trial in New York, *all* of it, got back here of course. Mr. Slocum wasn't a very popular man hereabouts when he died. Some people say it was a good thing he died—if he hadn't shot himself, someone else would have."

"I don't believe it."

"Believe it."

Hasher shook his head.

Worthy pointed across the room toward a side window. "You didn't know about that?"

Hasher walked to the window and saw a small hole in the lower pane. "Christ! A bullet hole?"

Worthy nodded.

"My God! When? Who?"

"When I can tell you," Worthy answered. "Who I don't know. Two months ago. Late one Saturday night he called me and I came out here. He'd been sitting over there"—Worthy pointed at the easy chair facing the stone fireplace—"and it went right past his head." He walked over to the fireplace and Hasher followed. Worthy put the tip of a forefinger in a jagged furrow at the top of a large chunk of granite. "Smashed the bullet. Made any ballistics test impossible. We couldn't even guess at the calibre."

"Did you find the gun?"

The Sheriff shook his head. "Where? How?"

"The lake, for a starter."

"If it's there, it'd be buried in muck. And if we found it, we still couldn't match that lump of lead with it." He looked at Hasher. "Does Vivian have a gun?"

Hasher had been about to ask the same question. "I don't know. I didn't even know that Lucius had one."

"He didn't," Worthy said. "Not until after that night. I suggested he might get one. Even went with him to pick it out." He looked down at the cold fireplace, laid with wadded paper and kindling and logs, as if the old man had expected to live to light it again.

Hasher felt sorry for Worthy and said, "It wasn't your fault."

"I never thought it was. Just bad luck."

"Are you going to mention my presence here in your report?"

"If you hadn't told me she called and you answered, I might have forgotten I found you here," Worthy said. "Now I can't." He paused to light a cigarette, then faced Hasher. "Vivian says the will's a fraud."

"Vivian says a lot of things—all lies."

"All?"

"Every single one."

The Sheriff shook his head bemusedly. "What'd he ever do to her? Not screw around certainly, not at his age."

"I don't know," Hasher answered. "Probably nothing.

She wanted the money and to get it she had to destroy him."

"Why'd he do it?" Worthy asked.

"Kill himself?"

"No, marry her."

"When she was so much younger?"

Worthy nodded.

"Who knows? He was lonely, probably figured he loved her and deceived himself into believing that she loved him. Happens all the time."

Worthy nodded.

Shrugging, Hasher asked, "Why does anyone marry anyone?"

Worthy nodded again, then grinned. "My old lady's younger than Vivian and looks twenty years older. Not even the cat would drag *her* in." He saw Hasher's surprised look and said, "Didn't you ever want a crack at her—Vivian, I mean?"

"My oldest and best friend's wife?"

"Apart from that of course," Worthy said hastily.

"I'd sooner fuck a pair of scissors," Hasher said.

Worthy laughed. "That bad?"

"The worst. I've known a lot of confused, nasty, ignorant, neurotic, vicious bastards but I've known only a couple of truly evil people. She's one of them." Hasher didn't mention that the other one was her lawyer, Marvin Rail.

"That black kid," Worthy said, "that was a lie, too?"

"Lyndon Johnson James?" Hasher stopped himself from pointing to the block of pictures on the wall.

Worthy nodded. "I got a hunch it was a black man who took that shot at Mr. Slocum. Not for all the other things they said about him stealing and such but for perverting that boy."

Hasher shook his head in disgust. "That boy is a thief. He's always been a thief. He stole from Lucius—not just his money and his possessions but his good name. That boy is no more a fag than you are. He's a junky. That's how they got him to tell those stories in court. He says what they want and he gets a lifetime fix." Hasher had no idea whether there was any truth to what he had said. Nor did he care. "Do you know what became of that boy?"

"One of my deputies saw him on the street in Poughkeepsie last Saturday night. The kid bolted."

"You were looking for him?" Hasher tried to suppress his excitement.

Worthy shook his head. "Harvey, the deputy, was off duty. But I'd like to talk to James. He was seen coming down the back path to this cabin the morning Mr. Slocum shot himself."

CHAPTER

2

At a little after eight o'clock the next morning, Hasher arrived at the Sheriff's Office and Worthy showed him into a small windowless room with a table in the center, four straight chairs tucked under its sides, and a bare bulb hanging overhead. On the table was a manila folder with a red tab: "Lucius Avery Slocum, Deceased" it said.

"This the interrogation room?" Hasher asked.

The Sheriff nodded. "We just wiped up the blood and hid the truncheons," he said, smiling. "You want anything, give a call." With that, he left, closing the door behind him.

Hasher had braced himself for what he was about to read. But he wasn't prepared for the photographs. The first one was taken from behind and above the body slumped at the desk, which was covered with newspapers, as was the floor under and around the chair he was seated on. It was so like him, Hasher thought, to want no mess left behind.

Forcing himself, Hasher carefully examined the dozen pictures, taken from different angles and distances, until the images on the paper were implanted on his memory. In time the revulsion he felt subsided and by the end he could almost ignore the subject of the photographs. Except for one—a close-up of the old man's head, with a dark hole burned through his thick white hair at the right temple. The eye on that side was open but the lips were closed. There was scarcely any blood, only a narrow trickle down the side of the face below the hole. Covering the desk top and the floor with newspapers had been unnecessary then, Hasher thought as he struggled to regain his composure.

He put the picture down and picked up the last one, which had been taken from a few feet from the side of the desk. The head was lying on its left side against the crook of the old man's left elbow, flat on the desk top; the right arm was extended with the hand down, the fingers spread; the pistol was just beyond them.

Hasher stacked the photographs and put them, face down, at one side. He picked up the next document in the folder: Sheriff William P. Worthy's report. It was briefer than Hasher expected and recounted how the Sheriff's Office had received a telephone call on the previous Monday, at 3:08 P.M., from Edward Wicknor, of the law firm of Wicknor and Pease, at 300 Park Avenue, New York City: "Mr. Wicknor represented himself as being Mr. Lucius Slocum's attorney (cf. affidavit of E. L. Wicknor before Coroner's Jury, appended)," Hasher read, "and informed this office that said Lucius Slocum had failed to keep an important appointment with him, said E. L. Wicknor, at the offices of Wicknor and Pease at 10:00 A.M. that day. Mr. Wicknor asked to speak to the Sheriff personally and said that he had spoken by telephone to Mr. Slocum over the weekend at his cabin on Lake Mercy. At Mr. Wicknor's request I immediately proceeded, with Officer Pacella, to the Slocum cabin."

The rear door to the cabin was unlocked, the account continued, and the Sheriff and Pacella found the body of Lucius Slocum slumped at a desk; a .32-caliber Smith & Wesson revolver was lying on the desk near the body and a single bullet was missing from the otherwise full chamber. Sheriff Worthy immediately called in members of the criminal-investigation division of his office, together with the coroner. A search of the premises and surrounding grounds had been conducted, after which it was concluded that the deceased had died by his own hand.

The next document was a single page—the criminal-investigation division's ballistics test, which showed that the bullet in Lucius Slocum's brain had been fired by the Smith & Wesson revolver found at the scene. The coroner's report was also brief. It stated that the cause of death was the penetration of a bullet into the right cerebral hemisphere of the brain. The approximate time of death was between 4:00 A.M. and 6:00 A.M. on the day the body was found. The last document was the verdict of the coroner's jury: death by suicide.

Hasher put the photographs into the folder and closed it. He sat back for a minute, staring at the wall opposite, then rose and went to see the Sheriff. Worthy was alone and waved him to a chair beside his desk.

"Satisfied?" Worthy asked.

"Let's say I found no suspicious circumstances. Do you have any doubts?"

Worthy grunted. "In this business everything is doubtful. Sometimes I even doubt that the sun rises in the east."

"But not that Lucius killed himself?"

"No reason to."

Hasher shifted in his chair as Worthy lit a cigarette and sat back and puffed at it, waiting.

"What about Lyndon Johnson James?" Hasher asked.

Worthy smiled fleetingly. "The identification wasn't definite. Maybe the person seen near the cabin that morning was him, maybe it wasn't."

"Why wasn't he mentioned in your report?"

"Why raise questions when you don't have the answers, when the case is closed?"

"Even if it might have been murder?" Hasher asked.

"No evidence of that at all," Worthy retorted mildly. "You read the report. Anything else?"

He was being dismissed, Hasher realized and said, "Isn't it unusual for a person who is going to commit suicide not to leave a note—some kind of last message to someone?"

Worthy squinted at him. "I got an idea you're a pretty good lawyer, Thomas." He smiled, friendly again.

"How long have you been a cop?" Hasher asked suddenly.

Taken aback, Worthy paused to think. "Sixteen years," he said. "Six as Sheriff. Why?"

"How many suicides have you investigated in that time?"

Worthy shrugged. "Don't know even roughly. Maybe fifteen to twenty."

"Did any of them *not* leave a note?"

Worthy rubbed his jaw in silence. "Only one I can recall offhand was old Thelma Nelson, over in Chambersville. Overdose of sleeping pills." He hesitated, squinting at Hasher through a cloud of smoke. "But she was so far gone with cancer her mind was affected. We couldn't figure if it'd been intentional or accidental. Since she took two-thirds of a bottle, we put it down to suicide."

"That's the only one?"

Worthy shrugged. "Far as I can recall."

Getting up, Hasher asked, "How much money did you find on him?"

Worthy drew on his cigarette without answering.

"Another thing you didn't mention in your report?"

Worthy smiled. "Not as much as you'd expect a man in his circumstances to be carrying."

"How much?"

"Now I know what it feels like," the Sheriff said, still smiling. "You want a job?"

Hasher waited.

"Twelve dollars and thirty-five cents," Worthy said at last. "As I mentioned, not quite what you'd expect." He shrugged. "Maybe he just forgot to go to the bank."

"Did you check?"

"Nope."

"Mind if I do?"

"Nope."

Hasher walked down the street and across the green to the First National Bank. Walter Stormont, its president and a high-school classmate of his, called for the Slocum account and within minutes Hasher had his answer: the old man had withdrawn $350 on Friday, less than three full days before his death. Hasher called the Sheriff and told him.

"You're thinking about that James boy, right?" Worthy asked after a moment.

"That's right."

"Say he got the money. It could have been blackmail. Or he could have taken it from the body. I told you, Thomas, the case is closed." Worthy was silent for a few moments and Hasher was about to hang up when the Sheriff said, "All the same, I'll put a call through to Poughkeepsie. If I find out anything, I'll let you know. Okay?"

Hasher hung up without answering.

The testimony of Lyndon Johnson James had come late in the trial, but Hasher read it first. Seated in the easy chair before a small fire in his cottage, he went through the bulky court transcript quickly, skimming the loosely spaced typescript until something caught his attention. Some of the testimony, he found when he read it carefully, was more horrifying than the pictures of the corpse that he had looked at that morning. And although Hasher had been present at the trial during a brief part of the boy's testimony—until it became clear that the old man wanted him to leave—the rest of it was far more disgusting, and damning, than he had imagined.

Marvin Rail, Vivian's lawyer, was a stocky man of about forty with thin blond hair pasted over the bald dome of his head and a puffy vulgar face. He had stalked back and forth before the witness stand and the jury box and as Hasher watched him perform he had seen that Rail had a suggestive way of moving his body to emphasize his witness's words. Hasher returned to the transcript:

Mr. Rail: So you and three other boys, members of the Boys Group, spent the weekend of August 3rd to August 5th at Mr. Slocum's cabin on Lake Mercy.

The Witness: We was supposed to stay the weekend,

but, as I said before, the other guys they had someplace to go Saturday night, a party or something, they said. I don't know—

Mr. Wicknor: Objection.

The Court: Sustained.

Mr. Rail: Did the other three stay or not?

The Witness: No, sir.

Mr. Rail: Did you stay?

The Witness: Yes, sir.

Mr. Rail: Just you and Mr. Slocum?

The Witness: Just me and him.

Mr. Rail: Where was Mrs. Slocum?

Mr. Wicknor: Your honor, I object to this—

The Court: Sustained. Mr. Rail, will you confine yourself to the issues before us?

Mr. Rail: Now, Mr. James, would you please tell us where you slept that night—if you slept?

Mr. Wicknor (rising): Your Honor, this is uncalled for—it's leading the witness.

The Court: It seems proper to me. Proceed, Mr. Rail.

Mr. Rail: Thank you, your Honor. Now, Mr. James, where did you sleep that night?

The Witness: In the study, Mr. Slocum's study. There was a couch there, like a bed. I mean, it was a couch daytime and you could open it out like a bed.

Mr. Rail: You slept there?

The Witness: Yes, sir.

Mr. Rail: On the opened-out bed?

The Witness: Yes, sir.

Hasher looked up at the fire and remembered how Rail at that moment had stuck his hands in the rear pockets of his trousers and thrust his pelvis forward in a slight swiveling motion as he continued.

Mr. Rail: How long did you sleep that night?

The Witness: How long?

Mr. Rail: Yes, how long?

The Witness: I don't know exactly. Like I went to sleep and all and a time later, I got no idea, I waked up.

Mr. Rail: Was there a specific reason why you woke up?

The Witness: Specific?

Mr. Rail: Was there a particular reason?

The Witness: Yeah. I mean, yes, sir. I was being blowed.

Mr. Rail: What?

Mr. Wicknor: Your Honor, this filthy, uncalled-for, unwarranted, immaterial slander—

The Court: Sit down, Mr. Wicknor. Now, Mr. Rail, if your witness might conduct himself more decorously.

Mr. Rail: I'm afraid this young man's life hasn't been very decorous, your Honor. He can only speak as he knows how—that is, to the facts presently before this Court.

The Court: Proceed.

Mr. Wicknor: I object. This procedure—

The Court: I told you to sit down, Mr. Wicknor. One more outburst from you will mean a contempt citation. Proceed, Mr. Rail.

Mr. Rail: Mr. James, do you know what the word "fellatio" means?

The Witness: No, sir.

Mr. Wicknor: Your Honor, may we approach the bench?

The Court: That won't be necessary. Bailiff, clear the courtroom. Until the Court rules otherwise, this proceeding will be conducted *in camera,* so to speak, except that the jury shall be present. There will be a half-hour recess.

That was when Hasher left. The last he saw was Lyndon Johnson James stepping down from the stand and grinning at the old man, who sat, unmoving and silent, alone. Even Wicknor had moved away from him.

As Hasher read on now, he was more frightened than horrified for he had begun to believe the boy. His testimony was too real not to believe—his broken, half-coherent story of how he had tried to get up and out of bed, to get away, but the old man had fallen on his knees, weeping, begging, offering him money. Finally, the boy went on, he had felt sorry for him and succumbed. He took the money and they repeated the acts many times— there in the cabin, in the Slocum apartment in New York, in the old man's car. Many, many times, the boy said and wept so uncontrollably the judge had to stop the proceedings.

Although the judge had closed the courtroom to spectators, he did not seal the evidence presented. The next day several reporters bought copies of the transcript and that was the virtual, if not the literal, end of the case. The jury awarded Vivian Slocum a divorce and $590,500. The judge, who was known for his hatred of the old-line legal establishment that Lucius Slocum embodied, let the verdict stand; so did the Appellate Division and the Court of Appeals. Two weeks after the last decision was handed down, Lucius Slocum died.

The telephone rang and Hasher put down the transcript and went to the extension phone in the kitchen.

"Are you all right, my darling?" Margaret asked.

He didn't answer.

"Thomas?"

"Sorry," he muttered. After a pause, he said, "Has it occurred to you that Lyndon James might have told the truth?"

Margaret gasped. "But you said—"

"I may have been wrong."

"What's happened? What've you found out?" she asked anxiously. "Are you all right?"

"You never read the transcript of the boy's testimony, did you?"

"No. Did you?"

"I just finished it."

"Where did you—? Oh. In his cabin?"

"Yeah." He took a bottle of Scotch out of a cupboard, some ice out of the refrigerator, and a glass off the drainboard. He poured a drink, added tap water, and took a long gulp. "I needed that," he said, knowing that the sounds were self-explanatory.

"Should I come back up there? Or will you come home —tonight?"

"No," he said quickly. "Tomorrow probably. I need time to think, maybe to make a call or two. Is everything okay at the office?"

Margaret didn't answer at once. Finally she said, "They're upstairs right now, talking about disbanding the firm. Sillitoe took his case away from me this morning. Some bastard at your club asked George Barker at lunch today if it was true that we had changed the firm's name to Pederast, Whitby & Barker."

Hasher swore.

"You should be here, Thomas. As a senior partner, you carry weight. You could stop it."

"I have no desire to stop it," he said curtly. "They got into this mess by believing Vivian instead of Lucius. I'll be damned if I lift a finger to help them now."

"Did you know that I was born in 1908?" Lucius Slocum had asked Hasher one evening, a month before the old man's death, as they sat on the creaky porch of his log cabin.

Hasher waited. Actually he had never thought about the year of his old friend's birth. It didn't matter, except that it had been a long time ago—a time that always conjured in his imagination a picture of quiet farm life and the shady streets of small towns, a time when people could go to and from work or come home alone at night without fear that they would be murdered.

"Most people were poor of course, but we didn't think much about that," the old man went on. "I don't believe I ever heard the word 'poverty' used when I was a boy. It wasn't a distinction, there was so much of it. There was also a great deal of drunkenness, drug addiction, whoring, and crime—far more than you might imagine. Possibly even more than there is today, though it's impossible to prove, given the fragmentary and unreliable statistics from back then." He paused to puff on his pipe and look out over the lake. " I suspect that if we could measure the old villainies, we'd be in for quite a shock. Still, there was a difference all the same—a basic difference in outlook."

Hasher took a swallow of his cold coffee and waited.

"People believed in decency," the old man said at last. "I don't know if they practiced it so much more than people do now, though they probably did, in small ways at least, out in the rural areas where most Americans then lived. But they *believed* in it. It was sort of an inspiration." He paused again and tamped his pipe. "Like hope, or God, or the spirit of humanity itself."

Hasher nodded, without speaking. He suspected that this was as close as his friend would come to the subject of what had been done to him. He had become oblique, as if that would deflect any direct hits.

But suddenly the old man leaned forward, facing him, and said angrily, "I've lost my faith, Thomas!"

Startled by the intensity of his voice, Hasher could only stare at him in wonder. Faith? In God? In man? he asked himself. Instead of asking the old man what he meant, Hasher only nodded and waited again.

"I'm a very great fool," Lucius Slocum said. "I really believed in it all."

Even then, Hasher hadn't understood. But now, as he sat bundled against the cold on his own porch, staring down the lake at the Slocum cabin, he remembered Margaret's words: "It's only a game. . . . He didn't know either." At last Hasher understood what the old man had meant. He had believed in that decency still, and in a flawed society that struggled to be just, in fairness between men, in a legal system, the basis of it all, that delicately balanced the various forces of society to bind men together and yet to keep them apart. Above all else, Hasher knew, Lucius Slocum had believed in the law. And he had discovered that it was all a game only after he had lost it.

Slowly Hasher's fingers tightened around the tumbler of whisky as a thought flashed into his mind. "Of course," he murmured, wondering how it was that he had not seen it long before. If Lucius Slocum had been guilty of the grave offenses he was charged with, he could never have spoken as he had to Hasher that day. He would simply have remained silent or talked about something else. Whatever he might have been he was not a hypocrite.

A moment later another thought, this one a question, occurred to Hasher: Why had Vivian been so intent upon getting him out of the cabin? While she was capable of trying to destroy the memory and the legacy of a dead man, like all bullies she usually had others do her dirty work—James, Rail, a hired hand.

Hasher got up and paced back and forth along the porch, his nervous excitement making his movements awkward. Finally he stopped to calm himself and stared down the lake once more at the log cabin. She had wanted to get him out of there badly enough to do it herself, or at least try to, over the phone. Why? Then he remembered that James was believed to have been at the cabin on the morning that the old man died. Why? Had he gone there, as Worthy suggested, to blackmail his benefactor one last time? Had he found him dead and robbed the corpse? Had he killed? . . . Hasher shivered.

Or had the boy been looking for something?

Hasher picked up his drink and was about to take a swallow when he paused to look at the cabin. James's picture and his horrifying court testimony, or a cleansed version of it, had appeared in the local paper. How would he dare risk being seen here after that? Unless his errand was crucial, Hasher thought and took a drink of whisky. Could he have known before he came that the old man was dead?

Nothing but speculation, Hasher told himself, and swore at his helplessness. Not a single hard fact. He went into the cottage. The fire was nearly out and he put some kindling and logs on it and stood there, staring into the smoke rising through them. He was puzzled, certain that something was wrong but having no idea of what it might be. Vivian? he asked himself. No, she wouldn't have killed her husband. No reason to, once she had ruined him and got his money. For her, it was better to let him die, alone and disgraced.

The fire was blazing now but Hasher didn't notice. A lurking thought emerged. He gripped the mantelpiece. She didn't care about the old log cabin. She wanted something *in* the cabin. That was why she vowed to fight the will, why she drove him out. The private papers that Lucius had left to Hasher under the will? *Something* in those papers? She had to have them! She had sent the boy to get them but he had found the body of Lucius Slocum, robbed it, and fled. So she had to drive Hasher out, she had to protect whatever was there until she could get to it herself.

He felt the heat and backed away from the fire. What was it—cash, negotiable securities, gold? Hasher dismissed the idea. Not the old man. Banks, safes, vaults—those were his repositories of wealth.

Hasher went to the kitchen to make coffee. He hadn't slept for more than two or three hours a night since he learned of the old man's death. Befuddled by weariness and frustration, he stood by the kitchen sink looking out the window at the dark trees as a gust of wind blew more yellow leaves off and the smoke from the chimney swirled and vanished among them. Something in the configuration brought back the photograph of the dead man slumped at his desk, the black hole in his white hair.

Hasher shook his head sharply to get rid of the image. He looked at his watch: 2:25. About four hours until dark—say three and a half hours before he would leave. He must get there before nightfall and it would be hard going through the woods.

Sleep, he thought groggily, I've got to sleep. He went to the bedroom and lay down but it was useless. The same thoughts, spinning in incessant repetition, were beyond his control. An obsession, he knew. Cursing suddenly, he sat up on the side of the bed. It was exactly that obsession which had killed the old man. Cursing again, Hasher stood up. He couldn't let it get him. Tonight he would find whatever it was they were looking for. Then he could sleep.

CHAPTER

3

Hasher took out the record book he had found on the bookshelf in the cabin and went back to his chair by the fire. Perhaps there would be a clue buried among the diary's legal details. But after his cursory perusal when he first found it, he doubted that it would have much to offer. Still, anything was better than sitting here, or pacing, or trying to sleep while the obsession and the fury hidden in him grew. He turned to the first page and began reading.

Nearly two hours later he closed the diary, dazed by the brutal story he had found hidden here and there, in isolated passages, among the legal facts and the theories of the case. The fire had almost gone out and Hasher realized that he was cold. But he was too stunned to stir and sat dumbly, trying to calm himself.

Why had the old man left the diary on the bookshelf, almost out in the open? he wondered. Was it a trick, like Poe's purloined letter—safer that way than if he had hidden it? The only secure place would have been a safe-deposit box but he would have known that state officials would impound its contents upon his death. Then he must have suspected that Vivian would contest the will. So he had left the diary for Hasher to find. . . . And to use?

He looked down at the book on his lap. Use how? While it damned Vivian irreparably, it contained no proof, nothing that would be admissible in a court, only the old man's unsupported claims. And, worst of all, he had revealed there that the one piece of evidence that might have saved him from her, that still might restore his good name, had been destroyed long ago—by his own hand. His innocence, his folly were nearly beyond belief, Hasher thought, for the old man had made no effort to protect himself.

Or had he? After all, there was the diary. Why else had he left it like that? Then, as Hasher looked at it again, he realized that maybe the old man had simply forgotten about it. In those final hours of pain, what could such a thing have mattered to him?

Hasher got up and threw more kindling on the low flames and picked up a log. Halfway toward dropping it into the fireplace, he stopped and straightened, still holding the piece of wood. Did they know about the diary or suspect its existence? he asked himself. He shook his head to dismiss the idea and put the log on the flaming kindling, then added another. Again he stopped. There had to be some reason that Vivian had been so anxious to get him out of the cabin, some reason for James to have been there the day the old man died.

The heat drove Hasher back to his chair. Picking up the diary, he stared at it, wondering if the old man had left it in the cabin for *them* to find. But why? he asked again.

He looked at his watch: 4:40. Whatever the answers to his questions, he had to have the story in the diary fully in mind so that he would be ready for them if they came. And he was sure that one of them would—tonight or tomorrow night.

Leafing through the pages of now irrelevant legal details, he found the first passage of the story and began rereading:

> When Vivian Trumbull came to work for me, she was twenty-seven years old. I was fifty-five and had been a widower for nearly ten years.
>
> Vivian was an extraordinarily lovely and graceful

woman, as well as the best secretary I had ever had. Careful yet quick, sensitive to the smallest problems of her work, and mine, she was also unfailingly good natured and kind. As time passed, she took over more and more of my lesser work, even drafting certain papers, handling leases, and managing several estate accounts. After she had been with me for a couple of years, I know that I could not function nearly as well professionally without her.

As time passed, I began to feel that old longing stirring in me, the desire that I thought had died with Mary, and I came to believe that I must have Vivian always at my side if I were once again to live as a man. But I knew I was far too old for her—twenty-eight years older. And yet! Ah, what pain those self-deceiving words "And yet!" have caused me.

I fought my desire until it obsessed me and I could scarcely resist my own demands and needs. But I had no will to fight hers. For, yes, it was Vivian who told me that *she* loved me! I was a vigorous, brave, vital, sensitive man in a world of callow boys and fools, she said. I was the youngest man in spirit she had ever known. I could not believe her, but I did. And so we wed. I was sixty-one, or a month short of it, and Vivian was thirty-three. I was the happiest, and the proudest, and the most foolish man alive.

His face drawn, Hasher looked up at the fire just as the phone rang. He got up and crossed the room to the telephone stand in the corner by the front windows. But when he answered, the line went dead.

Vivian, he thought, then realized that it could have been any one of them. They were planning the visit to the cabin and had to know if he was still at the lake. Would they postpone the search now? No, he decided, if he was there the urgency would be even greater to find whatever they were after before he did. He went back to the chair and picked up the diary. Was that what they wanted? he asked again—and again saw that his question was pointless. He would find out soon enough.

He opened the diary and found the next passage in the chronology:

The Lindsay estate, actually that of Thomas Benton Lindsay, was the largest that our firm ever represented. At the time of his death, it was worth a little over $22,000,000. Despite inheritance taxes, the combination of Alma Lindsay's miserliness and a rising market has increased the estate to nearly twice its original value at the time of his death. As Tom Lindsay's friend and attorney, I, of course, personally handled the estate— or, perhaps I should say, mishandled it through my own blindness.

The thefts from this estate within our firm came to a total of $271,560. These thefts occurred during the fourth and fifth years of Vivian Trumbull's service as my secretary, before we were married.

When my wife charged in her divorce complaint that I had far greater assets than I admitted to, I had no idea what she meant, and concluded that her claim was based on nothing more than Marvin Rail's ingenious capacity for deceit. But when she stated in court that she had suspected I was stealing from at least one of the firm's clients when she was still my secretary, I was dumbfounded. Her further claim that she had spoken in confidence about her suspicions to our senior colleague, Harold Whitby, who was by the time of the trial conveniently dead, convinced me that she had herself stolen the money. Harold was utterly incapable of behaving as she testified—namely, by scoffing at her suspicion. However much Harold might have believed that such a claim was nonsense, he would have instantly ordered an audit of the estate, just as I would have in his place. His concern for the reputation of the firm would have transcended any desire to spare my feelings or to protect me.

Hasher paused, remembering how the senior partners of Slocum, Whitby & Barker had ordered an audit an hour after Vivian Slocum's testimony about the Lindsay estate. In two weeks, the accounting firm reported that $271,560 had been stolen from the estate during the period that Mrs. Slocum claimed in her testimony she had become suspicious of her employer. Two hours after the audit report came in, Lucius Slocum offered his resignation. He was innocent of any theft, he said quietly, but he was culpable in neglecting to oversee his own work properly. His partners accepted the resignation and ignored the explanation. Hasher had angrily beseeched the old man to defend himself but he refused.

Hasher turned back to the diary:

During the last two or three years of Vivian's service as my secretary before we married, she frequently gave me papers to sign. She was, as I have noted, extremely able, extremely dependable as far as I knew, extremely loyal to the firm and to me, so I signed. Of course, most of the papers I signed were legitimate. But a few others —the transfers of one stock into another, then another, then into government securities with no listed owner— constituted the theft. If you examine the audit, as I did before leaving the firm, you will see that she started out on a modest scale: first $1,000, then $1,500, then $4,000; when she felt safe, the sums became $30,000 and $45,000 and $80,000.

Although Vivian stole the money, I was responsible. Moreover, there was no way later on that I could prove her guilt and my own innocence. After all, the signatures on the transfer documents were unquestionably mine.

Now, of course, the Internal Revenue Service has moved in to get its share, on the ground that I failed to report this stolen money and to pay taxes on it. They are certain to prosecute me, and the little I have left after Vivian gets her court-ordered portion will be nearly exhausted. So, after fifty years of honest labor, I die a bankrupt and a criminal.

Hasher got up and went out to the front porch for some air. Standing with his fists clenched by his sides, he stared down the lake at the log cabin. It would be dark in an hour. He had to leave soon. He went back inside to get ready.

He changed into dark-brown corduroy pants, a blue sweater, a navy windbreaker, and heavy walking shoes. Looking at the bottom of the closet where the shoes had been, he nodded to himself and knelt by the closet and dragged out all the remaining shoes and boots. Running a hand back across the rear right corner, he found a protruding nail head and lifted it. Half the closet floor came up with it. In the small cupboardlike enclosure below was a steel file box. After lifting it out, Hasher took a minute to remember the combination, then dialed it and opened the lid. Inside was a cardboard shoebox and inside that was a cloth bag of the kind used to protect silverware. He took out the bag and loosened its drawstring and removed a nickel-plated snubnosed .32-caliber revolver.

Sitting down, Hasher examined the gun. It was fully loaded and the safety was on. He turned it over and over in his hands, wondering if he should take it along. He wouldn't need it if Vivian or Rail came, or even both; he could handle them with words. But James . . . a vicious kid who might be armed himself. . . . The feel of the gun comforted and excited him; he stuck it in his jacket pocket, closed the secret door, and shoved the boots and shoes back on top.

One more section of the diary and he would be ready. Returning to the living room, he sat down and began reading again:

Now for Lyndon Johnson James—an inaptly named young man if there ever was one. He once told me that his father chose that name because President Johnson's anti-poverty program had provided the father with a job and enough money to set up housekeeping with Lyndon's mother. Apparently this "family" arrangement lasted until the "war on poverty" ended, when the father vanished.

Or so Lyndon said. But then Lyndon said many many things that hadn't the faintest truth to them. I had known that for a long time, almost since the day he was brought to me, at the age of thirteen, by the minister near Lake Mercy, the Rev. Jonathan Dollwin. By then, Lyndon had been in the reformatory twice, once for holding up a gas station at knifepoint and once for slashing another boy in a fight.

Allowances must be made, of course. We have exploited black people for three hundred years and have ourselves driven them to their desperate acts. I ignored Lyndon's deceit and I ignored his thefts from me—small amounts of money from the cabin, a silver cigarette lighter there, a rather expensive fishing rod, a costly camera from the apartment in New York. One has to be patient with such boys and provide them with an example. Or so I believed.

In any event, Lyndon's deceit turned out to be like Vivian's deceit—bottomless. The story he told on the witness stand about my seducing him when he was thirteen was the same story, almost word for word, that he had told me one day in a confessional mood about another older man. I cannot bring myself even now to mention his name, but I imagine you will easily guess it. I don't know whether that story was as much a lie as the story he told about me, but it no longer matters.

Hasher looked up from the diary. It must have been the Reverend Dollwin. There had been rumors about him for years and when he and his wife died in a fire that swept through the rectory, firemen found pornographic magazines of men and young boys hidden in the Reverend's workshop above the garage.

My God, Hasher thought, had James set the fire? Realizing that he might find the answer later, Hasher returned to the diary:

Two years after Vivian and I married, she decided that it was unsuitable for the wife of a senior partner to go on working as a secretary at the firm, and became a fulltime wife. We lived quietly and congenially, and I confess that to this day I can find no fault with her conduct as a homemaker and a mate.

It was just a week past my sixty-eighth birthday when one morning the secretary who replaced Vivian, Miss Morley, came into my office. Her face looked as if it were about to burst into flames, and she was trembling so that she dropped the letter she was there to deliver. It had arrived in the mail that morning, addressed to me, and since it wasn't tagged as personal, she had opened and read it, or part of it, until she realized what it was. Miss Morley stammered out an apology and fled.

The letter was from Lyndon Johnson James. He was seventeen or eighteen then, I think, and had been in and out of my life for five years, more often than not to my regret. The boy was made for trouble and always found it. His letter was nearly illiterate, but it was clear enough—all too clear. He had been arrested again, this time for shoplifting, out in Detroit, and he wanted money for a lawyer who promised to get him off for a thousand dollars. That was a familiar tale, for Lyndon had tried to touch me twice before on similar grounds, although only for two or three hundred dollars each time. On both occasions I had refused.

To get this over with (it is hideously painful to me even now), he wrote that he had been Vivian's lover from the time he was thirteen years old, only weeks after I had taken him into my house. Thirteen! They had, as he put it, "fucked all the time"—at the cabin, in the woods, in her car, at our apartment in the city. He claimed he had a note from her to prove it, and he quoted from it. Forgive me for repeating the words, but they are burned into my soul like the fires of hell.

If I write them down, the pain may ease a little. Even if it doesn't, at least you will finally know what has happened to me. Her words were: "I must see you tomorrow—must! must! must! I can't wait another day. I want you in my arms and your great black cock pulsing, throbbing, flaming inside me. I must have it! Oh, Lynny my sweet, I will take you in my mouth afterwards and drink your passion like nectar!"

Hasher got up and went to the window overlooking the dock. At least he had one answer, he thought, and remembered the time, a Saturday morning a few years before, when he had been sunning in a pair of shorts out there. He had seen something in the water a couple of hundred yards away and figured that it was a dog or a beaver. But it had been neither. In a few minutes he saw that it was Vivian. She had swum the length of the lake and when she pulled herself up, panting, onto the dock, Hasher went to help her.

"I thought I'd drop by for a drink," she gasped, smiling, as she sprawled out on the warm boards of the dock, her long body in a little black bikini glistening with drops of water in the bright summer sun.

Margaret and Lucius planned to come up to the lake together that afternoon if they finished their work on an urgent case.

"Did Lucius call yet?" Hasher asked.

Vivian shook her head. "A drink and a towel," she said. "I'm freezing."

Hasher got up quickly. "I bought too many oranges at the market this morning," he said. "How about a fresh screwdriver?"

He wasn't certain but she seemed to stare fixedly at his groin before she smiled and said, "Perfect!"

He brought her a towel and went back to the cottage. When he came out with the drinks, Vivian was lying, face down, on the towel without the top of her bikini. As he gave her a glass and she reached up to take it, most of one breast was revealed. He turned away and went back to his chair.

Hasher had seen Vivian in a bathing suit before but never in a bikini and certainly never in half a bikini. He wondered how she intended to get back to her cabin. He could drive her in the car or take her in the canoe. The canoe, he decided; that way, they wouldn't have to pass through the cottage—dark and cool and inviting—and nothing could happen in a canoe.

A moment later he asked himself if that was what he wanted: nothing. And, a moment after that, he knew that was exactly what he wanted from his oldest and best friend's wife: nothing. Nervously Hasher began chatting, all the while trying not to look at her more than glancingly. It was not easy. Vivian was beautiful, she was nearly naked, and it was not easy. From time to time, she brushed a hand back over her thighs or her half-bare buttocks to flick away an insect and her movements —full of grace in her impatience—silenced him each time. Then she raised a delicately arched foot and bent her leg. Again he looked away.

Suddenly Vivian cried, "A bee!" and sat up, facing him. Her breasts were almost too big but not quite. She waved her small hands in the air and squealed, "Get away!" Hasher couldn't see any bee.

Abruptly Vivian stopped. "Oh, God," she said, "I forgot." Demurely covering her breasts with her arms, she smiled and said, "Don't be such a prude, Thomas. They're just fucking tits."

As he looked at her, she took away her arms. She was right, he thought, they surely were fucking tits.

"Now you've seen them, that's over. So I can sun myself on the front." She lay down on her back, squirming a little as she stretched out on the towel. "Nice," she murmured and closed her eyes.

It wasn't now, Hasher told himself, it was never. He looked down at her and felt his cock swelling.

Vivian's eyes opened. "Don't worry, Thomas," she said. "Life is full of surprises."

"Time for a swim," he said. Jumping up, he took three running steps and flung himself into the cold water. It worked. Five minutes later he climbed back onto the dock and found Vivian wearing both pieces of her bikini. She smiled and handed him the towel. As he dried his face, he heard her say, "Don't forget, dinner at eight," and looked up to see her execute a fine racing dive and swim away.

Since then, he had wondered a hundred times whether she had been making a pass or merely flaunting her beauty to win his admiration. Now, as he stared out over the dock and remembered that day, he knew the answer. Or part of it. He still didn't know if she had really wanted him or had only meant to humiliate him, to make him betray his friend, to show him that he was no better than she was, even worse. Had she been angry at his rejection, he wondered, or did she hate him now only because he had refused to be like her?

Hasher shuddered slightly at the question—at the magnitude of this woman's wrath—and poured a small glass of straight whisky. When he went back to the diary, he noticed that the handwriting was different after the passage about her note to James—uncertain, wobbly. Stricken by the dead man's agony, Hasher wondered how he could have been sure that the boy hadn't lied. But as soon as Hasher resumed reading, he found the answer:

I knew then that it was true, that the words were Vivian's, for she had once spoken those final words to me, and I had never forgotten them. Besides, I remembered incidents that I must have repressed—her touching him when there was no need to (beyond her own passionate need), how she had accepted, and even encouraged, his presence in our life (actually far more than I did), and, above all, how I had once caught her looking at him with a kind of rapacious greed that I only now recognize as lust.

In his wretched letter he vowed to send Vivian's love note to the newspaper here unless I sent him $1,000 at once. I knew, of course, that the paper would never print it and that, in all likelihood, John Patterson would destroy it as soon as it reached his desk. But I also knew that others would see it before then, on its way to the editor, and that they would talk. I would have to give up my life here. And yet— Again those lulling words "and yet"! I could not allow myself to be blackmailed. And yet. . . .

I was aflame with passion—the passion of hatred. That I had never known such ardor from my own wife! But enough of that. I knew that I could not survive the scandal of revealing her behavior, whether I did it through a divorce suit or James did it in some other way. And I knew that my wife's "honor" was in actuality my own. In the end, there seemed only one choice: to buy my wife's note from James. On a pretext—I could barely endure speaking to her on the telephone— I flew at once to Detroit. James had told the truth about being in jail on a shoplifting charge, but the rest of what he had written was only partly true. The lawyer, a common hack of the sort to be found hanging around just about any criminal court in the hope of picking up a client he can fleece, had asked James for only $500. I paid him that and for another $200 James gave me Vivian's note.

I returned on the next flight to New York, went home, threw the note in her face, and moved into a hotel.

Hasher slapped the diary shut. He knew the rest all too well and it was time to go. Striding back to the bedroom, he hid the diary in the metal box under the closet floor. As he straightened up, he noticed his old canvas fishing creel hanging by its strap on a coat hook. He took it to the kitchen and packed it with a thermos of hot coffee, a couple of cheese sandwiches, and some candy bars.

He looked out the window over the sink. It was nearly dark.

CHAPTER

4

Hasher entered the darkening woods and headed off at a slight angle away from the lake. After a hundred paces, he told himself, he would cut back to the left and follow the shoreline a few yards inland and out of sight from anywhere on the lake. But a few paces farther on he lost count as his mind returned to the story he had read. If Vivian had been a fool to write such a note, the old man had been a worse fool to give it back to her, whatever his rage or his fear that any use of it would bring scandal down on his own head. And the letter from James. . . . Why had the old man destroyed that? For the same reason—

Hasher stopped. *That* was what they were looking for —the letter! James must have told Vivian about it. . . . But, no, he would hardly confess to her his blackmailing betrayal. . . . Then Vivian had learned somehow—maybe the old man had told her in his rage when he left her and had forgotten to record that fact in the diary. . . . No, no, too unlikely. He hadn't forgotten anything, not Lucius in his obsessed state. . . .

Hasher took a few steps and stopped again, cursing himself for the delay but unable to resist the questions that could be crucial if one of them came to the cabin that night. Perhaps Vivian knew nothing about the black-mail letter but only feared that the old man had left behind something incriminating to her. . . . That at least would explain her attempts to drive Hasher out of the place. . . . If only James knew about the letter, then he would be the one to come. . . . But why? What could he fear now? Surely not scandal, not a thief and self-confessed male prostitute like him. He would glory in the liaison with a beautiful white woman.

Hasher cursed his confusion and headed on through the woods. All he knew for certain was that the letter no longer existed. The old man had described in the diary how he had called his secretary into his office after he read the letter that she had inadvertently looked at and instructed her that she had never seen, never heard of such a letter. Then he had burned it in front of her and said, "It did not exist."

"Oh, Lucius, Lucius, Lucius," Hasher muttered in despair at the old man's folly. He had meant to protect himself by protecting his wife but had only saved her and destroyed himself.

Pausing to get his bearings, Hasher started off at an angle to the left, toward the lake. When he saw it at last ahead of him, gleaming black in the night, he swung to the right and followed the shoreline from behind a screen of pines. It was hard going, totally dark now, and twice he fell. After the second time, he lumbered to his feet and climbed over a rocky abutment to higher ground and sat on a flat stone to rest. He was in a small clearing.

He stiffened as he heard a sound—like something solid hitting wood. Someone on the porch of the cabin, he thought as he slid off the stone and moved forward, in a simian crouch, toward the lake. It was only twenty feet away but the distance took him several minutes as he inched along, trying to make no sound. If he had heard that noise, a branch cracking beneath his foot could give him away.

When he reached the rocky shore at last and peered through the darkness, Hasher saw the darker bulk of the cabin only thirty yards away. Suddenly he caught a glimmer of light flash across a window that faced onto the front porch. Someone was in the study with a flashlight!

He crouched down, then flattened out on the rocks, with only his head raised. Now it was too late. One of them had got there first. He swore softly. He would crawl back into the woods and go home. They had won, it was over, the old man was dead, go home.

Hasher took several deep breaths, holding each in for a long time and letting it out slowly to ease his pounding heartbeat—a trick he had learned in Vietnam. But that was too long ago, he told himself. He hardly remembered. . . . A surge of shame welled up in him. . . . He hadn't forgotten that. How he had frozen in terror the first time out on patrol, hiding in the undergrowth as his men moved on past him toward the enemy . . . then joining them when the fight was over for a futile burst of gunfire into the empty jungle. They had avoided him for weeks after that but he had finally made up for it. . . . He was as ashamed of that—his crazed heroics—as of his cowardice. . . . In the end he had fought for an absurdity: his comrades who had died.

Hasher raised his head. It was the same now, he thought. He had failed his friend when it mattered but he could not fail him when it no longer did.

He got to his knees, then his feet, and moved back into the woods and started toward the cabin. He emerged in a small clearing near its rear corner, at the opposite end from the study. His heart was pounding again and his breath came in short shallow gasps. Moving quickly across the last few yards of rough turf, he pressed his body against the wall of the cabin, feeling the curve of a cool log against his cheek and smelling creosote. He slipped the creel off his shoulder and quietly lowered it to the ground.

Again Hasher wanted to flee but again he forced himself to go on, knowing that he couldn't live with another betrayal. Taking out the pistol, he gripped it tightly, reassured by the feel of the weapon, and crept forward around the back corner of the cabin, past a small attached shed, and up to the rear door.

He stopped there. If it was locked from the inside, as

it would almost certainly be, he would give up and leave. Or should he hide there in the dark, he asked himself, and wait until whoever was inside came out? It might be only a prowler but he could be armed. Hasher gripped the gun.

He took the doorknob and turned it slowly. When it stopped, he pulled it gently toward him. The door swung outward silently.

"Shit!" he whispered.

There was a crashing sound as something fell or was thrown onto a floor.

He looked down at his shoes and wondered if he should take them off to muffle his entry but decided against it; he would need every weapon he had. Releasing the safety catch on the gun, he opened the door further and slipped into the dark kitchen. As he did, there was another crashing sound.

Hasher crept across the large kitchen to the door into the living room. Once there, he paused to recall the exact layout. Around the round oak dining table, which he could just make out to his left in the dim light, then straight on to the study door. Now he saw that it was open, as a splash of light spilled out over the doorsill into the living room, then vanished.

Praying that a squeaky board wouldn't give him away, Hasher moved slowly, a few inches at a step, across the living room and at last reached the wall beside the study door. He stood with his back to the wall, breathing deeply and slowly again to still the frantic beat of his heart. All right, he told himself, all right. He had the advantages—the gun, surprise. . . .

A male voice cursed and Hasher realized that it was books that were being thrown onto the floor. That would be the time to make his move, he thought; he must be ready for the next time. A flash of light again spilled out of the doorway and he froze, gripping the gun and wondering if he could use it. He listened to the shuffling sound of books being shoved around on the floor. Or was it something else? Some papers he had missed being searched through? He waited. He would know soon enough.

A minute later another batch of books crashed to the floor and Hasher turned and walked into the study.

Lyndon Johnson James was sitting on the floor amid a litter of books and loose pages that had fallen out of some of them. He was wearing blue sneakers, jeans, and a black jacket. He stared at the figure in the doorway, his eyes very white against his dark skin, his pink mouth hanging open. Clearly he couldn't see in the dim beam of the flashlight, which was turned away from the door.

How old is he now—nineteen, twenty? Hasher wondered absurdly.

"That you, Sheriff?" James asked in a trembling voice.

Hasher moved further into the room, now in a half-crouch, holding the gun out with both hands.

"Shiiiiit!" the boy said in contempt. "It's only Hasher." He started to get up.

"One more move and I'll blow your rotten fucking brains out!" Hasher snapped. "Sit down!"

The rage and determination in his voice stopped the boy. He sat back down. Then he smiled. "Fuck you, Hasher. You ain't got the guts." But he didn't sound sure. And he didn't move.

Hasher desperately tried to keep the gun steady; any wavering, any sign of uncertainty or weakness could mean doom. He glanced covertly at the flashlight lying on the floor a foot or so from the boy's right hand, which was resting on his right knee. Hasher took another step forward. If James turned off the light or even knocked it away, he could be on his feet, with a gun or a knife in that hand, in seconds. Lithe, fast, ruthless—a deadly child.

Hasher saw the hand clench the knee, then relax. James was going to make a try. Suddenly, just as the hand darted toward the flashlight, Hasher took two running steps forward and kicked the boy in the face.

He screamed and the flashlight slid across the floor as his hand struck it. Hasher stooped down and grabbed it as it rolled past. He flashed it on the boy, who was lying on one side, his hands over his face, blood streaming out between his fingers onto the litter of loose pages covering the floor. Hasher stood still, holding the light on him steadily, then bent down and frisked him for a weapon. Nothing. He stepped back out of reach.

James groaned and rolled onto his back and slid his bloody fingers down enough to see over their tips. "Motherfucker," he moaned.

Hasher smiled. "You still think I don't have the guts?"

James slowly propped himself on his elbows and spat out a front tooth. Then he sat all the way up and reached into his mouth with thumb and forefinger and pulled out another one. He looked at Hasher with murderous hatred.

Hasher moved closer and stuck the muzzle of the gun an inch from his bloody lips. "You're going to talk, sonny boy. If you do—*everything!*—we'll see about your future. If you don't, there won't be one." Quickly he moved back and dragged a wood chair across the room to its center. Sitting down on it a few feet from the boy, with the gun now in one hand and aimed at his belly, he held the flashlight in the other hand.

"Okay," Hasher said after a moment, "let's start with what you're looking for."

James stared at him in silence, his bruised thick lips open, the gap in the upper row of his teeth visible, his eyes bulging with fury. There was dark blood, drying now, on his chin and hands. "Go fuck yourself!" he snarled.

Hasher smiled. "You want more?" He brought the gun back as if to pistol whip him. James cringed. "Do you?" Hasher cried.

The boy lowered his head, looking down at his lap, but didn't speak.

Slowly, clearly Hasher quoted from Vivian's impassioned love note to James, as written in the old man's diary: " 'I want you in my arms and your great black cock pulsing, throbbing, flaming inside me.' "

The boy's head snapped up and he stared at Hasher in astonishment. Amused now, Hasher realized that he thought a homosexual pass was being made at him. Hasher calmly went on: " 'I must have it—must! must! must! Oh, Lynny my sweet, I will take you in my mouth afterward and drink your passion like nectar.' " Hasher paused and grinned down at the boy.

James's face registered his dawning awareness of where the quoted words came from with all the subtlety of a silent movie double-take. He tried to conceal his surprise by saying, "You faggot!"

Hasher's grin widened. "I see you remember Vivian's words. So that's what you're looking for."

James tried to curl his lips in contempt but it didn't work; he was too simple, too unpracticed to pull it off. That he was there for exactly that reason was registered on his face like a drawing. "I don't know what you're talking about," he mumbled, surly now.

"I'm afraid it's not here, Lynny my sweet," Hasher said. "You were a little too late."

James glared at him ferociously. "You stold it!" he cried.

Hasher knew the boy would kill him instantly if he got the chance. Anxious that his main advantage besides the gun—the boy's fear—might dissipate unexpectedly, Hasher leaned forward and waved the gun in his face. "Talk or I'll beat you to death—very slowly and very painfully."

James looked doubtful, then afraid.

"I also know, and can prove, that the story about your homosexual affair with Lucius Slocum was true in every respect except that it was between you and the Reverend Dollwin." He paused to note the look of uneasiness on the boy's face, then hurried on, "I can also prove, and will prove to the police unless you talk, that you started the fire that killed Dollwin and his wife."

James grunted.

"Did he refuse to pay any more blackmail money?"

"It was just a fire!" the boy cried. "It wasn't my fault they got trapped. *I* didn't kill them!" Suddenly he stopped and glared again at Hasher. "You got a fucking gun, you got fucking facts, you got the fucking letter, so what else you want from me, motherfuck? Leave me be!"

Hasher ignored the outburst. "You say you didn't mean to kill the Dollwins but the law says that if somebody dies because of a felony you commit, that's murder. Arson is a felony." He paused. "Sheriff Worthy doesn't like you, Lyndon. You'll get life."

"What d'you want?" the boy shouted.

"I want to know what happened."

Afterward Hasher had no way of knowing whether what the boy finally said was true or not. Clearly afraid of a murder charge, he refused to say anything more about the Reverend Dollwin. Nor would he talk about his relationship with Lucius Slocum. "You say you know all that, so why ask me?" was all he would reply to Hasher's questions about the two men. But he was more than willing to discuss his affair with Vivian, which, he confirmed, had begun when he was thirteen and had lasted, off and on, for close to six years. "Man, she wore me out," he said, grinning. "Three, four, five times a day when we was together. She near fucked me to death. They oughta make her register that pussy as a dangerous weapon." He had, as Lucius wrote, blackmailed his old benefactor for $700. And now he had come here in search of the letter and her note.

"Why?" Hasher asked. "Blackmail?"

"Call it that," the boy said with a scowl. "I got up there in that courtroom and say what they tole me and after she won, she laughed in my face and tole me to git! She say I come near her or even her place ever again, she call the cops and tell them I tried to rape her. So I come here to get the letter you already got." He glared at Hasher as if he were Vivian's protector.

"They promised me a third of what she got from old Slocum. Then she laughs at me. 'Begone, little nigger,' she says. She don't need me no more. She's got that bastard Rail." He paused and looked away, then turned back. "You maybe think niggers is no good shit. There never been a nigger in the world bad as that shit Rail. You even pass him on the street, you get covered with shit." He lapsed into a moody silence.

Hasher contemplated telling him that there was no letter, that the old man had destroyed it, and that Vivian had the note she had written her lover. That way, James would be deprived of any hope of blackmail and might seek more direct revenge on her and Rail. He had as good as murdered the Dollwins. For what? Probably the good rector had refused to pay blackmail or had tired of the boy. Or he had stopped paying. Whatever the motive, it wasn't as strong as this—her contemptuous use and rejection of her young lover.

But Hasher stopped himself. Something was missing. Could the letter actually not have been destroyed? He stared at James and demanded, "What were you doing here last Monday morning, the day he died? *You* killed him, didn't you?"

Fear flickered across James's face again and he waved his hands back and forth to dismiss the accusation. "I didn't even know he was here. I come looking for the note and letter. I see his car out back and peep in. that window"—he pointed toward the window behind the desk—"and he was there. First I think he's sleeping. Then I see the gun. He's dead."

"So you robbed the body."

James shrugged.

"Why should I believe you—a perjurer, an arsonist, a murderer?"

James shrugged again. "You say you want the truth. You got it." He stared at Hasher with contempt and hatred, then his face softened. "You let me go now?"

Hasher was surprised by the question. It hadn't occurred to him that he might let the boy go. And yet he wasn't sure what else he could do. His word alone about the fire that had killed the Dollwins wouldn't be enough for an arrest, let alone a conviction.

Hasher got up and shoved the chair to one side and stepped backward carefully several steps, his arm out with the gun aimed at James. "Up," Hasher ordered. "Slowly. No tricks. I'd hate to kill you before I get the Sheriff over here."

Suddenly the phone rang. Vivian again! he thought and turned, startled, toward the door. When he turned back, only a couple of seconds later, Hasher saw the boy hurtling across the room toward him, a gleaming knife in one hand above his head, his face contorted. As Hasher swung the gun toward him, the boy screamed in fury and flung himself forward. Hasher fired.

James grunted and slumped to his knees, the knife clattering across the wood floor, and then he slid forward and lay face down.

Quickly rolling him over with a foot to stop the blood from spreading on the floor and to make certain he wasn't faking, Hasher shone the light on the boy's face. His mouth and eyes were open. He was clearly dead. Kneeling beside him, Hasher saw a small hole in the left breast of his black jacket. Only a little blood had oozed out and he knew there wouldn't be much more now; the bullet had gone directly into his heart and stopped the pump.

When Hasher stood up, the room careened before him and he bent down again quickly to restore the bloodflow to his head before he fainted. He tried not to look at the corpse but did and tasted vomit in the back of his throat. Slowly he stood up, trying to get hold of himself. It was different now; this wasn't Vietnam, the dead boy was someone he had known, there were laws. He was a murderer.

The phone was still ringing, he realized. He shook his head to clear it and winced as a brief stab of pain flashed through from one temple to the other.

"The knife!" he said aloud, over the jangling phone, and swept the beam of the flashlight back and forth across the floor until it glinted on the blade halfway across the room. The boy must have had it hidden under his leg, he thought. Abruptly Hasher turned to the door and shouted at the telephone, "Fuck off!"

It stopped. He grinned at the coincidence. But as he

looked again at the body the grin trembled and disappeared. Shock, he told himself, that was all. In a few minutes. . . . It had been far worse the first time in Vietnam. A boy younger than James. Hasher had vomited afterwards and been sick for days. They had assured him that it would get easier each time. It had—all too easy.

Self-defense, he told himself quickly. If he hadn't fired, James would have killed him. Hasher stared at the body and shook his head. He had wanted to kill James, had come here armed and ready, and had killed him. Whatever a jury might say, he knew, he would always know.

Suddenly he thought of Margaret. How could they live with this?

Feeling sweat on his face, Hasher put the gun and flashlight on the chair and took out a handkerchief. He dried his face and the back of his neck as he walked out of the study and through the living room to the kitchen. Moving easily in the dark, he found Lucius Slocum's favorite whisky—Bell's twelve-year-old Scotch—and filled half a water glass and drank it straight down. He shuddered slightly from the drink but felt better almost at once. Standing by the counter with the empty glass in his hand, he stared out at the black night, wondering what it was that Margaret had said about him. At last he remembered some of it, the part about the fury hidden in a dark place deep inside him.

Hasher nodded. It was true. But there was less of that in him now. Had he satisfied the rage burning there with that bullet? He didn't know. Maybe all men had such fury within them. Like rats hiding in the night; one knows they are there but rarely sees them.

He poured another inch of whisky into the glass and lifted it in a silent toast to the old man.

CHAPTER

5

As a young man, Lucius Slocum had been a commander in the Navy and a junior aide to Admiral Nimitz in the Pacific during the Second World War. There were trophies and memorabilia from that period in the cabin—his framed commission, innumerable photographs, unit citations, his Silver Star and Purple Heart, a long jagged fragment of shrapnel that had pierced his thigh and fallen, spent, at Nimitz's feet. There were also more useful objects, such as some Navy blankets (now threadbare from use), coils of various gauge rope, several bundles of canvas for the sail of the boat the old man had never got around to building, lanyards, boxes of brass screws, hooks and eyes, and grommets, along with other nautical supplies.

When Hasher ran across the canvas and grommets in a large closet, he paused, something tugging at his memory, and then remembered. Quietly he let himself out the front door onto the porch and through the screened door to the ramp leading down to the dock. He jumped off the ramp into the long grass at the side. Heading back toward the cabin in a half-crouch, he ducked between two upright logs supporting the floor of the cabin, which at that point on the slanted shore was about four feet above the ground. It was darker there under the porch, without the dim light of the night sky, but by edging along with his hands out he finally felt the rowboat. It was a relic from

Admiral Nimitz's flagship. Slocum had managed to buy it years after his war service when the great ship was decommissioned. He had lovingly cared for the little boat, sanding and refinishing it outside and in every couple of years—painting the hull a gleaming white and varnishing the stained wood inside.

Hasher dragged the boat out from under the porch. Standing back to look at it, he was aghast at how it gleamed even in the dark. Once in the water, it should be less visible, he thought, but then shook his head in despair as he visualized the gleaming hull's reflection on the black water. He shrugged. He had no choice.

The boat's top was covered with a taut canvas tarpaulin, made to order and fastened at the gunwales with brass grommets and turnbuttons. Moving around the boat quickly, Hasher turned the buttons and lifted the canvas off, folded it, and tossed it back under the porch. He clambered into the boat and opened a small wooden cupboard under the partly enclosed bow. The rubber sheet that the old man had used when fishing in the rain was neatly rolled up and tucked away there. "Better than any raincoat," he'd told Hasher when they got caught in a cloudburst on the lake one day and huddled together under the black rubber sheet. "Gives you plenty of freedom to move about and isn't as hot as one of those slickers."

Now Hasher took the rolled bundle and hurried back to the cabin. Inside the front door, he stopped and listened intently, his heart pounding again and the blood throbbing in his temples. A car motor? Worthy! Panicked, Hasher looked wildly around the room. Had he left the door to the study open? He could see in his mind the body of Lyndon Johnson James lying on its back, the eyes and the teeth so white against the dark skin.

Hasher ran the length of the room, flung the rolled rubber sheet into the study, and yanked the door closed. Leaning against it and trying to get his breath, he realized that the kitchen door was unlocked—the way he had found it, the way James had left it. The boy must have taken the key from its hiding place under the eaves. Now where was it? Hasher asked himself frantically—in the lock on the inside of the door or in one of James's pockets? Either way—! He swore viciously. Whoever was coming might know where the key was kept. When it wasn't there—! He swore again.

Hasher nearly screamed when he realized that he had left the gun on the chair in the room behind him. He turned to go back and get it but stopped as it occurred to him that if it was Worthy, he would surely spot the gun's bulge in Hasher's pocket. But then if it was somebody else—Vivian or Rail or Rail's agent—and they had a gun. . . .

"It's over," Hasher whispered.

A car door closed, then another. He ran to the kitchen and peered out through the window over the sink. A white car, its parking lights on, stood a hundred yards down the rutted drive to the cabin. A few feet closer was the wavering beam of a flashlight. It must be a police car, Hasher decided.

He found the key inside the lock on the kitchen door. Pausing a second, he yanked it out and shoved it into his pocket. He grabbed the bottle of whisky and the glass he had used and ran back to the living room. Putting them down on a table beside the big chair facing the fireplace, Hasher took a box of kitchen matches off the mantelpiece, knelt down, and lit the wadded newspaper under the kindling and logs. When the paper was burning well enough, he slid the cover off the matchbox and shoved both box and cover into the flames. A moment later, the fire burst into a roaring crackling blaze. Quickly then, Hasher moved back and sat, slumped, in the big easy chair and poured some whisky into the glass. He took a swallow and waited.

If they looked around the outside of the house before coming in, they would find the boat of course. If it was the Sheriff or Vivian, either one would be suspicious at that. Then they would want to come inside. And there was nothing to stop them. Hasher jerked forward an inch and muttered, "Oh my God!" He slumped back into the chair and let his head sink into the thick soft cushion and closed his eyes. He had forgotten the creel lying by the side of the cabin. Once again, he was sure it was all over.

Hasher was gazing pensively into the leaping flames a few seconds later when the beam from a powerful flashlight swept over his face. As terrified as if he hadn't set the scene, he leaped to his feet, dropping his glass and crying out, *"Who's there?"*

There was no answer.

Blinded by the light, he put a forearm over his eyes and waited in terror.

There was a click and a lamp beside the great stone fireplace went on.

Hasher lowered his arm and stared wide-eyed at Worthy. *"Jesus Christ!"* he cried, enraged. "Are you trying to give me a stroke?" Hasher looked down at the broken glass on the hearthstone, then back at the Sheriff, and slumped down in the chair. "I know, I know, I'm not supposed to be here."

"I thought we had an agreement," Worthy said mildly. He went out to the kitchen and Hasher heard him say to his deputy, "It's okay. Go cover the radio."

Worthy came back carrying two glasses. He scuffed the broken glass on the hearth into the fireplace, handed Hasher one of the glasses, and sat down in the other chair facing the fireplace a few feet away. Hasher poured a drink for himself and handed the bottle to Worthy, who carefully poured an inch or so of whisky into his glass and sat back. The two men looked at the fire in silence. Hasher examined it nervously, looking for traces of the match box. There weren't any but the fire had dwindled from its first blaze and the biggest log on top was hardly scorched.

Worthy took a sip of his drink. "You haven't been here long, have you?"

All that Hasher could think of was the boy's eyes in the room behind them. "I don't know how long," he said. "Half an hour. An hour. Why?"

Instead of answering, Worthy asked, "Why are you here at all?"

Hasher shifted in his chair so that he could see him. "I'm in trouble, Bill."

Worthy waited for a moment, then asked, "What kind of trouble?"

"Bad trouble."

Worthy continued to stare at him but didn't repeat his question. Finally, he turned back to the fire and took another drink.

They were silent for awhile until Hasher quietly said, "It may sound trite but he was a father to me. He practically brought me up after his wife and my folks were killed. You know all that."

The Sheriff nodded.

"Whatever I am, whatever I have I owe to him."

Worthy didn't speak for a long time but at last he said, "I liked Mr. Slocum, too. A lot. You may not know it but he made a hefty contribution to both my election campaigns."

Hasher hadn't known it and looked surprised.

"He was a decent man, it seemed," the Sheriff went on hesitantly. "Decent to me anyway. Decent to the town, even though he didn't really live here full time. Decent to the people. The Boys Group—" He broke off, embarrassed, then gave Hasher a sudden sarcastic look. "Are you trying to commune with him? Have you gone batshit?"

Hasher feigned a look of surprise. "Not commune, actually. No spirits or anything crazy. Contact is all. I need the contact. I thought if I came here and sat by the fire with a glass of whisky, the way he did—put myself in his place, that is—I might get an idea, an insight, a hint, some kind of clue." He thought about the body in the next room and repressed a shudder.

"A clue about what?"

"I don't know. If I knew, I wouldn't be here."

Worthy got up slowly and leaned against the mantelpiece with his back to the low fire and looked around the

60 /

room carefully—all too carefully, Hasher thought in fear. Had the door to the study been closed when they left the cabin together the day before?

"You still think they killed him?" Worthy asked suddenly.

Hasher shook his head. "I don't know. I admit it doesn't look like it. All I know is that what happened doesn't make sense. It wasn't like Lucius Slocum to take his own life. Something's wrong."

Worthy walked to the front window and stood with his back to Hasher, who was terrified that he would see the rowboat. Apparently, though, the reflective glass of the window, the dark porch, the screens enclosing it, and the darkness beyond obscured his view. He turned. "You're a a lawyer. You know what happens when a civilian interferes with the police."

Hasher nodded.

Worthy came back to stand by the fireplace as before. "Don't get in the way, Thomas. You have any suspicions, any facts, any evidence, you come to me. In these parts I'm the law. Don't get in my way."

"Is that a threat, Bill?"

Smiling for the first time, Worthy took out a pack of cigarettes, lit one, and threw the match into the fire. "You've known me for going on thirty years," he said. "We played together as kids. Now, would I threaten you?"

Hasher smiled up at him. "I believe you would." He paused, then asked, "How come you just happened to come by while I was here? The lights weren't on. Was it the smoke from the fire?"

Worthy's lips tightened around the end of the cigarette as he inhaled. "Vivian Slocum asked me to check on the place every day."

"I thought *you* were the law around here," Hasher said with a smile.

Worthy's face went hard and Hasher realized that he had gone too far. He mustn't antagonize this man. Hastily he went on, "You know, Lucius used to talk about the law a lot. He loved it—I believe more than anything in the world except Mary. He lived by it and through it, he believed in it the way some people believe in God. And he was destroyed by it."

The hard set of Worthy's face eased. "How?" he asked. "I thought he destroyed himself. You said it was all lies but he didn't even try to defend himself."

"He couldn't," Hasher said. "He didn't have the proof. He had destroyed it to protect Vivian, and through her himself, from scandal."

"Can you prove that?"

"I don't know. But I'm going to try. I couldn't save his life but maybe I can save what it meant."

"Fair enough," the Sheriff said, looking relieved. "As long as it's all legal and above board—or even legal and below board. But don't get any ideas about taking the law into your own hands—not in my bailiwick anyway."

Again Hasher smiled. But an instant later he remembered the corpse in the next room and said, without thinking, "The law is a beast."

Worthy looked surprised—and hostile. He threw his cigarette into the fire.

Hasher couldn't stop himself. "It's simply an instrument by which people with power keep it. The law corrupts and finally destroys everyone who gets near it. It's an inferno of deceit." He was aghast at his words but they were out and he couldn't take them back.

"You prefer disorder, every man his own law?" the Sheriff asked, with a smile, as if the subject wasn't worth discussing.

"If that's the only way," Hasher answered, surprised at his calm certainty. "When society destroys its people or when it fails to protect them, they owe it nothing."

Worthy looked amused. "They don't have much choice."

Hasher knew that he had to stop. Turning away, he nodded, as if conceding defeat. "I'm bushed," he said. "I walked over here by the road and I don't feel much like walking back. How about a lift?" He drained the whisky left in his glass and felt his hand trembling.

"By the way, we've got a lead on James," the Sheriff said.

"Oh? Where?" Seeing the body in the next room, Hasher exerted the last bit of self-control he could muster as he looked directly at the Sheriff.

"Poughkeepsie. The police got a tag on him through an informer—"

"But you don't suspect him in Lucius's death."

"I still want to know what he was doing here that morning."

"Just as you want to know what I'm doing here now?"

"Yeah," Worthy said, smiling. "By the way, have you told me?"

"I thought so," Hasher answered, "but you didn't seem to want to understand." He turned away and picked up the whisky bottle and two glasses and walked to the kitchen. "Get the light, will you?" he called back.

He heard the fire screen sliding into place, then the light went out, and a moment later Worthy joined him at the back door.

"Where's the key?" Worthy asked.

Hasher took it out of his pocket and handed it to him. The Sheriff locked the door and Hasher said, "It goes up there, under the eaves. Here, I'll put it back." He held out his hand.

Worthy slipped the key into his pocket. "I'll keep it this time."

They turned and walked to the police car.

CHAPTER

6

For an hour Hasher waited, aching with the tension of
what he had gone through and was going through now as
he listened for the sound of a police car outside. If
Worthy had, on second thought, gone back to look around
the cabin, it would be over soon. Any plea of self-defense
would be futile now, Hasher knew. That might have held
up—but only after a police investigation, a long trial, and
sordid publicity—if he had called the police immediately.
But now the Sheriff had been sitting in the cabin, drinking
while on duty, with a corpse that was still warm lying in
the next room. Worst of all, he had been made a fool of.

Hasher went to the kitchen and heated a can of soup
and made some toast. He poured a glass of milk and sat
down at the small table in the corner. He knew that he
must eat, that he would need all the strength he could
drag out of himself for what lay ahead, but the food
nauseated him and he shoved it aside after a few mouth-
fuls.

With a groan he got up and went into the bedroom and
lay down. The face of the dead boy—the luminous eyes
and the white teeth—loomed before him in the darkness.
Hasher moaned and turned over, huddling under the comforter, trying to empty his mind. At last exhaustion drove
him into a fitful sleep. He mumbled disconnected words
and phrases and once he screamed as a rat sprang out
of the night at his throat. When he heard a siren, he cried

out and leaped off the bed and stumbled about the room in confused terror. The telephone rang several times before he realized that it wasn't a siren.

"I'm sorry I woke you," Margaret said when he answered groggily.

He looked at his watch: 10:32. It was time to get moving.

"I'm so worried about you," she said. "Why don't you come home? What good is it being there alone?"

From the start he had told himself that his vengeance on them would drive him away from Margaret. But he had believed it only in passing and in the back of his mind. He could not give her up, he told himself now, and yet knew that he already had.

"What?" she asked.

Hasher didn't answer. He only wondered if he had spoken his thoughts. "You can't demand that someone love you," he said finally, his voice angrier than he intended.

There was the sound of a gasp cut off. "Is that what you think—that I *demand* your love?" Her tone was angry now too.

"You didn't let me finish," he said hurriedly. "You can't demand that someone love you when they're all wrapped up in something else."

"Like hatred?"

"Maybe." His regret over what was happening, his helplessness nearly choked him. He had to save the little he had left. "I love you," he said softly.

There was silence on the other end. "Me too," Margaret said in a faint, trembling voice. "Come home. I need you."

"Me too," he repeated. "I'll be there soon." He hung up, despising himself.

This time he forced himself to eat. Afterwards, he found an old pewter flask in a drawer, filled it with whisky, and stuck it into his jacket pocket. He mustn't forget to retrieve the creel, he thought, and turned out the kitchen light.

Pushing the canoe into the water, he eased it alongside the dock and clambered in. As he paddled away, he felt the colder air rising off the water. He dipped a hand into it. *Jesus,* it was ice water! Could he do it? he asked himself. Whether he could do it or not, he knew that he had to try. It was his only chance.

Hasher was so absorbed by slipping the paddle into the water—silently—and pulling it back, taking it out—silently—and reaching forward for the next stroke that he nearly ran the canoe into an outcropping of rocks on the shore a hundred or so feet to the right of the cabin. Furiously digging the paddle into the mucky bottom, he stopped the canoe inches from the rocks and backpaddled until he was clear of them and headed for the dock. He came up to it slowly, careful not to make a sound, and took hold of the rough planks and pulled the canoe toward the shore. As it plowed into the reeds and wet earth, he clambered out and dragged it up beside the rowboat. He couldn't use that now, he knew; while it would have been far more suitable, he no longer had time to row it back here, now could he risk leaving his canoe at the cabin during the time the task would take. Running up to the porch, he grabbed the tarpaulin he had tossed there earlier and fastened it over the top of the rowboat, then shoved the boat back into its place under the porch.

Hasher let himself into the cabin with his own key, which the old man had given him many years before, locked the door, and stood in the dark kitchen, his heart pounding again. He had no more time to waste, even on fear, he told himself. Besides, if Worthy had found the body, he wouldn't be sitting here waiting for the murderer to return.

Crossing the kitchen, Hasher walked carefully through the dark living room to the study door. He paused there, then cursed himself for his weakness and entered the room.

"Jesus Christ!" he muttered in disgust. He had left the flashlight on. It was lying on the seat of the straight chair, its beam aimed directly at the door and lighting the corpse on the floor. If Worthy or his deputy had made a circuit outside the cabin before coming in and seen the dim light from the study window on the porch. . . . If Worthy had glanced at the crack under the study door and seen light there in the moments before he turned on his own flashlight and then the lamp by the fireplace. . . . Hasher cursed his own folly.

"Hopeless!" he muttered.

Moving quickly now, as if to restore his confidence, Hasher searched the boy's clothing for anything that might identify him. All he found was a cheap worn wallet containing a driver's license (in someone else's name); eight stubs from welfare checks, each in the amount of $42.84; torn slips of paper with names, addresses, and telephone numbers; other slips with only numbers; a good-luck charm—a sleazy aluminum horseshoe; and $62 in cash. He shoved the wallet into his own back pocket and got up.

Looking at the dark rectangle of the window behind the desk, Hasher saw that although there were no curtains, there was a curtain rod along the top. If he hoped to do the job quickly, he would need more light than the flash provided. Closing the study door behind him, he went to the closet beside it and took out one of the Navy blankets. After he had hung it over the curtain rod, he put the desk lamp on the floor in front of the desk's kneehole, switched it on, and hurried out to the porch in front. Only the faintest glimmer of light was visible at the top, not enough to be noticeable unless someone was standing on the porch. And if someone was standing on the porch. . . . He shrugged and went back inside.

Within twenty minutes Hasher had the body rolled up in the rubber sheet and bound with some of the medium-gauge rope from the closet. The face had been the worst part, especially the eyes. He'd had to cover the face with a small towel from the closet before he could go on and he knew he would never forget. The hands were difficult too—long narrow sensitive hands with rose-colored nails. He had tied the wrists together and then the ankles before wrapping the body in the sheet, to prevent a limb from flopping loose and blocking the entrance of the body into the hole in the rock.

With this, the most revolting part of his task, completed, Hasher stood up, feeling a little better. But as he glanced around the room and saw all that was still to be done, the feeling vanished. He shook his head. Cleaning up would have to wait. The body was first.

He cut off another length of rope, about twenty feet long, doubled it back on itself, and tied the ends together and then to the rope around the foot of the bundled corpse. The simplest way would be to drag the body along the floor of the study and living room, out across the porch, down the ramp to the dock, he told himself but then realized that splinters of wood would get embedded in the rubber and if the corpse were found, the police could easily trace the murder back to this spot.

He flicked on the flashlight, turned off the lamp, and opened the door. Moving back to the body, Hasher knelt on his right knee and slipped one arm under the boy's neck and the other under his knees. With a slow lugging movement he lifted the bundle a few inches off the floor. Then, with a grunting lurch, he got it onto his knee. He paused to get his breath. Rising upright suddenly, he flung the body up and over his right shoulder, the head over his back, the legs hanging in front. He turned and staggered to the door, then slowly, carefully made his way in the dark down the length of the living room toward the dim light of the windows and the door between them. He almost fell once but stumbled on, opened the door with his left hand, crossed the porch, shoved the screen door open, and half ran with his burden along the ramp and to the end of the dock.

Hasher let the corpse roll off his shoulder. It landed on the planks with a thud. Taking the looped end of the rope he had tied to the ankles, he shoved the bundle with one foot. It rolled over. He shoved it again. It rolled over and with another thrust of his foot he pushed it into the water, then tied the rope to an upright support beneath the dock.

Kneeling on the planks, Hasher peered down in the dark. The white rope was barely visible as the bundle floated submerged a few inches below the surface. The air inside the wrapping, he thought, and the air in the boy's lungs. That was fine, exactly as he wanted it.

He got up and ran back into the cabin. Taking the flashlight from the study, he went into the kitchen and found two plastic shopping bags. He returned to the study, closed and locked the door behind him, turned the lamp back on, and went to work. First he replaced the books that James had pushed or flung onto the floor. Some were in sets and, cursing the lost time, he put them back in the best order he could manage, for he knew that Worthy, or even Vivian, might notice, since they knew how tidy the old man had been. Next Hasher swept the loose pages that had fallen out of the dry old books together into a pile. Fitting those back in place in the books, he knew, would have taken hours; anyway, who would notice, except possibly a secondhand bookseller months later if the books were disposed of? And by then some missing pages from some worthless books could hardly be incriminating.

As Hasher picked up a handful of the pages from the floor, he felt something sticky and looked at his fingers. It was half-dried blood, still moist from being between the pages. He shuddered and wiped the blood off onto some clean pages. It must have been from when he kicked the boy in the mouth, he thought. Then he saw the two teeth. One was stuck to a page near his knee, the other was at the foot of the bookcase.

Suddenly he leaned forward, gagging, and vomited into one of the shopping bags. All that he had thrust out of his mind—the boy's bloody mouth, his contorted face as he flung himself screaming, the gleaming knife poised above him, the roar of the gun, James slumping to his knees, his dead eyes open in the half-dark—all of it spun madly through Hasher's mind. He knelt, retching time after time, until, drained and exhausted, he fell to the floor and lay, moaning, his knees drawn up foetally.

At last the seizure passed and with a groan Hasher raised himself to his knees. He covered the teeth and the blood-smeared pages with other pages, wadded them up, and thrust them into the clean bag. He tied up the bag he had been sick in and dropped it in with the papers. Then he quickly swept the remaining pages on the floor together and put them in the bag, together with the few remaining feet of rope that he had used from the coil and the boy's wallet. He knotted the top of the shopping bag and placed it by the door.

Hasher crawled around the room searching for any telltale signs. All he found were three dark-brown spots, each the size of a nickel, lined up in a row about six inches apart, near where the boy had fallen when he was shot. Hasher peered at them. They seemed too dark for freshly dried blood but he couldn't be sure, so he gently scraped the surface above one of them with James's knife. Wax, he saw as he examined the blade. The spot was intact underneath. Blood or not, it was old.

The knife—slender, with a five-inch incredibly sharp blade and a black handle—seemed more deadly to him now than the gun as he remembered that flashing blade above him. He figured out the switch mechanism and swung the blade back into its handle, snapped it out, and swung it back again. It was paltry evidence now, he knew, but it was the only evidence that he might have acted in self-defense. Slipping it into his pocket, he looked around the room again. Everything seemed all right, just as it had been before. He was desperately anxious to get out of the cabin but, recalling his earlier carelessness about the flashlight, he forced himself to examine every inch of the room again.

When he finished, he turned off the lamp, put it back in place on the desk, and climbed up to take down the blanket. He folded it and stuck it under one arm, then shone the flashlight around the room one last time, picked up the shopping bag and the gun, and left, closing the door behind him. He locked the front door to the living room from the inside, walked carefully through the dark cabin to the kitchen door, unlocked it, stepped outside, relocked the door, and ran around the side of the cabin toward the dock.

Halfway there, Hasher went sprawling. He lay on the rough turf for a few moments, cursing his clumsiness, until he discovered the cause of his fall. The creel. "Jesus Christ!" he muttered. He had forgotten it again and if he hadn't fallen over it, he would have left it there for someone, probably Worthy, to find.

"Hopeless, hopeless, hopeless," he said softly and got up. He stood motionless for a minute, wondering if he was trying to get caught before he killed again.

It was colder on the lake now than it had been an hour earlier. Hasher tested the water: forty-five to fifty degrees, he calculated, and shivered. Peering through the darkness, he searched for the darker shore and the great rock. If he came out above it—or, worse, if he didn't know where he was—he would have to paddle back and forth along the bank until he found the place and the body might get entangled in branches of the trees that had fallen into the water along the shore.

He swore softly.

For the twentieth time, Hasher craned around to see if the doubled rope was still tied to the crossbar at the rear of the canoe. It was. He slowed his paddling, then resumed it rapidly, to see if the body floating, half-submerged, ten feet behind the canoe tugged at the rope. It did. He pulled the paddle back in too shallow an arc and icy water splashed onto his face and dripped down the front of his jacket. His knees were already soaked from earlier splashes. Again he wondered if he could do it and again he knew that he had to.

Something white appeared ahead and Hasher stopped paddling. As the canoe drifted closer, he saw that the object was the trunk of a large birch tree that had fallen into the lake, its roots still clinging to land. A moment later he remembered the tree and that the rock was beyond it, perhaps a hundred yards farther on. Swinging the canoe around and paddling back out into the lake to avoid the submerged branches at the tip of the tree, Hasher passed that hazard and swung back toward the shore. A few minutes later he saw the great rock, its white surface gray in the darkness, looming ahead. He stopped paddling and let the canoe glide toward it. Now the worst part of all, he thought. Then it would be over.

Once he had moored the canoe and tied both ends of it to small trees so that the craft was parallel to the bank, Hasher climbed to the top of the rock. Staring down at the water ten feet below, he tried to remember how old he had been when he discovered the place. Twelve? Probably. How often had he gone in there? Half a dozen times a summer perhaps, until he was fifteen. It was about then that the reeds had begun growing on this side of the lake, spoiling it for swimming. Hasher stood, wondering if it was the same now, twenty-five years after he had last been there. As far as he knew, no one else had been aware of the place when he was a boy and he had kept his secret. If anyone had learned of it, it wouldn't matter since no one swam in this, the reedy part of the lake, anymore.

Sitting down on the rock, Hasher took off his shoes and socks. He stood up, shivering, and pulled the jacket and sweater over his head together. Then he slipped out of his corduroy pants. He left on his shorts; the thought of the reeds or something slimy on his genitals was too much. Shuddering now in the cold, he slid down the side of the rock to the bank, at a spot just behind the canoe, rose to his toes, and made a shallow dive over the rope holding the bundled corpse.

For an instant he thought he had struck something but realized that it was only the shock of the cold water. Dazed, he surfaced and as his body swung downward he felt the reeds tangling his legs. Jesus, he thought in panic, he and James might stay here together. Turning around, he swam back to the rock, grabbed a tendril of a root, and felt it pull loose from the earth. He grabbed a thicker one; it held. Again his legs swung down into the reeds. He thrashed about frantically, then finally got hold of himself. Panic was his worst enemy, he knew. It could kill him.

"So could this fucking water!" he muttered. He had never been so cold. Paddling back to the canoe, he reached over the side and fumbled around the bottom until he found James's flashlight. It was encased in rubber and to his relief it worked under water.

First he must find out if the place was the same, before he took the body in; otherwise he could never be sure that it wouldn't be found one day. Hasher knew he didn't have much time. After the initial shock of his immersion in the icy water, he had temporarily recovered and now even felt reasonably comfortable. But the cold was slowly numbing his nerves and muscles, impeding his movements, confusing his perceptions. He didn't have much time.

Staring up at the great rock rising above to get his bearings, Hasher lifted his head, took a deep gulp of air, and dove down directly through the reeds toward the submerged center of the rock. The rock was murkier than it had been when he swam there as a boy and the reeds were so thick that the flashlight was nearly useless; it was nothing like the filtered sunlight of the bright sunny day years ago when he had discovered the cavern.

Still, he found the hole in the rock almost at once, some four feet below the surface, and shone the light into it. As far as he could tell, everything was the same, although the hole itself was smaller than he recalled. Of course it would seem so, he told himself; he had been only fifteen then. He pulled out as many of the reeds rising in front of the hole as he could manage and rose to the surface.

Paddling there to keep afloat, he looked up at the domed white rock and remembered that he had thought of it as a head. The round top was the bald pate; the sloping narrow seam that came down from its forehead to the water was the nose; below the waterline—three feet below, he remembered now—was the hole, or lips, as he had once thought of them. They were about a foot thick and beyond them was the cavernous mouth inside the stone head.

Hasher took another gulp of air and dove. He went directly through the lips—suddenly terrified that he would get wedged in them and die there. But he slipped through easily and once inside the mouth, a cavern within the rock, he pressed his feet against the inner wall beside the hole and thrust himself upward, toward the airspace at the top. As his flashlight struck rock, he lowered his arms and raised his face. He breathed through his nose and inhaled water. Choking and gasping desperately, he swallowed water and more went into his lungs. Instantly he realized in horror that the water level of the lake had risen. There was no air space! The domed inner crown, some eight feet across and a foot high in the center and formerly filled with air, was now filled with water.

Frantic, Hasher put his feet against the stone roof and thrust himself downward to find the exit. His lungs were bursting and he knew he was close to death. But there was no hole! He must have got turned around. No more! No more! he screamed to himself in terror.

In a final desperate act, Hasher rose like a rocket to the top and pressed his lips against the domed ceiling. Air! He gulped it, coughing and gasping and choking. It was fetid dead air but air nonetheless. Shining the light above his head, he saw that he had been right: the lake had risen and so had the level of water inside the hollow rock; now the open space was reduced to a two-foot circle at the very center of the dome and it was only three or four inches high at its highest point.

He breathed slowly, deeply, trying to calm himself and restore his lung capacity. Realizing after a minute that the air probably contained little oxygen and that at this rate he would soon deplete what was there and black out and drown. Hasher took one last gulp and dove back for the hole. This time he found it at once, squeezed through, and shot to the surface of the lake. Nothing had ever tasted as good to him as the night air and nothing had ever looked as beautiful to him as the dark sky.

What an idiot he had been to go inside the cavern at all! he told himself. As he clung to the side of the canoe to rest, he imagined, for the first time, the mad folly of the twelve-year-old child who had entered the cavern without a thought of the danger, without any awareness that unless there was an air space inside, he would perish and never be found.

It took Hasher four dives before he got enough of the reeds out to clear the mouth of the entrance to the cavern. Then he took the bundled corpse down and got its feet and lower legs into the hole. The body was rigid now, for rigor mortis had begun to set in, but Hasher managed, in two more dives, to push the body all the way through except for the shoulders and head. He realized now that he had wrapped the rubber sheet too many times around that part—in an unconscious attempt to conceal the face —and he went up for air three more times and dove again and again before he had freed the rope around the end sufficiently to unwrap part of the sheet. At last the body slid into the hole. But as it did the rubber flapped loose and James's face appeared, his great white eyes staring into the dim beam of light toward Hasher. A moment later the face vanished as he gave one last shove to the soaked and matted hair of the boy's head.

Hasher rose to the surface and took several deep breaths. His eyes were starting, his mouth contorted in horror. Suddenly he buried his face in the water and screamed.

CHAPTER

7

The apartment, on East 73rd Street, was fairly large and very comfortable. On the twelfth floor of a solid brown-brick building, which had been erected when walls were walls, it contained a good-sized white-marble-floored foyer; a capacious living room with a fireplace and an elegant carved green-marble mantel; a kitchen that was big enough for two people to move about in and, if they liked, to take breakfast or lunch in at a small round table in one corner; two full baths, each with a large deep tub and a big old-fashioned basin; and three bedrooms. The furnishings of the main room were in the mode of what decorators like to call "traditional"—big soft easy chairs, a highbacked down-cushioned sofa, some antique tables and wood side chairs, bulbous china and slender brass lamps, a gray-and-blue-and-gold Chinese rug, dark and bright fabric coverings, warm yellow curtains, and many pictures and books.

Margaret Green and Thomas Hasher had signed the lease together, they had searched for the furnishings together, they had split the costs and paid all the bills together, and now, as usual after a meal, they were washing the dishes together.

Hasher was glumly regarding a dirty frying pan when Margaret said, "It didn't go very well, did it?"

Hasher shook his head without speaking. The brunch with the Wilsons had gone worse than not very well. After returning to the cottage and disposing of the evidence from the old man's cabin, Hasher had bundled up in warm clothes and sat by the heater drinking hot whisky and lemon juice. Exhausted, he had slept only three hours, got up with a sickening hangover, called Margaret to say he would be there in a few hours, taken the diary, and fled from Lake Mercy.

As soon as he arrived at the apartment, half an hour before the Wilsons, he made a huge pitcher of Bloody Marys and gulped one down when Margaret went to answer the door.

Sam Wilson, a tousled and deceptively jovial man, had made a fortune in New York real estate and had retained Slocum, Whitby & Barker to set up various trusts for his children and a tax-free foundation to keep his money from what he called "the I.R.S. rapists." Hasher didn't like Wilson but, as Margaret had reminded him, the man was his biggest client; losing him would be a disaster, for both Hasher and the firm.

He couldn't help himself. He had hoped that the Wilsons would distract him—and delay the conversation he was going to have to have with Margaret—but instead his own distraction ruined the affair. Gloomily silent during most of the brunch, he forced himself to eat the kippers and scrambled eggs and hashed-brown potatoes that ordinarily he would have consumed with pleasure. He had two more Bloody Marys and three glasses of white wine and then wanted only to go to sleep.

Wilson tried to get him to talk about "the Slocum scandal," as he put it, and Hasher retorted curtly, "That will be cleared up soon, I assure you, to your own satisfaction." When pressed to explain, he said that he couldn't just then. Margaret looked at him in alarm and curiosity but Hasher would say no more.

Wilson fell silent then, too, and the room reverberated under the noisy chatter of Betty Wilson, a foolish bleached-blonde woman of fifty, of whom Hasher had once said, "She's had everything lifted except her mind."

Now Margaret faced him determinedly. "What is it, Thomas?"

"What is *what?*" he said angrily and began scrubbing the frying pan furiously.

"You know what! What did you find up there?"

He turned on her and said through clenched teeth, "Can't you see I'm exhausted?"

"I see that," she said calmly. "I also see that something terrible has happened to you. I have a right to know, a *need* to know. Naturally I wasn't as close to Lucius as you were but I'm closer to you than he was. If we're going to be together, we're going to be together all the way or not at all."

She was right, he knew at once, she nearly always was. He had hoped to find some way of not telling her what he had learned because it would drag her into it and might even lead her to suspect him later on when he moved against the others. About Lyndon Johnson James's death, he was determined to say nothing. But he realized now that he would have to tell her the rest—and soon.

Hasher looked at Margaret and saw that she knew she was losing him, probably had lost him; he saw too the helplessness in her eyes, the pained weariness in her face. Again he was overcome by his own agony of regret over what he was giving up. Suddenly he grabbed Margaret and clung to her, as if for the last time, and buried his face in her hair so that she couldn't see his eyes.

"I'll tell you all about it—tonight," he said. "But now I've *got* to sleep."

Has mankind devised anything more wondrous than this—the bed? Hasher thought, as he slipped, naked, between the fresh cool sheets. Birth, dreams, illness and recovery, escape, thoughts and ideas, sex, sleep, and death all took place here. It seemed miraculous to him that so much of one's life, and what was most crucial to it, passed in one place. He pressed his head into the soft comfort of the pillow and pulled the covers up to his neck and waited for the only solace he could hope for now. Almost at once it came and he fell into a deep sleep.

He awoke four hours later when Margaret slipped into bed, also naked, and embraced him. They held one another caressingly, murmuring of their love. He put a hand between her legs and found that she was ready and entered her. They moved together in a slow rhythm for a long time, almost without passion, until she reached her climax in a rising moan of wonder. "Oh. Oh. Oh. Oh. Oh. Oh. Ohhhh." He held her closely, as her back arched and she nearly pulled away from him, to enjoy her pleasure fully, and then he plunged fiercely into her and cried out in his own joy. They lay silently afterward, consoled for now, and when he turned to kiss her he tasted her tears.

Was this the last time? he wondered, sinking into empty despair. He was glad he hadn't thought of that at the start.

They lay still, in silence, until he felt himself drifting back into sleep. He groaned and got up. "I'm hungry."

Margaret laughed. "That's news?" He was always hungry after he made love.

They fixed supper together—cold roast beef, dark bread, cheese, a salad, and a bottle of red wine. When they finished eating, she poured more wine for both of them and sat back, glass in hand, and said, "I'm ready."

Hasher nodded. He dreaded the recital of all that deceit and malevolence and pain for what it would cost him in telling it. But maybe if she understood what had happened to Lucius, she would understand what was happening to him. Leaving out everything about finding James at the cabin, Hasher told her about Vivian's telephone call, about Worthy's arrival at the cabin, and, as concisely as he could manage, every detail in the old man's diary.

Margaret listened in silence, except for a few brief questions as he went along, and he saw on her face all of the emotions that had affected him when he had read the diary: astonishment, disgust, anger, pain. At the end he saw that she was silently weeping.

"That poor man," she murmured. Looking across the

table at Hasher, she shook her head. "And you too. . . .
I'm so sorry, Thomas."

When he realized how this sharing had brought them
together, he wished he could go further and tell her the
rest. But he knew he couldn't. Getting up, he started a
fire, and stood for a minute with his back to her and
watched the flickers of flame gathering.

"You're going to Judge Manelli with this, of course,"
she said.

"I don't know," Hasher answered.

"But why not? My God—"

He turned. "You didn't go to the trial or read the
transcript. Manelli was against Lucius from the start. He
ran the trial as if he was on Rail's payroll." He paused
and shrugged. "Maybe he was. It happens. They're just
people too."

"Wicknor then?"

Hasher nodded. He would have to go to the old man's
lawyer first, if only for the sake of legal propriety, but he
hadn't much hope there either. It would mean asking
Wicknor to buck the system, to get up and say that a
court had permitted a grave and unnecessary injustice, a
grievous wrong, that it had allowed an innocent man who
lived at the heart of its own system to be driven to his
death. No, Hasher thought, Wicknor was not one to rock
boats.

"And your partners?"

"I have to tell them of course." Hasher watched her
somberly. "When I submit my resignation—tomorrow."

Appalled, Margaret could only stare at him in silence.

"After Lucius devoted forty years of his life to the
firm, they wouldn't even listen to him. How could I
possibly go on working with such men? I have no choice."

"But what will you do?"

"I'll manage. Over the years I've put a good bit aside
and my investments have done pretty well. If I had to,
I could live quite awhile without working."

He looked at the fire and wondered if James's death

had left him with a debt owed to society. But the idea seemed absurd; it was, in truth, only a game.

"All I know is that I'm through with the law," he said, turning back to Margaret. "It sickens me."

"Thomas, you've got to get hold of yourself."

"That's exactly what I'm doing—for the first time in my life," he said, angry now.

They were silent and at last she asked, "What about me?"

He looked at her in surprise. "How does that change anything for you? With Lucius and me gone, they'll have to promote a couple of associates. Who better than you?"

"Won't they punish me?"

"After I tell them they're a pack of scoundrels?"

She nodded.

"It's likelier they'd punish you for their own cowardice. But I don't think they'd dare. I might talk. A word here, a word there about how they let an innocent man—a friend, a colleague, in some cases the man who had personally hired and trained them—how they let him be destroyed."

Again they were silent, staring at the fire, until Margaret spoke: "It seems so drastic. Shouldn't you wait? Cool off?"

Hasher shook his head firmly. "That wouldn't change anything. I know what I've got to do."

She sighed. "I'll miss you so during the day."

He looked at her and saw her lips tremble as she tried to smile. God, I love her, he thought, and turned away in pain.

They finished their wine and he made coffee and washed the dishes while it brewed.

When he handed her a cup of it, she said, "I put your mail on your desk."

Hasher stood by the fire, smiling down at her fondly, amazed again at her tact and how well she knew him; she sensed that he wanted to be alone.

The two extra bedrooms had been fixed up as studies, so that they could work in peace or escape each other into solitude. His desk was a plain pine table and in the center of it he found half a dozen letters, an announcement of a lawyer friend's move to another firm, a fall catalogue from L. L. Bean, and a padded envelope-bag of the kind that books are mailed in. He glanced through the letters quickly and turned to the bag. There was no address sticker on the front, only his name and address hand-printed in block letters directly on the bag itself.

He looked more closely at the letters and gasped. They had been printed by Lucius Slocum. The postmark was blurred but it seemed to be dated the previous Saturday, two days before the old man's body was found. The bag had been sealed with staples and masking tape. Hasher smiled as he opened it, remembering that the old man always instructed the firm's secretaries to seal such bags with masking tape so that postal workers wouldn't scratch themselves on staples.

Inside the bag was a large manila envelope and a smaller letter-sized white envelope. His hands trembling, Hasher opened the first and pulled out what he quickly saw was a Xerox copy of the diary he had found in the cabin. The plain envelope contained a letter to him:

My dear Thomas,

By the time you read this, my dilemma will have been resolved. Yours, if you see it that way, will just be beginning. Whether or not you choose to act must in no way seem to you an obligation to me or, even more, to yourself. Remember always that as an old man my life, while still precious, hadn't long to go on anyway, while yours is full of the richness of hope and challenge, possibility and fulfillment. You owe me nothing, except a decent memory. I beg of you: Do not lose what you have and may have for that which is already lost.

Enough of that; you are a grown man, a strong man, an independent man, and will do as you see fit.

If you did not find the diary that I left in my study in the cabin, you will not know what the enclosed Xerox copy is. I left, at the far right end of the second-from-the-bottom shelf on the bookcase in the study, a diary written in an old-fashioned, red, imitation-leather record book, stuck between Hawthorne and Melville. On the shelf directly below are all the court papers in Slocum vs. Slocum.

Hasher paused, wondering when the old man had written these words. A day, two days before he shot himself? My God, he thought, the equanimity, the poise he'd had as he faced death. Or had it been only weariness, despair? Hasher went back to the letter:

My reasons for leaving the diary there and sending you this copy, rather than simply sending you the original, were, first, to lead you to understand most of what had happened and, second, to mislead anyone else (James or Rail or Vivian) into believing that they now possessed, and could destroy, the only remaining "evidence" of their misdeeds.

The truth is somewhat different from what I wrote there.

Stunned, Hasher sat back. "The truth is somewhat different. . . ." My God, he thought, sickened, had he killed someone out of a mistake? Quickly he read on:

Everything I wrote in the diary was true, except for two points: I did not burn the blackmail letter from Lyndon Johnson James, and I did not fling Vivian's love note to him in her face when I left her. The piece of paper I burned for Miss Morley's benefit was from a ruled pad I had in my desk; I had merely scrawled on it in pencil, then held it up before her—it was similar enough to the original to deceive her in her bitter embarrassment—and burned it. The note from Vivian, fortunately (or unfortunately now for you, perhaps), had been written in black ink on a smooth piece of white paper, admirably suited for Xeroxing; the copy, which I flung at her, was indistinguishable from the original, except for a few smudges from James's hand; I even creased and recreased and pressed the copy in a curved state to make it appear that it had reposed in the boy's wallet for some time.

Hasher sat back, smiling in wonder. He had fooled them all! But then Hasher wondered why he hadn't presented the boy's letter and her note to the court? Or at least to her and Rail? Wouldn't that have been enough? He turned back to the letter:

You are wondering, of course, why I didn't use these documents to defend myself in the divorce suit. The answer is: I did. I gave copies of them to Mr. Wicknor. He pointed out, after careful consideration, that if he presented the originals to the court—say during cross-examination of James and my wife—it would be impossible to prove when they had been written (since neither was, of course, dated), that the blackmail letter had been written by James voluntarily (rather than, for example, under some kind of coercion from me), or that Vivian's note had not been written much later than it was (that is, long after our separation). Beyond these persuasive points, Wicknor assured me, as I already knew, that it would take handwriting experts, on both sides, days in court, and we would almost certainly end up with an inconclusive debate about whether the documents had been written by the hands we claimed. Finally, he observed, even if the jury believed us, that would serve only to besmirch my wife for her sexual misconduct and James for his greed. It would not wholly destroy the boy's claim about the homosexual affair, if it affected that claim at all. And it could not conceivably disprove Vivian's charge that I had stolen from the Lindsay estate, since my signatures were, as I had already testified, on the documents by which the money had been withdrawn.

All that Wicknor felt he could do with the letter and note was to show copies of them to Rail and say that we were fully prepared to use them in open court. Either Rail didn't believe they were authentic or he didn't care. He merely laughed when they were shown to him and walked away.

Hasher sat back for a moment to rest and consider what he had read. If they hadn't cared then, why did they care so desperately now? And that they did was made clear by Vivian's attempt to drive him out of the cabin. Or was it for some other reason? More bewildered than before, Hasher went back to the old man's letter:

In the end, I decided that the letter and note should not be used. I could see no advantage to myself, beyond adding the word "cuckold" to those already being used to describe me.

However, Thomas, the papers may be of some advantage to you.

Hasher put the letter down and picked up the envelope it had been in. But the documents weren't there. Nor were they in the book bag or the envelope with the copy of the diary. Had the old man forgotten, in his last fearful hours, to include them or had he hidden them somewhere else? Perhaps the letter would say:

If you have removed the diary, Thomas, I would suggest that you replace it. My only purpose was for them—or, most likely, Vivian—to find it, which would falsely reassure her that they are now safe, since it states that the only remaining evidence against them has been destroyed. I had to do that to protect you, the only part of my life I regret, and so deeply, leaving behind. If they believe that the letter and the note had survived me, they would never rest until they had them. They would contest my will to deprive you of the cabin and my books and papers—and at almost any cost. However little these documents may have been of use in a court of law, they would be deadly weapons in the hands of someone willing to use them in a public forum in a manner that I was unwilling to. Since I alone know the vicious lengths that these people will go to gain their ends, I alone can protect you from them, even now. Beware, Thomas, beware!

Now Hasher understood their desperation. They knew that he wouldn't hesitate for a moment to use the documents to avenge his old friend. But why? Hasher wondered. Why hadn't the old man told him all this and given him the diary and the blackmail letter and the note Vivian had dashed off in her sexual frenzy? Why now?

Hasher put a hand to his forehead and found that it was wet with perspiration. His neck and shoulders ached painfully and he wiped his face and leaned back in the high desk chair to rest. Dazed by what he had read, he gave up trying to solve the puzzles it created and went back to finish the letter:

I beg you to understand, my old and only friend: I am *not*, like Hamlet's father, returning now as a ghost to prompt your revenge. I am dead, Thomas, and I would be in peace.

All I want, all I ask, all I can hope for, in these last hours of my long life, is the remembrance and trust and love of the only person who matters to me now: Thomas Hasher.

Goodbye, my son.

As he looked at the final words—"Yours in memory"— and the firm signature of Lucius Slocum, Hasher felt tears running down his cheeks. He bowed his head and let them flow.

When he recovered at last, he sat for a long time pondering the questions raised by the letter—above all, the whereabouts of the documents, those "deadly weapons in the hands of someone willing to use them." Their absence infuriated him. Had the old man mailed them separately for safety's sake? But that would make no sense. If someone intercepted this parcel and found the documents missing, they would intercept a letter following as well. He sat forward. Was that what had happened? Then he shook his head in disgust with himself. A follow-up letter would be intercepted only if this had been intercepted first. He would get nowhere if he was as muddle-headed as that. Again he went through all the envelopes and the bag but found nothing. He slowly leafed page by page through the copy of the diary with no more success.

Finally he went back to the living room, where Margaret was reading some legal papers, and asked if she had given him all of his mail. She put her glasses on the top of her head and looked at him, puzzled, and nodded —as if to say no, she hadn't hidden his mail from him. Chagrined, he went back to his study and reexamined all the envelopes and all the mail that had been stacked there. Nothing.

He grabbed the book bag, clutched it furiously, and flung it across the room. Then he stared at it in the corner and went to retrieve it. Smoothing it out, he felt around it until he came to what he had sensed as he crumpled it before: a slight stiffening near the opening. Going back to the desk, he removed the staples in that portion and found, in the padding inside the bag, a slit about five inches long, Slipping a thumb and forefinger into the opening, he felt a paper packet and carefully eased it out. It was a small ordinary envelope. His name was written on the front in the old man's script.

Inside were three pieces of paper: James's blackmail letter, scrawled in pencil on green-lined paper torn out of a cheap notebook; Vivian's passionate plea, signed with a flaring V that she had filled in with tiny curlicues, like pubic hair; and a message signed "L. S.," which read:

Forgive the melodrama (or paranoia), Thomas, but it seemed wiser to hide these crucial papers additionally, in case someone else happened to open the bag before you got to it. Furthermore, I had to pass on to you this warning as secretly as possible: Vivian informed me, through Rail, after the trial that she possessed similar "evidence" about your having stolen money from a trust fund set up for the Poulson family, under your supervision. I can only assume that you unwittingly signed financial transfer papers in the same manner as I did.

She, again through Rail, warned that if you interfere with either of them in any way at any time in the future, this "evidence" will be transmitted immediately to the firm and to the District Attorney.

I cannot know if this story, or threat, is as fabricated as their "evidence." All I can do is tell you what I was told, and beg your forgiveness in having, however innocently, made you subject to their vicious blackmail, too.

Again, beware!

That was all. Hasher read the message with mounting anger and then fear. He tried to recall whether Vivian had ever given him papers to sign when she was the old man's secretary but it was too long ago, too many papers had crossed his desk for him even to hope that he might remember.

He put the papers back in the small envelope and sat unmoving, numbed by his helplessness. My God, she was clever, he thought. She had been aware, even years ago, that only he stood in her way, that only he would fight for the old man. And now he could fight no more. The trap had been laid and one step— He swore viciously. If he resigned from the firm now, that would solve only part of the problem, by far the lesser part, for then they would go to the D.A. He swore again. If only the old man had told him all this long before, during the trial, they could have fought it together. That way, they might have. . . . Hasher shook his head as he thought of Judge Manelli; it would have ended the same way.

Margaret knocked and came in to say that she was

going to bed. He nodded, scarcely hearing her. But when he saw her look of concern, he said that he would be along in a minute. As she smiled gently and pursed her lips in a kiss, he was stung again by a sense of loss. Before this final message from the old man, she might have been able to help, because Hasher, still the lawyer, had a slim hope that he might restore Lucius Slocum's good name through the law. Or, if not that way, then through publicity of some kind. Margaret could have helped there even more for she was a writer of uncommon skill and had an uncanny feel for when and where and how private matters should be made public.

He sat with his head in his hands at the desk, befuddled by weariness and despair. Those courses were closed now, he knew. The slightest move and Vivian and Rail would attack and it would be over. He had to give up. He could quit the firm—if there was a firm to quit—but that was all. Surrender and forget it. Let Vivian have the cabin and everything else. Take Margaret and go away. Give up. Forget it.

Again he saw the boy's great staring eyes in the dark water as the corpse slid into the stone tomb.

CHAPTER

8

The mood at Slocum, Whitby & Barker was apparent
to Margaret and Hasher as soon as they crossed the reception room and said "Good morning" to the young
woman at the desk. A lovely creature with long red hair,
she was ordinarily a person of indomitable cheerfulness
but now she gave them a glum look and a glummer
"Morning" and looked away.

They had been Lucius Slocum's close friends, so they
were responsible, Hasher thought as he paused at the first
turn in the inside corridor to say goodbye to Margaret.
She touched his arm and said, "Remember, Thomas."

He managed a nod and a smile. At breakfast she had
spoken at length, almost a lecture, about how Lucius
would have wanted above all that the firm be saved.
Hasher hadn't been at all sure about that, not after the
way the members of the firm had behaved, but he heard
her out and even acted as if he agreed. The only way to
save the place, she had gone on, was by his telling the
partners exactly what had happened. He had the diary,
the only weapon left, and now was the time to use it.

Hasher also had doubts about the effects of such a
course. These people were concerned only with saving
themselves. And even if he could persuade them to save
the firm instead, or at least to try, how could they convince their frightened clients, or the gossips at their clubs,
or the legal world at large that the old man had been

vilely traduced and was innocent of all charges? As Hasher parted from Margaret, he was almost certain that it was too late. They wouldn't listen. He could imagine their reactions to his bizarre story: doubt, suspicion, disbelief, fear of the consequences of libel and slander suits by Rail and Vivian.

One of the partners, Will Moss, had apparently asked to be told when Hasher arrived for he came into the office a minute after Hasher sat down.

"Hello, Will."

"Thomas," Moss said and slumped into a deep leather chair. He looked ill—his eyes red, his face puffy and gray, his hands shaking—but then Hasher realized that he was merely hungover.

"It's that bad?" he asked.

"Worse," Moss said. "Where the hell have you been?" Before he got an answer, he waved a hand to dismiss the question. "It doesn't matter. Not a damn. Nothing can save the firm now."

"Where I've been and what I've been doing might," Hasher replied calmly. He hadn't expected to say that; in fact he hadn't planned what he was going to say.

Moss looked surprised but doubtful.

Suspecting that he had been too hasty, that some background would have to be laid first, Hasher backed off. "It's not clear yet," he said. "But I'm on the track. . . ." He shrugged and looked at the mail on his desk and wished he had at least had a chance to go through it, some time to collect himself. It was all too quick.

Moss waited and when Hasher didn't go on, said, "I wouldn't tell this to anyone else, Thomas, and I'd appreciate it if you don't either. I'm looking for another job."

Hasher stared at him impassively, thinking, There it is.

"Some of the others are too, I hear," Moss went on nervously. "Wheeler, Cohen, and Willoughby hope to start their own firm. A client of mine tipped me off. They're trying to get his account."

That was it, Hasher thought. It was over. He stared at

Moss, without trying to conceal his contempt, and waited.

Moss colored. "I'm sorry. I know how you felt about Lucius."

"How I felt is how I feel," Hasher said mildly.

Moss's eyes widened. "Still?"

Hasher nodded. "What she said was all lies."

Moss sat forward. "You can prove that?"

"Do you mean, have I got the smoking revolver?" Hasher asked.

Again Moss waited.

"My evidence depends on how willingly it's listened to," Hasher said. But he knew it was hopeless. He was too late. These men were lawyers and wouldn't blindly accept the old man's unsubstantiated claims in the diary—especially not after their lack of faith in him had led him to blow his brains out; they would never be able to admit they'd been so wrong as that.

But still Hasher knew that he must try. "Call a meeting for six this evening," he said. "All the partners—except Paul Wheeler. I don't trust him. Never have. Everyone else. Okay?"

Moss slumped back in his seat. "We've got such a meeting already scheduled." He looked at Hasher for a minute. "Except you're the one who was to be excluded."

Me?" Hasher rose halfway out of his seat. Then he understood and slowly sat back. He had been too close to the pederastic old thief to be trusted! Rage blazed through him. They would never listen, not to him. The ship was sinking and they were scurrying about the decks, searching for a hawser to crawl down. He got up and faced Moss. "Please tell my colleagues at the meeting that I have resigned, as of now."

Moss looked surprised, then amused. He got up too. "I've always disliked you, Hasher, and now I can say it: You're a moralistic son of a bitch!" He grinned. "Like that pious old fraud Slocum. Ever since the trial I've wondered —just how close were you two?"

Fury burst inside Hasher like a grenade. He smashed a fist into Moss's face and the man fell back into the leather chair, blood spurting out of his mouth. Hasher turned and walked out.

On the drive north, he tried to calm down but only inflamed himself more. All the mutual respect, the concern for clients, the honor of the firm, the high ethics of practice, and his own integrity. . . . He struggled to recall Margaret's words, then remembered: "only a game." Those men were hyenas, sharks in three-piece pinstriped suits. Yet, as angry as he was at his partners, Hasher knew that he had behaved about as badly as one could. Despite Moss's filthy innuendo, when Hasher had struck him, he saw now, he had abandoned all pretense at being a civilized man. With that single blow, he had demonstrated that the rationality, coolness, objectivity that were supposed to typify men like him did not exist in his case—perhaps never had.

His fury had burst free and now he was as frightened of himself as Margaret was. Had he released a demon, that rat of his soul, when he killed James? he wondered.

He shivered and turned up the heater and drove on, grimly angry with himself, through the cold blustery day. He had not even stopped on his way out of the office to speak to Margaret. He should have called her at least before leaving town. But he hadn't been able to bring himself to; she would be furious, appalled, embarrassed, and there would be no way he could explain or make it up to her. Now, even if the firm survived, she wouldn't. Unless she broke off with him. . . .

When he reached the lake at last, he turned quickly into the drive to the old man's cabin, to avoid being visible from any passing car. The drive ended a hundred yards from the cabin—as close as the old man would allow cars to be parked—and Hasher pulled up under an old lean-to that had been put up years before.

Hasher took a brown paper bag containing the original diary from the seat beside him and got out. He hurried to the cabin but when he was a dozen feet away, he stopped. The back door was barred by two heavy planks nailed across it. The Sheriff's office, he thought. Vivian of course. Then she was truly desperate to keep him out. He smiled: she had him locked out when all he was trying to do was put back in place what she had the cabin locked up to protect.

The front door of the porch and the inside door to the cabin itself were also barred. With an oath, he examined the windows on one side of the cabin; they were locked—probably nailed shut from inside too, he thought. "Shit!" he hissed.

He stepped back from the building to get a full view of it. Hands thrust in his raincoat pockets, he stared along the thick log walls, underneath at the crawl space, and up at the roof. Then he grinned. He had all but forgotten of course. . . . Twenty-five years since he had tested it with the old man.

Turning, Hasher hurried to the side of the front porch and the trellis there. It was unusually sturdy, built that way on purpose to hold a grown man's weight. He took off his coat and dropped it on the ground and stuck the paper bag halfway down under his belt at the back of his trousers. Then he quickly climbed up the trellis and crawled onto the roof. Its slant was shallow and he had no trouble climbing up it to the chimney.

Immediately beside it was a two-by-two-foot trapdoor. He remembered how the old man had made him use it one day on his own, in a suddenly announced fire drill. Praying that the hinges hadn't rusted shut, Hasher took hold of the small brass handle at the top of the square and yanked it. It didn't move. Swearing, he took it with both hands and pulled. With a screech of corroded metal, the door opened. He swung it back so that it lay flat on the roof, and peered down into the hole. There, a couple of feet directly below, was the cabin's great center beam. Hasher lowered himself onto it, then put a foot on top of the bookcase built into the wall beside the fireplace. Again he remembered the old man's pride in the arrangement—especially the extra-strong shelves with steel braces under each so that they could be used as a ladder.

Seconds later Hasher was on the floor of the living room and in less than a minute he had stuck the diary back where he had found it in the study. He quickly checked the room again to see that he had left no traces of Lyndon James's presence, and death, there. Then he left by the way he had come. It all took no more than ten minutes.

In less time than that, Hasher drove around the lake to his own place and parked and went to the back door. As he unlocked it and stepped inside, he knew instantly that something was wrong. He stopped and listened. Nothing. Realizing that if someone was there, his entrance would have frozen them into silence, he waited. At last he crept forward and took a large knife off a magnetic rack behind the butcher-block counter and moved on toward the hallway to the living room. He paused at the half-closed door to the bathroom, then suddenly shoved it open. He waited a moment and felt a wave of shudders move up his back. Suddenly he jumped into the bathroom, knife raised, and looked wildly around. Nothing. He flung the shower curtain to one side. Nothing.

His heart pounding, Hasher moved back to the hallway and along it to the living room. It was half-dark there and for a moment he thought he saw a figure slumped on the sofa. It was only a mound of dark pillows. He turned on a light and exchanged the knife for the fireplace poker. Slowly he went on to the other hall and the first bedroom, which he and Margaret used. The door was closed. Trying to recall whether he had left it that way, Hasher paused, turned the knob, and flung the door open so hard that it crashed against the wall. He reached in to switch on the light, half expecting a roar of gunfire. Again there was nothing.

His nerves were going, he realized and leaned against the wall to rest for a moment. He had almost recovered when he heard a sound—like something small and hard dropping in the back of the house. He froze. He wanted to flee—to run out to his car and speed away, to leave for good. . . .

But he forced himself back into the hallway and through the same motions as before—flinging open each door, to the other bedrooms and their closets, to the closets in the hall; switching on lights; looking everywhere, even under beds. He found nothing.

Nerves, he thought, swearing softly. He must have imagined the sound. Or a mouse. It was the time of year they came inside. He must remember to put down poison.

When he finished with the last room, he stood at the rear of the hall and stared up at the only remaining place to search: a square frame in the ceiling, a trapdoor into the attic, which let down an aluminum ladder when it was opened. He shook his head. Nothing in the world would induce him to go up there.

As he turned, he paused and sniffed once, then again. An odd smell that he couldn't place lingered there. He frowned and tried to recall what the odor reminded him of, but now it had vanished, if indeed it had ever been there.

It was time for his final chore: the ashes in the fireplace, where he had burned the bagful of loose pages, leftover rope, and the boy's flimsy wallet with everything but the money in it. Hasher swept the ashes onto a small shovel and dumped them into an empty scuttle. He took it outside to the dock and emptied it, in a swinging arc, over the water. He watched as the ashes littered the surface, then slowly absorbed and sank. He rinsed out the scuttle and went back to the cottage.

At the door he paused and looked back at the lake. Something was wrong, missing. . . . Oh, my God! he thought as he realized that the boy's teeth had been in the bagful of stuff he had burned. He looked down at the scuttle. They weren't there. Staring at the lake again, he tried to remember whether he had heard the tiny splashes they must have made. He couldn't. "You idiot!" he muttered. Now they were in the shallowest part of the lake. But the bottom there was muck too, he thought, and if anyone found one of them, it would be taken for some long-dead animal's tooth.

Suddenly he remembered the aluminum good-luck piece in the wallet. That would have made a noticeable sound as it hit the water. Maybe it hadn't been swept up . . . or the teeth. He hurried back into the cottage and the fireplace and got down on his hands and knees and searched the hearth and floor of the fireplace with care. Nothing.

At the sound of two sharp raps on the back door, he stiffened, then jumped up and dusted off his hands. He put the firescreen in place and turned. There were several more raps. Hasher took the poker again and went to the kitchen. Pulling aside one half of the curtain over the window in the rear door, he saw an enormous policeman.

"Mr. Hasher?"

He opened the door. "Yes? What can I do for you?"

"The question is can I do anything for you?" the man said. Hasher looked at him, puzzled, and he went on, "We got a report a man was seen near here. On foot." He jerked a thumb over his shoulder toward Hasher's car. "You weren't on foot, I assume." Then he noticed the poker in Hasher's hand and looked at him inquiringly.

"That's right," Hasher said, "but I don't understand—"

"Sheriff Worthy said he understood you had left here yesterday, so we figured maybe a prowler. A stranger was seen coming down your drive on foot by Mrs. Crow, from up the road. She called us."

Hasher propped the poker beside the door. "When was the report?"

The officer shrugged. "Maybe half an hour ago."

That noise in the back of the house, Hasher thought. Jesus, was he in there right now? The attic? Again all he wanted to do was flee the place. Panicked at the thought of someone inside . . . armed . . . gunfire. . . . "That's about how long I've been here," he said quickly. "I forgot some papers and drove back up this morning. If you'll just wait a minute, I'll get my things and leave with you."

"One moment, please," the policeman said as he moved his huge bulk into the kitchen, seeming to fill the room. "Would you mind showing me some identification?"

"In my own house?" Hasher asked incredulously.

"That's all I want to make sure it is. Since I don't know you, I'd look pretty silly if I left a burglar behind who claimed to be Thomas Hasher."

Hasher smiled. "Of course," he said and took out his billfold. He handed the officer his plasticized I.D., with his photograph on it, as required by the building his office was in, for night and weekend entry.

The policeman took it with a hand the size of a baseball glove, looked at the picture, then at Hasher's face, and back at the picture again. He handed him the card and grinned. "You are you all right. Sorry."

"I'm grateful for your precautions," Hasher said. "And for looking after the house while I'm away."

"No need to be," the man said mildly. "Part of our job. We check these places nearly every day." He turned to go.

"If you'll wait, I'll be right with you," Hasher said anxiously. "That report kind of bothers me."

The policeman turned back and nodded.

Hasher hurried into the living room and grabbed an envelope without knowing what was in it; it didn't matter. Just so he got out of there. He took his coat and rejoined the man at the door. Hasher locked it behind him and walked beside the officer to his car; a few yards behind it was a police car with a man sitting behind the wheel. Hasher got into his car and rolled down the window. "Best to the Sheriff. And thanks."

The officer touched the brim of his campaign hat. He walked on to the other car and squeezed into the passenger seat.

At the end of the drive, the driver of the police car tooted his horn twice briefly and turned to the left, toward the village. Hasher returned the signal and swung to the right, toward the city. He had meant to do one more thing: check the area around the great white rock to make sure he had left no sign of what had happened there. But now he was too afraid and told himself that it was unlikely anyone would go there this late in the year. And soon ice would form around the rim of the lake. It would be spring before he would have anything to worry about.

"I don't care *what* he said to you!" Margaret cried. "Are you going to smash in the face of every vicious fool you come across? My God! Can you imagine what they're saying about you?"

He had never seen her so angry. "I know," he said contritely. "I know." But then anger rose in him too. "It can't be any worse than what I've said about them."

"But, Thomas," she cried, leaning forward in exasperation, "you're only one man. *They* are a law firm! They can do you untold damage—and will."

He glanced at his watch. "They won't be a law firm for long. They're meeting in less than two hours. To disband the firm."

Margaret wasn't listening. "Moss swears he's going to sue."

"Just talk," Hasher said. "That's all he's good for. What he said to me is clearly 'fighting words,' under the law. You know that. I was justified—"

"So you were justified!" Now she was nearly screaming. "Fuck justification! Do you want to get up in court and have all that filth about Lucius raked over and heaped on *your* head now?"

Hasher hadn't thought of that. "He wouldn't dare," he said.

"You don't even realize what you've done. You broke his jaw!"

"Oh my God," he said softly.

Margaret slumped into a chair. He went to her and put a hand on her shoulder but she pulled away. She was truly afraid of him now, he realized—afraid even of his touch. He looked down at her for a moment, then went to the kitchen and poured a drink. It was foolish, he told himself; he hadn't eaten since early that morning and it was now past four. He emptied the glass anyway in one swallow and refilled it.

When he went back to the other room, Margaret looked up at him. "What's happened to you?"

She had forgotten the story in the diary already, he thought. "It didn't happen to me," he said and sat down across from her. "It happened to Lucius."

"For God's sake!" she shouted. "Lucius is dead! Let him go!"

"I can't."

She stood up and faced him. "You've got to make the choice: a dead man or a living woman." She left the room.

Surprised and then angered by her threat, Hasher stared at the empty doorway she had left by. As if he had a choice! he thought. Before he had learned the truth, there had been no need to make a choice. And after he had learned the truth, there had been no way for him to go except the way he had gone, so he hadn't chosen anything. In fact, he realized now, he hadn't even considered any alternatives once he finished the diary. And then James's death. . . . There was no going back from that.

To accept what had happened, to keep his silence, perhaps to ask Margaret to move somewhere else with him and start over, would, he knew, destroy him. If he failed Lucius now, he would fail himself in a way that he could never escape. He would blame himself and then he would blame her because he would have made *that* choice to keep her. In time they would have little of their love.

Anyway, he told himself as he stared at the doorway and waited for her to come back, now the choice was hers, not his. Maybe she could hang on, maybe it would all pass, maybe they would once more have. . . . Hasher felt tears come to his eyes as he contemplated a future without Margaret. Angrily he wiped them away with his fingers. There was no other way, he knew, no choice. For the first time in his life he understood the word "fate."

The telephone rang. He waited until it was clear that she was not going to answer and went to take the call. It was Sheriff Worthy. "Hello, Bill," Hasher said nervously. "What's up?"

"The police officer who came by your cottage today, Tiny Timmons—"

"Why does every giant in this country have to be called 'Tiny'?" Hasher asked, pleased with the casual note. "What about him?"

"An hour or so after you left, Tiny and his partner went back to recheck your place. When they got to the back door, a man ran out the front way and into the woods."

"My God!" Hasher's heart pounded; then he had been right—someone had been there. He might have been killed. "Did they catch him?"

"No. But they fired at him—the damn fools. All I need before the election is a murder charge against my men. Anyway, they checked the inside of your cottage as best they could. Everything seemed in order, except for one item."

Hasher waited.

"Did you leave the folding stairs to the attic down when you left?"

"No. I haven't used it in months."

"Well, someone else did. It was down when they went inside. He may have been up there in the attic, hiding, when you came in this morning. You're probably a very lucky man, Thomas."

It'll be the first time, Hasher thought. Even though he had been sure someone was there when he was, this confirmation frightened him badly. He tried not to show it. "Why would anyone want to break into a place like that? There's not a thousand dollars' worth of stuff in the whole house."

"Maybe he didn't know that until he got inside. Maybe he was casing the place when you arrived and he had to hide. We've got a lot of thieves stealing antiques out of summer homes up here."

That couldn't be it, Hasher thought. A glance through a window would show that the only antique was the plumbing.

"Or maybe some guy on the run," the Sheriff went on. "It could seem like a good spot to hole up in and rest for a day or two. Isolated, a gas heater that wouldn't show smoke, some food. Ideal. Anyway, I thought I'd let you know in case you want to come back up and check. Strictly speaking, the officers had no legal right to go inside, even to check. Hope you don't mind."

"Of course not," Hasher said quickly. "I'm grateful." He waited a moment, as if thinking, then said, "I can't get back up this week, I don't think. But I'll let you know when I can."

"Do that," Worthy said. "Seems there's been an unusual amount of coming and going these days at Lake Mercy. Funny, a quiet place like that."

Hasher went back to his chair and sat, staring at the amber liquid and half-melted ice in his drink as he held it, distractedly wondering if this latest event had anything to do with the rest of what was happening to him. He took a swallow of the whisky and tried to dismiss the thought. Paranoia, he told himself. It was the pressure.

A minute later Margaret came back into the room and handed him an envelope. Seeing that it was addressed to him at the firm and that it had been opened, he looked up at her in surprise.

"They gave your secretary instructions to open *all* your mail, even when it was inscribed 'Personal.' Only stuff not related to the firm is to be sent on to you."

Hasher started to swear but stopped himself as he took the envelope and saw that it was from the law firm Cutter & Raskovsky. He took out the letter inside and glanced at the signature; as he expected, it was from Marvin Rail, dated four days earlier.

Dear Mr. Hasher:

It seems only proper to inform you at once that I have today filed papers before the Surrogate, County of New York, contesting the will allegedly written by Lucius Avery Slocum, deceased, on behalf of his former wife, Vivian Trumbull Slocum. Said papers will be forwarded to you in the usual form. I have also petitioned for an order to seal the property jointly owned by Lucius Avery Slocum and Vivian Trumbull Slocum at Lake Mercy until the issue of the alleged will has been finally settled.

Mrs. Slocum has advised me that in order to facilitate bringing this unfortunate dispute to an amicable close, she would consider settling the issue by relinquishing her rights to said property if a suitable arrangement can be reached between her, the rightful heir, and you, the putative heir.

Should you be interested in pursuing this suggestion, kindly let me know, and I shall arrange a meeting.

In my opinion, such a settlement would be to everyone's advantage. In the hope that you concur, I am

> Yours truly,
> *Marvin Rail*

Without a word, Hasher handed the letter to Margaret and finished his drink. While she was reading, he went to the sideboard and refilled his glass.

"Give up your claim, Thomas," she said. "Otherwise it will never end."

He didn't answer. Vivian and Rail had no intention of actually trying to beat the old man's will, he was sure. They were stalling, buying time, waiting until they could make certain that there was nothing among the old man's papers in the cabin that could be used against them. She must know about the trap door in the roof too, he thought. They would send someone. If the diary was found, they would think they had it all. Then they'd drop the suit contesting the will.

"What are you going to do?" Margaret asked.

Hasher went back to the telephone and took out the directory. Then he put it away and asked, "What's his number on the letter?"

Margaret looked at him in surprise. "Why?"

"I'm going to make an appointment with them."

CHAPTER

9

"*Herbert J. Lime—Confidential Investigations*" *the black* letters on the opaque-glass-paneled door read. Hasher opened it and entered a small room occupied by a brown plastic sofa and wooden-armed chair flanking a white Formica table that held several old and tattered copies of *Playboy* and *Penthouse;* facing the door at the opposite side of the room was a pale-blue Formica desk and sitting behind it was a plump frowzy woman with matching hair.

Hasher identified himself and said that he had an appointment with Mr. Lime. A couple of minutes later, just as he had taken a seat and opened the nearest magazine to a full-page, rearview picture of a young woman wearing only black boots and a black cowboy hat, with her face turned coyly over one shoulder and her sumptuous ass thrust out toward him, a door beside his chair opened and a man came in.

He was in his mid-fifties, of medium height, with curly gray hair, thick bifocals, and a lot of teeth. His trousers sagged beneath a small but prominent belly. "Herbie Lime," he said, with a toothy smile. He reached out a hand but when Hasher tried to shake it, Lime took the magazine from him and appraised the photograph.

"You too?" he asked, looking at Hasher. "Me, I'm an ass man all the way." He drew his head back a few inches to focus better on the picture. "Nice. Nice but not the best." He put the magazine, opened, down on the table and bent over it. "Now if it were more like this," he went on, enlarging the outer curves of the buttocks by tracing his forefingers around them, "that's the best. An ass like that, with the same small waist—Jesus!" He shook one hand as if it had gone to sleep. "Like peaches! I'd trade all the tits in the world for one like that. Jesus!"

Hasher glanced at the woman behind the desk. She seemed not to have heard and he gathered there probably was a lot she didn't hear in this office. He wanted to leave but a moment later the man closed the magazine and took his arm.

"Come in, come in," he said, flashing his teeth again. *"You've* got a problem, *I've* got a solution."

As Hasher reluctantly entered the office, he felt as if he had walked onto a set for a Raymond Chandler movie. The room was small and badly needed painting. On one side was another brown plastic sofa and matching chair, on the other side were several metal filing cabinets (one with a brown hat on top and, Hasher suspected, a bottle of bourbon inside), and in front of the single dusty window was an old scarred wooden desk with a wooden swivel armchair behind it.

Lime waved him to the sofa-chair side and sat down behind the desk, leaned back, and clasped his hands over his belly. "Speak to me," he said.

Again Hasher wanted to leave but then remembered the words of the fellow who had recommended Lime to him: "His appearance, his manner, his office, his speech will put you off. Don't let them. He's as good as they come. Herbie would like to be a crook but he's too honest. So he knows how it's done but won't do it himself."

Awkwardly Hasher recounted the story he had decided on an hour before: that Vivian and Rail were trying to blackmail him and that he needed comparable evidence against them to stop it.

"Mind telling me what their blackmail's about?" Lime asked, serious now.

"Not at all. I'm told I can trust you absolutely."

Lime displayed a large crescent of teeth. "Don't believe it. Trust nobody absolutely, not even yourself. Maybe especially yourself. Go on."

With a nervous smile, Hasher said, "They've concocted a story about my stealing money from a client. Oh, I forgot. I'm a lawyer."

"An easy thing to forget. I'd like to forget what I am at times too."

"The story's not true," Hasher added.

"True or not doesn't matter," Lime said. "A charge like that could wipe you out. The Bar Association. Rumors. Gossip. Clients getting nervous and taking their business away from you."

"Exactly."

Lime took a toothpick out of his shirt pocket and began digging at his teeth.

Staring just past his head at the dirty window, Hasher went on to explain that he had an appointment with Vivian and Rail the following afternoon, at 4:30, and thought it might help if he had on him a concealed tape recorder in case they said anything incriminating.

"They won't," Lime said flatly and put the toothpick back in his shirt pocket. "At least *he* won't. She may try but he'll stop her. Anyway, wiring you is easy."

Hasher wanted to explain that Vivian was the smart one, the more evil of the two, though it might seem hard to make that choice, but he refrained. It was irrelevant and there was no point in telling this man too much. Instead, he explained that he also wanted Vivian and Rail followed for, say, three days immediately after his meeting with them.

"He's married and has children and I understand he and Vivian are having an affair," Hasher said.

Lime made a clucking sound of disapproval and said, "What's this world coming to?"

Irritated by having to defer to this man because he needed him, needed his confidence and discretion, Hasher snapped, "It should be enough to stop them."

"You mean, stop him, don't you? How about her?"

Hasher sighed. "Nothing will stop her."

Lime thrust his jaw forward quickly and pulled it back. "How about some home movies?"

Hasher looked at him, nonplussed.

"A movie complete with sound track, made in her bedroom—or wherever they release their steaming passion," Lime said and displayed his teeth again.

Hasher sat forward. *That* had never occurred to him. "You can arrange it?"

Lime shrugged and ducked his head to one side. "It's illegal of course. Illegal acts have a disagreeable way of costing more." He raised a hand, palm outward, to stop Hasher from replying and went on, "Not to me. I play it legit. Oh, now and then, maybe a tiny corner gets cut, maybe I don't see something or hear something. But legit. Still, there are guys. . . ."

Hasher slumped back in his chair. "Where? That's not my kind of world."

"Unfortunately it happens to be my kind," Lime said. "You finger the two of them for me. Somehow the rest will get done."

Hesitating, Hasher thought for a few moments, disgusted by what was being offered but knowing that he was going to accept it. "How much?" he asked at last.

Lime picked up a pencil and began jotting down figures on a small pad. "Wiring, three-day surveillance"—he paused and looked up, saying, "That means two men," and returned to his figures—"plus the rest." He wrote some more, then finished with a flourish. "Four of the big ones should do," he said. "Three of them up front."

Hasher winced. But after a minute he nodded and took out his checkbook.

"Uh uhn!" Lime said, waving a hand. "What if later they subpoena your canceled checks? Then you've got to explain or, worse, *I've* got to explain." He smiled. "I don't mind lying but not under oath. You can lie, a client can lie, and nothing's likely to happen. But judges don't like people in my line. And ever since I was a little tot I've had an aversion to bars. Besides, there's my license."

Hasher nodded and got up. "What time tomorrow for the wiring?"

Lime got up too. "You're due for the appointment at four-thirty, come here no later than three. With three."

"What size bills?"

"Hundreds are nice," Lime said. "I always thought Benjamin Franklin was an asshole but I like his portrait. A lot." He grinned.

Hasher shook hands with him. "Thanks, Mr. Lime."

"Herbie," he said.

"Marvin, you really must do something about these dreadful furnishings," Vivian Slocum said. She was seated on a low sofa, her lovely long legs crossed, one arm languorously stretched out along the top of the cushion beside her, and her small hand, with its slender fingers dangling like petals of a flower, moving slowly, suggestively.

Hasher, sitting on a low uncomfortable upholstered chair across from her, glanced with distaste around the large office. Its furnishings were modernistic, sterile and tasteless. He looked back at Vivian and marveled again at her calm and her beauty. She would look like the Duchess of Alba on a subway car, he thought.

Marvin Rail smiled at her and ignored the taunt. Turning to Hasher, he said, "Shall we proceed?"

Hasher nodded without speaking. When he had come in, a minute before, he had barely been able to manage a mumbled "Vivian" to her and a nod to Rail, who had proferred a hand, then withdrawn it as Hasher sat down. He was surprised and upset by his own behavior, for he had determined, before entering, that he would behave as he always behaved with professional adversaries: polite, correct, cool without being unfriendly. But he hadn't been able to and now he feared that he might arouse their suspicions of him unnecessarily.

Rail patted the top of his head, as if checking to make sure that the few strands of blond hair he had left were still there, and said, "Mrs. Slocum feels, and I'm afraid

I'm inclined to agree with her, that her husband's will is one final attempt to have his revenge upon her—from, so to speak, beyond the grave."

Hasher grunted softly, with disgust and astonishment. But then he saw that the remark was precisely typical of Rail: combative, deceitful, and disarming. Suddenly he remembered Lime's instructions to switch on the tape recorder as soon as the conversation got down to business—but no sooner, since the device recorded for only half an hour unless there was an opportunity to reverse the cassette. Hasher reached into his inside breast pocket, flicked the tiny switch, and pulled out a notebook and a pen. "I trust you don't mind if I make notes," he said.

"Not at all, not at all," Rail answered, smiling broadly.

Hasher pulled his French cuffs out slightly so that the goldmesh cufflink microphones would pick up the voices, and opened the notebook. He looked back at Rail.

His puffy face had darkened slightly. Apparently he had hoped to set an angry tenor to the meeting, Hasher thought, so that he could later blame his opponent's intransigeance for any breakdown in negotiations. Even the most experienced lawyer could be susceptible to such tactics, if they were used astutely. But there was nothing astute about Rail; it was all bullyboy stuff, Hasher thought and relaxed a little.

Rail waved a pudgy hand with its small manicured nails and said, "As you well know, Mr. Hasher, this case has been very long, very unpleasant, and very painful for everyone—not just for your late colleague and, I assume, yourself but for Mrs. Slocum above all."

Unsettled by the man's relentless audacity, Hasher glanced across at Vivian, who was watching him with a gentle smile. Again he was astonished by her. Then he imagined her with Lyndon Johnson James's cock in her mouth, and instantly felt better.

Rail cleared his throat for their attention and when Hasher looked back at him, he went on, "It seems clear that Mr. Slocum's alleged will could not stand up in court. It was written only two weeks before he took his own life. A man so distraught by events as to be deranged."

"You mean it's deranged not to want to leave the little you have left to a wife—or an ex-wife, rather—who has taken the rest of all you had?" Hasher asked.

Vivian laughed softly.

"If that's the way you want to approach this matter—" Rail began angrily.

"And you also mean that you can be as rotten as a man can get but if I respond with common sense, then my conduct is inexcusable?" Hasher snapped.

"Enough!" Rail shouted. "We had hoped to discuss this matter amicably and now you—"

"Bullshit!" Hasher said.

Vivian looked at him in surprise.

Rail hunched forward over his desk. "All right, then, here are our terms. I've had a tentative appraisal made of the property at Lake Mercy. The figure was seventy thousand dollars."

Hasher snorted.

"To expedite matters and settle this disagreeable case once and for all, Mrs. Solcum has consented to drop her contesting of the will and sell *her* property there to you for fifty-five thousand dollars. A handsome offer by any measure."

"I thought you had something to discuss," Hasher replied, getting up. "If that's all, we can stop now."

"That's *not* all," Rail said, glaring at him. "There's a matter of culpability involved."

It had worked, Hasher thought, delighted. Rail's own tactic had worked against him. Hasher waited for a moment, then said, "On whose part?"

"Yours, I'm afraid," Rail answered and smiled nastily. "A slight shortage in an estate under your administration."

Hasher played it as he knew he was expected to: He sat down. "I don't understand."

Rail could not restrain a triumphant pause. Then he

said, "The Poulson estate. Some seventy thousand dollars is missing from it."

"That's nonsense!" Hasher said.

"Is it? I would suggest you conduct a private audit except that I understand you have resigned from Slocum, Whitby & Barker." Rail grinned at him.

Nothing unusual about his knowing that, Hasher assured himself. It had been three days and in his world bad news about anyone traveled faster than electricity. So the old man had been right; Vivian had trapped him too. He waited.

Certain that he had the upper hand now, Rail sat back and opened his arms expansively. "There's no need for all this hostility. Essentially you and Mrs. Slocum have a common interest: to settle this disagreeable business and get on with your lives."

"By?"

"By your agreeing to buy out Mrs. Slocum's interest in the Lake Mercy property for fifty-five thousand dollars, and by her agreeing to drop the suit against her husband's will and. . . ." He stopped.

"And the culpability?" Hasher asked. "The so-called culpability?"

An uneasy glance flickered through Rail's eyes. "That, too."

"In other words, blackmail," Hasher said, getting up again.

"That's an ugly word," Rail said. He looked menacing now.

"You're an ugly man," Hasher said calmly. He had it now. He turned to go.

"The Bar Association will be most interested," Rail said.

Hasher stopped and turned back. "Let me know when you've run out of blackmail." Still, he hesitated. He knew he must not break off with them; above all, he had to have reason to keep in contact.

"That's your final word?" Vivian asked suddenly.

Hasher looked at her with hatred. "No," he answered.

"I'm not the least bit afraid of your talk about alleged culpability. Nor am I the least bit afraid of either of you—though God knows I should be, given your vicious destruction of Lucius. For his sake, to stop any more slime being poured over his name in another lawsuit, to settle this thing once and for all, I'm making you an offer for the Lake Mercy property. It's firm and final: forty thousand."

Rail sneered. "And the Bar Association?"

Hasher smiled. "Apparently you heard only half the news. I resigned not only from the firm but from the bar. I've had enough of filth like you."

When Herbie Lime leaned out of the window of a car parked in front of the building on the street below, all Hasher could see were his teeth.

"Got it?" Lime asked.

Hasher nodded.

"Let's hope the recorder picked it all up. Get in the driver's seat."

Hasher walked around the car and got in. As he did, he saw there was someone in back—a nondescript man of indeterminate age with a camera on his lap.

"Meet Touchy," Lime said.

Hasher turned back to shake hands and realized that he had already forgotten what the man looked like. Perfect, he thought, a fellow who had been born for this job. Then he noticed his fingers—those on one hand tapping and moving around the camera and those on the other stroking his knee—and understood where his name came from.

Touchy rolled down the window and looked through the viewer of his camera, pointed at the entrance to the building, and adjusted the lens. Then he lowered the camera and picked up a piece of white cardboard from the seat and fitted it over the lens, which fit snugly into a hole in the center, with the viewer opposite another hole.

When Touchy turned the cardboard over, Hasher saw

the lens protruding from a hole in a letter "O" of a hand-painted sign that said "Repent now, Ye Sinners, or Forever Burn in the Torments of Hell." Touchy raised the sign and stuck it in the open window, which it fit exactly.

Hasher laughed.

"Touchy's from the South," Lime said. "He always wanted to be a preacher."

The three men waited in silence, watching the entrance to the building. Hasher glanced at his watch after a few minutes and saw that it was just past five. Soon hordes of people began leaving the building. He swore under his breath. If Vivian and Rail left now, they might be lost in the crowd. But he was fairly sure they wouldn't leave during the rush period; she hated being jostled, he knew, and she hated even more being in a situation where she didn't stand out.

By five-thirty the departing workers had thinned out to a steady but modest trickle. A couple of minutes later Hasher said sharply, "There! The man in the black rain-coat and the woman in white."

She wasn't wearing white actually; rather she had on a pale cream-colored knitted wool coat and a matching cap. The coat was fitted and clung to her sinuously.

"That's her?" Lime asked. "Crikeys, who could blame him? Got them, Touchy?"

The answer from the back seat was a click, then another, and, as the couple came toward the car, then turned, only a few feet away, and Hasher averted his head to avoid being recognized, still another.

Lime turned around and said to Touchy, "The usual. Give me the camera and I'll have the shots ready for Harvey when he spells you. Call me at the shop or here."

For the first time Hasher noticed a telephone receiver hanging below the dashboard beside him. A moment later he heard the rear door open and close. Lime took out a notebook, glanced at his watch, and wrote down the date, time, and place. Then he faced Hasher and showed his teeth. "That's the only blackmailer I've ever seen I wanted to fuck," he said.

"You'd probably get the clap."

"Worth it," Lime said.

Hasher took a manila envelope out of his inside breast pocket and handed it to him. "Count it."

"I'll do that," Lime said with a grin. But he counted the thirty $100 bills rapidly and carelessly, then looked up. "It's Friday evening. You think they'll spend tonight together, maybe the weekend?"

Hasher shrugged. "That's your job." He couldn't resist adding, "Herbie."

"If he's still living with his wife, they won't—anyway, not likely. Guys don't take 'business trips' on weekends. What's the layout of her place?"

"A triplex," Hasher answered. "The top three floors of a townhouse on East Eightieth Street. I gave you the address."

"I need the layout for the hear-evil, see-evil."

Hasher frowned in puzzlement until he realized that the words were an absurd code for the sound and video bugs. Reminded of the recorder in his pocket, he undid the cufflinks and pulled them up his sleeves by the fine wires attached to the tape recorder. He removed that and slipped out the cassette and handed the machine to Lime.

"Their first floor is the parlor floor of the house. It has an entrance hall, a dining room, and a kitchen—in that order, front to back. On the second floor is a large living room facing the street and a study in the rear, looking out on the garden. On the top floor are two large bedrooms and two baths."

"No bathrooms on the lower floors?" Lime asked. "Some interesting things happen in bathrooms."

Hasher avoided looking at him. "I forgot. On the parlor floor there's one off the foyer. None on the second floor."

Lime wrote in the little book. "You said the ground floor is used for a doctor's office, right?"

Hasher nodded.

"Good. No one there at night. You drive."

"Where?"

"Wherever you're going. I've got to make floor plans."

Hasher drove in silence, carefully, so he wouldn't make it difficult for the detective to do his drawings. Finally, Lime closed the notebook and sat back and sighed. "I always know when they're special," he said, as if he were talking to himself. When Hasher didn't speak, he explained, "Women like Vivian Slocum. . . ." His voice trailed off into another long sigh. "When you see them, you only look at their faces. No tits, no ass, no legs—just faces. Jesus, hers took my breath away!"

Hasher turned and saw his sadly pensive look and realized that the man had never had a woman like that. Unexpectedly Hasher saw Vivian as she had looked, lying on her back, stretched out on his dock in the sun, wearing only the bottom of her bikini, taunting him. He grinned as he imagined what Lime would have done under those circumstances. But Lime would never have had the chance. Was that why she hated Hasher so, he asked himself again—because he'd had the chance and turned her down?

CHAPTER
10

It was nearly six-thirty when Hasher unlocked the front door to his apartment and went inside. He stopped. Margaret should have been home by then but there were no lights on, no call of greeting. He put his coat in the foyer closet and went into the living room and turned on some lights.

"Margaret?"

There was no answer. He went back to the bedroom and saw, to his surprise, that the bed was unmade. She always made it before they left in the morning, he knew. Then he saw a pile of clothes flung into a corner and went over to them. A brown wool skirt and a tan wool shirt. Hadn't those been the clothes she had worn that morning when she left? He stopped, his heart pounding, as he assured himself that they were. *Her* clothes, like that? Never! Then he saw her brown shoes by the foot of the bed and nearby a pair of panties and, tangled around them, pantyhose.

"Margaret!" he cried.

There was no answer. He ran into the bathroom and saw that it was empty. So was the kitchen. He tore open closet doors, expecting to see her body tumble out each time. No one. At last he went to her study and found the door closed. He opened it slowly, fearfully. It took a few moments before his eyes adjusted to the dim autumn light coming in through the two windows. And then he saw her, slumped in the large wing chair in the far corner. He ran to her, crying "Margaret, what is it?" even while he feared that she was past answering.

Her legs were tucked under her and she was wearing her blue cashmere robe. He saw her feet, bare, and her hands, clasped tensely in her lap. Her eyes were open but not looking at him. Her face was wet with tears. He bent over and kissed her forehead. It was warm, hot even, and he knew that she was alive.

Hasher fell to his knees beside the chair and took her hands. They remained clasped and he couldn't free them. He stared at her face and finally she turned her head and looked at him through her tears.

"Oh, my darling, my darling," he said softly. "What happened, what is it?"

She stared at him, seeming to see something else, and a sob escaped her.

Hasher waited a moment, then said again, softly, beseechingly, "What is it?"

This time she shook her head—slowly in one direction and slowly back, half a dozen times, as if beyond all words.

He rose and sat on the edge of the chair and took her in his arms. Then, at last, she burst and the sobs tore out of her as she wept, half-screaming, and clung to him desperately, crying, "Thomas! Oh Thomas! Oh Thomas!" over and over. He felt her tears washing down his cheek and his neck and soaking his shirt collar. And still she wept, her body heaving convulsively, her fingers digging into his back. It was hysteria, he knew, true hysteria. He had never seen it before and it was the last thing he would have expected from Margaret. He waited, knowing that was all he could do, holding her and murmuring "My love, my darling, it's all right, it's all right."

After ten minutes or so, her tears and sobs subsided and finally she was silent and unmoving. She clung to him still though, and he waited for another few minutes before slowly pulling away from her. He took out his handkerchief and gently dried her face.

"What happened, my darling?" he asked.

A great sob shook her body and she stared at him, horror-stricken, then shook her head, this time rapidly, from side to side. "I can't!" she cried. "I can't! Oh, Thomas!" Again she wept. At last, after more tears and more silence, she slumped back in the chair and buried her face in her hands.

"Would a drink help?" he asked, stroking her dark hair.

She shook her head, still in her hands.

"Tea?"

She nodded and slowly he got up, stared down at her for a minute, and hurried out to the kitchen.

When he returned and she took the tea and sipped it slowly, staring off past him, her crumpled face inconsolably woeful, he drew a small chair up beside her and sat down and waited. At last, half an hour later, she told him what had happened.

She had left the office early, to escape the gloomy mood of the place as the firm slowly collapsed. Stopping at the neighborhood butcher shop for some duck pâté and a brace of quail for a special dinner—"Good food always cheers you up," she explained through a trembling smile—she had got home a little after three. She put the groceries away and went to the bathroom. As she sat there, trying to decide whether to order a Pommard or a Châteauneuf-du-Pape to go with dinner, suddenly there was a terrible pain in her head and she blacked out. When she came to, she had no idea how much later, she was on her bed, face down and naked. Her head throbbed and there was a great weight on her and a fierce stabbing pain in her anus. As consciousness came fully back to her, she nearly screamed as she realized what was happening to her. She was being buggered.

"Oh my God!" Hasher said, choking with fury. He took her hands and held them between his, again murmuring, "Oh my darling, my love." He was trembling so that he could only with difficulty remain on the small chair.

Margaret pulled her hands away and covered her face with them and cried, "Oh it hurt so—oh my God! Oh Thomas! Help me, help me!"

He couldn't. He was frozen with horror and rage. He pulled her wet hands away from her face and leaned forward. "A drink," he said. "You need a drink."

Margaret shook her head. "You have one," she said brokenly.

Grateful, he jumped off the chair and ran out to the sideboard and in a few moments was back with two glasses and a bottle. With shaking hands he poured both glasses half full and held one out to Margaret. Again she shook her head. He drank the contents of that glass in two gulps and put it on the floor.

In a minute she went on with the ghastly story. She had managed—how, she didn't know now—to control herself and not let on that she was conscious. "I was sure he would kill me if I saw his face," she said, shaking again with terror. "I thought he had a gun or maybe a knife because once or twice I felt something cold, something metal, against my arm."

Hasher grimaced and took a drink from the other glass, then held it out to her once more. This time she took a swallow of it and shuddered.

Calm, calm, she had told herself, trying to repress the screams of pain and horror tearing at her throat. She felt the man's hands clutching her breasts and heard his soft moaning and felt his hot breath on the back of her neck and the side of her face, and, at last, barely restrained herself as he shrieked, like an animal, and came in her ass.

Now she wept again and buried her face in her hands once more.

Hasher began pacing. He was shaking with rage—and disgust. He tried desperately to rid his mind and heart of that, the disgust, because it was for her, for Margaret, and he was horrified at himself but couldn't help it. He stopped and faced her. "Go on," he said angrily, unable to help that either. "All of it. Get it over with. For God's sake be quick about it!"

Margaret looked at him, puzzled at first, then gradually awareness and disbelief came over her face. Hasher ran to her and kissed her wet hands and wet face. She stared stonily at him as he said, almost pleading, "It's all right, it's all right."

Her body was stiff in his arms. He backed away, sensing that she didn't want him to touch her. "Did you see him?" he asked.

"His hand." And before he could ask the next question, she added, "He was white."

"That's all you saw?"

She nodded slowly and a moment later said, "But I smelled something—on his breath."

Hasher repressed a shudder; the word had drawn a picture for him of the man lying on her as the rest of her description hadn't. Now he could almost feel and smell the hot breath on her neck.

"Cloves," Margaret explained. "The odor of cloves."

Looking away, she went on in a low voice to describe her worst terror—when he got off her and she lay still, unmoving, unable to see, certain that now he would kill her. "I swore to myself that if I lived, I would make every moment of my life count." Finally she had heard the bedroom door being unlocked, opened, closed. A little later she thought she heard the front door click. She had remained on the bed for a long time until she was sure that he had gone. Then she had wept—quietly at first, stifling the sound as long as she could but finally letting go uncontrollably.

"I got up then," she said and rose now. She wobbled unsteadily and Hasher moved forward to catch her. But she backed away. "I felt something wet on my legs." She opened her robe and touched the inside of her thighs. "It was his semen."

Trembling, Hasher stared at her, wondering why she was telling him all this. But then he knew: she was flaunting his own disgust. Ashamed again, he waited.

Margaret let her robe fall closed. "I wiped it off with some tissues. I went and double-locked the front door so he couldn't come back. I took four hot baths. Each time I got out of the tub, I still felt him all over me. I tried to douche my ass but it hurt too much."

She buried her face in her hands and Hasher took her in his arms. "Being a victim is horrible—horrible!" she cried in his ear and pulled away.

"Oh, my God," Hasher said softly, helplessly.

Margaret looked up suddenly and glared at him with hatred. "Men are hideous beasts," she said through clenched teeth. "They would torture God."

"The word is that they did," Hasher said and immediately regretted the attempt at levity.

But she didn't seem to have heard. She took the glass of whisky he had left for her on the desk and drained it. He went to the phone and dialed 911.

Margaret grabbed the receiver away from him and slammed it back in its cradle. He looked into her furious eyes. "Haven't I been humiliated enough?" she cried.

"I thought—"

"Jesus Christ!" she screamed, "I didn't even see his face!"

"I'm sorry," Hasher said. He moved toward her but she rushed out of the room. He followed her slowly and found her in the kitchen, slamming dishes into the sink. "Forgive me," he said. "I can't stand what happened to you. I. . . ." He couldn't think of anything more.

She turned on him. "To me or to *you?*"

As he looked at her, she seemed to him deformed. He turned away. He knew that she was right but he couldn't help himself. A moment later she took his arm and pulled him around gently and embraced him. "It's all right," she said.

Here she is, comforting me, he thought and buried his face in her hair. Then he kissed her forehead and her cheeks and, at last, her lips. His eyes were closed and when he opened them he saw that she was staring at him. He released her.

"At least let me call Dr. Lamb," he said.

Margaret went on staring at him for a few seconds as if she were seeing something else. "All right," she replied at last. "But only tell him I was raped. I didn't see his face. He had a mask on or something. All I know is he was white." She left the room.

Their doctor lived in the same building and arrived in a few minutes. By then, Margaret had stripped the bed and remade it. She flung the sheets and pillow cases she had taken off in the hall and called out, "Throw them away!" Shuddering with disgust, Hasher wadded them up and put them in a paper bag and dropped it in the waste can in the outer rear hall. As he came back into the kitchen, the front doorbell rang.

"What happened, Thomas?" the doctor asked as he came in. "You said rape? In *this* building? Where was the doorman?"

"I haven't asked. She refuses to let me call the police."

Dr. Lamb nodded. "You know how they act sometimes. She's had enough as it is."

Hasher led the way to the bedroom and left the doctor there, saying, "If there's anything you want. . . ."

The doctor dismissed him with a nod and closed the door. Hasher went out to the kitchen and washed the dishes that Margaret had left. Then he filled the ice bucket and a pitcher of water and took them into the living room. Twenty minutes and two drinks later the doctor joined him.

"She'll be all right—physically at least," he said, declining a drink. "I gave her a sedative to make her sleep. And a massive dose of penicillin. Those guys usually have syphilis."

Hasher tried not to show his revulsion.

"No intercourse for ten days," the doctor said. "In a week I want her at my office for a blood test."

Hasher nodded dumbly. Sex? he asked himself. Would she ever want it again?

"The rest is up to the two of you. It can be difficult."

He picked up his bag. "Try to understand, to sympathize. In a way, it's worse for the man."

Again Hasher nodded. He couldn't imagine making love to her.

Vivian's nipples were red and erect. He slid down her naked body and began sucking one and caressing the other with a thumb and forefinger. She moaned and he pressed his hard cock against her thigh. "Oh Thomas!" she cried softly. "Fuck me!" He decided to make her wait a little, to build up her desire, and moved to the other breast and took her nipple in his mouth. "Oh Thomas!" she cried again. "Please!"

The bell rang and Hasher jumped up. "Rail!"

"What?" she asked.

The light went on and Hasher found himself staring at Margaret, lying beside him in their bed. He mumbled incoherently, desperately wondering what he had said in his sleep.

"Rail?" she asked. "Is that what you said?"

The bell rang again and he realized that it was the telephone in the living room. He had pulled out the phone plug in the bedroom and shut the door but the ringing was still loud, shrilly persistent.

"I was dreaming," he said and got up.

It was Herbie Lime. "Sorry if I woke you but it's important."

Hasher looked at the clock on the mantel: 7:40—not all that early. "What's wrong?"

"Touchy. Your friends went out last night and he went in. Its being Friday, he figured they'd be out for some time. An hour was all. He'd done only the sound—in the bedroom."

Alert now, Hasher asked, "He was caught?"

"No. Went out through a skylight and over the roof-tops."

"Did anyone spot him or guess he was there?"

"Yeah," Lime answered. "He walked back past the house, on the other side. A police car was in front."

"What now?"

"For starters, I give you back one of the big ones. Maybe two if what he planted was found. I won't know until he calls in to report whether it's working."

"If it isn't?"

"We wait—at least a month. Or give up."

"It's got to be right away, no waiting," Hasher said, angry at the detective for his airy indifference to the way the job had been botched.

"No way," Lime said. "Can you imagine Touchy in jail?"

"Maybe he ought to go into another line of work."

"Shouldn't we all," Lime replied. "I'll let you know soon as I've got more." He hung up.

Hasher stared at the buzzing receiver and wondered, with a start, if it was tapped. As soon as Lime called back, he would meet him somewhere and arrange to have the apartment electronically swept.

When he got back into bed, Margaret was asleep.

CHAPTER

11

She spent all of that day, Saturday, in bed—sleeping a lot, reading a little, and staring off at nothing. Twice Hasher thought he heard her weeping and went to stand by the door: only silence. He made some soup for her and tea and toast but she scarcely ate and after he had gone to sit by her bedside and talk a couple of times—brief, stilted conversations—he gave up. He paced the apartment in his soft-soled slippers, full of guilt about his behavior. Finally he gave that up too.

Telling Margaret that he was going out for a walk, he went to a nearby neighborhood bar, ordered a mug of ale, and used the phone to call Lime.

"Either they found the tap or it was installed wrong," Lime said. "Anyway, it's not working."

Hasher swore under his breath. "What next?"

"It's your shot."

"My own apartment," Hasher said. "Somebody broke in there yesterday. Nothing taken. He sapped my woman when she came in early. He got away. Unseen. No identification."

Lime gasped. "She's all right?"

"A headache is about all," Hasher lied, and immediately remembered, even more guiltily, that he hadn't even asked about how her head felt after the blow. "Scared of course—scared as hell. Me too," he added.

"It's the emotional side that counts now," Lime said,

sounding like the doctor. He paused and asked, "What can I do?"

Hasher paused too, then said, "It seems odd that he didn't steal anything."

"Maybe he didn't have time. He got there just before she did. She came in. He panicked and bopped her. Could have tied her up and burgled at will but too scared. Ran."

The man hadn't been scared at all, Hasher thought. What he had done took time. Besides, he'd apparently had a gun. He was ready. If Hasher had come in . . . they'd both be dead now. "I've got a feeling," he said.

"Listen to it," Lime said quickly. "Always. Speak."

"Maybe he was there for another reason."

"Like?"

"Like planting a tap or bug," Hasher said.

Lime whistled. "Rail," he said. "I like it."

"I don't." Hasher was angry again. "I want the place swept, just to make sure."

"That I can do. When?"

"Monday? How long will it take?"

"Depends on the wiring in the walls, electrical equipment around, TV antennas. Could be three hours, could be eight. And it costs—a good part of that big one I owe you back."

"That's all right." He hesitated, still angry at the man but not wanting to cause a break with him. "Do you do it yourself or hire someone?"

"A specialist—called the vacuumer," Lime answered without any sign of taking offense. "The best."

"Monday then?" Hasher asked. "After ten?"

"I'll have to check with the man. If you don't hear from me, we're on."

Hasher gave him his apartment number and hung up. He finished his ale and left. On the street he felt anxious and looked behind him nervously. He was being silly, he told himself; it was the pressure again. But still he walked rapidly and looked back a couple of times as he crossed the streets on his way home.

When he got there, he heard Margaret talking on the phone to her mother. He went to the kitchen to see what was in the refrigerator for dinner and saw the pâté and the brace of quail. Not those, he thought and shoved them out of sight behind some jars; they would only remind her of coming home.

Margaret came into the kitchen in her robe. "Mother asked me out," she said. "I think it might help."

Hasher turned to her and nodded. Her mother, a pleasant chatty woman who lived an hour away on Long Island, would be just the person for her to be with. "Are you sure?" he asked, hoping that she would say yes. She did and he relaxed, only a little guilty now. He had failed her, he knew, but that didn't mean he must go on failing her. Given a little time, he would pull himself together. Until he did. . . .

"You're not going to tell her, are you?" he asked.

She smiled, dismayed at the question. "After ten years of trying to convince her that I'm perfectly safe in the city?" She opened the refrigerator and peered inside. "Let's have the quail," she said.

At ten o'clock the next morning Hasher put Margaret on the train at Penn Station and was so relieved by her departure that he felt worse than ever. He would go to his office, he decided, and begin clearing out his things. Dreading that too, after his schoolboy brawling, it still seemed better than returning to the apartment and sitting around uselessly. He would check the register downstairs in the lobby of the office building before going up, to make sure no one he didn't want to see was there. That included just about everybody; they would all know about his hitting Moss and quitting.

Hasher shrugged and headed east on 34th Street, glancing at Macy's windows and ignoring the derelicts here and there. His pace quickened in the next block and he gawked like a tourist at the Empire State Building across the street. By the time he got to Fifth Avenue, he felt better and decided to walk the twenty blocks instead of taking a bus or cab up Madison. He would pack up for three or four hours, then go have a couple of drinks and a good lunch somewhere.

He turned north on Fifth, paused to look at Altman's window displays, and continued on until he got to 40th Street. For him, the Public Library was even more impressive than the Empire State Building and he kept glancing across the street at the lions in front and the broad steps leading up to the squat handsome house of books. Hasher loved the inside of the place even more, with its marble halls and great arched and vaulted ceilings, its prints and dark paintings and statuary, and the long rows of shiny tables in the reading rooms.

Since it was Sunday and still early, there weren't many people on the street. At the corner of 42nd, Hasher stopped and tried to decide, while he waited for the light, whether to continue on up Fifth or swing over to Madison, where the shops were more interesting. He looked back the way he had come and saw a man in a tan raincoat and a brown hat suddenly turn from where he was standing and begin examining the wares in a store window.

Hasher felt a tremor of fear and told himself that he was being absurd. He decided to take Fifth and quickly crossed 42nd and briskly headed on. At the next corner, though, he made a quick turn toward Madision. Halfway down the block, he looked back and saw a man in a tan raincoat and a brown hat just rounding the corner. There was some construction over the sidewalk ahead, so Hasher crossed the street to avoid it. He didn't look back again at the corner but turned north. Then, at a tobacconist's two blocks farther on, he stopped to look at the array of pipes in the window and glanced back the way he had come. The man was there.

Frightened now, Hasher crossed Madison and started back south, toward the man but across the street from him. The man stopped and examined a car, a very ordinary car, and started across the street. Hasher quickened his step and when he reached the corner of 43rd Street, he turned and ran to the entrance of the Hotel Biltmore.

Instead of mounting the steps to the lobby, he turned to his right and hurried along a short corridor, through another door, and entered the westernmost portals of Grand Central Terminal. He ran down the stairs and into the lower waiting room. It was deserted. He turned to the right and ran on, past the empty shops and around the square pillars, without looking back. At last he reached the main rotunda and stopped behind a display to see if he had been followed.

No one resembling the man appeared. Hasher realized that he was holding his breath and let it out shortly. After a minute, he went on, toward the escalator leading up to the Pan Am Building, and when he got to the top he looked down at the great rotunda. He saw no one suspicious. To be doubly safe, he went on through the Pan Am Building to the northern exit, at 45th Street. Looking back once more, he was sure that he wasn't being followed now—if indeed he ever had been. Coincidence, he told himself; it happened all the time.

Now he felt like a fool and didn't look back again. At his building entrance he again refrained from checking. That sort of thing could get out of hand, he told himself; in time he would be afraid of every turn, every unfamiliar face.

He signed the Sunday registry page and looked at the names entered for the firm. There were half a dozen, only two of which he recognized. They would all be young associates, he knew, there to meet their quotas of an average 2,000 hours each annually, which could be billed to clients. At a fee of $70 an hour, that came to $100,000 a year per associate for the firm after his or her salary was paid. It was a vicious system; it corrupted young lawyers in their first jobs and it cheated clients because most of the work was as useless as it was profitable. This was the point at which fresh law-school graduates learned what none of their professors had ever taught them: how legal practice actually works.

High-class thievery in thick-carpeted paneled rooms, Hasher thought. At least he was out of it. He remembered

Moss's epithet: "a moralistic son of a bitch," and wondered what he could do now for a living. He had enough to live on for two or three years . . . if he lived. Any plans for the future would have to wait.

Hasher showed the guard at the receptionist's desk his identification and went on to his office. As he closed the door behind him, he realized that he felt safe for the first time in days. The prowler at the cottage . . . the rapist at home . . . the man behind him on the street. But the feeling vanished as he recalled his encounter with Moss and the partners' exclusion of Hasher from their crucial meeting on whether or not they should disband the firm. He had more enemies here than anywhere else.

Hasher looked around the handsomely appointed room: the red-leather sofa and easy chair, the mahogany desk and tall swivel chair upholstered in black leather, the one wall covered with shelves of law books from ceiling to floor, and, with a brief smile, the deep-red carpeting and the dark-oak paneling. Sixteen years—a lot of work, a lot of cases and clients, a lot of disappointments, a lot of money. And some satisfaction. "Only a game," he thought again. Let the bird-dog associates have it. They would deceive themselves endlessly, struggle to rise, devote themselves entirely in mind and spirit and body to gain a room like this. And one day, probably not until old age made them more honest, it would be poison in their throats.

Hasher took a partially filled cardboard file box and emptied it. He put it behind the desk and began going through the drawers, sorting out what belonged to the firm from what belonged to him. To his surprise, he finished the task in less than two hours. He sat back and again surveyed the room—this time slowly and precisely, as if to fix the place in his memory. Noticing the pictures and diplomas and scrolls framed on the wall behind him, he rose and took them down: the baccalaureate from Dartmouth, the LL.B. from Columbia, the document attesting to his passage of the New York State bar exam and admission to the bar, and a large photograph of him standing proudly between Lucius Slocum and Chief Justice Earl Warren, his two heroes.

He put the frames on the papers in the box and turned to the top of the desk itself. It was fairly clean, with few articles—a blotter in a leather-cornered frame, a pottery jar with pencils and pens, a tobacco humidor and a rack of pipes from the days when he smoked, a calendar, a digital clock in a brown imitation-wood case, a letter opener, a green-marble pen stand with a glass inkwell, and a red-leather address book.

But it was enough to require another box. He got up and left the room for the stockroom halfway down the long corridor, hoping that he would see no one. He didn't and on his way back to his office with a smaller box than the one he had already used, he paused as he recalled Rail's threat about his "culpability" in handling the Poulson estate. Hasher turned and went back a few doors to one with a sign saying "Files Section: Authorized Personnel Only." Hasher had a key to the room and quickly let himself in. The room was dark and he found the switch behind the door and flicked it. Fluorescent lights flickered on, off, on. Grateful that no one was using the files, Hasher hurriedly went to the Ps and found the Poulson file. He stuck it inside the box and left.

Back at his desk, he opened the file and took out the folder dating from the last year that Vivian Trumbull was the old man's secretary. All the documents seemed in order. He took out the file from the previous year— the period in which she had stolen the $270,000 that she had blamed her husband for. Again there was nothing suspicious. They were bluffing then. It was unlikely that she would have begun by stealing from an estate that he, rather than her boss, handled, and it was even more unlikely. . . . But as he leafed through the file from the year before that, he soon saw he had been wrong: there was a discrepancy in the accounts of. . . . He paused and jotted down a column of figures: $70,248. He looked at his signatures on the three crucial transfer documents; they were unmistakably his.

Hasher sat back in his chair. He had let her make a fool of him not once but three times. My God, he thought, and ran a hand over his eyes. He rechecked. He had been right the first time: three almost identical orders for negotiable government bonds, payable to bearer—with no bearer named. A ten-year maturity date. She could have cashed them in immediately, and probably had, to avoid the risk if anyone noticed the discrepancy and sent out the bonds' registry numbers to alert federal banks.

He swore ferociously and slapped the file closed. He sat back with his elbows on the chair's armrests, his fingers pyramided under his chin. Finally he nodded, sat up, and opened the address book before him to "W." Between "Western Union" and "Wilson, Samuel" was "Wicknor, Edward," with both his home and office numbers. As the old man's lawyer, he would know, or at least should know, more than anyone else.

As it happened, Wicknor was working at his office, half a dozen blocks up Park Avenue, and suggested that they meet in fifteen minutes at the Bull and Bear, in the Waldorf, for lunch.

Hasher hung up, thought for a few moments, then removed the three incriminating transfer orders from the Poulson file, folded them, and slipped them into his pocket. Then he wrote out a request for the office manager, asking that the box of personal possessions be wrapped and delivered to his home. He got up and looked around his office for the last time.

"Fuck it!" he said.

He picked up the Poulson file to return it to the Files Section, then patted his breast pocket to make sure that he had the papers. First murder and then assault and now grand larceny, he said to himself. What next? He grinned. He had forgotten about breaking and entering. Before he knew it, there would be a ticket for double-parking.

Wicknor, a burly man with thick dark hair and heavy jowls, was hunched over half a Bloody Mary when Hasher arrived and sat down across the small corner table from him. After ordering a Bloody Mary for himself, Hasher tried to think of a place to start. Wicknor seemed uneasy and Hasher wondered if he would prefer to forget about the case of Slocum vs. Slocum, which he had lost about as badly as a lawyer could. Not that there had been any way to win it, Hasher knew, but he might have finessed a settlement or flung enough dust in his opponent's eyes to confuse everyone. Perhaps it wasn't the case at all, Hasher thought as his drink came and he took a taste; perhaps Wicknor had heard about his resignation and Moss.

Finally Hasher decided to go into the subject directly. Without mentioning the diary or the posthumous messages from the old man, he recounted the story he knew as if Lucius had told it to him as it unfolded. Wicknor confirmed it, with nods and grunts, in every detail and when Hasher asked why he hadn't introduced James's blackmail letter and Vivian's love note in evidence, he shrugged heavily and glowered across the table.

"Useless," he said. "Worse than useless. In a case like that, the best you can do is get it over with as quickly as possible. End it and mend yourself. It was a no-win from go."

Hasher nodded. He didn't want to antagonize this man any more than he obviously had. "I'm not questioning your defense, I just wanted to make sure I understood. That's how I understood it."

Wicknor seemed to relax a little. "I hear you resigned," he said.

"Rather more vigorously than I should have," Hasher replied with an attempt at a smile.

Wicknor nodded. "Moss is a prick."

"They're all pricks."

"Because they let Lucius down?" Wicknor watched him now.

"That mostly. But there are other things. You know what law firms are like."

Wicknor laughed shortly. "Like whorehouses," he said.

Hasher was surprised at his candor and decided to tell

him the rest—why he had asked to meet him. He told about the old man's warning that Rail claimed to have evidence that Hasher had also stolen from his clients' estates.

Wicknor was surprised. "How much?"

"A little over seventy thousand."

"It's not true of course," Wicknor said and lowered his eyes.

"No more than it was true about Lucius."

Wicknor looked up at him without speaking.

After a moment's hesitation, Hasher took out the documents that he had removed from the Poulson file and handed them across the table. Wicknor examined them carefully, then re-examined them.

"The same as with Lucius," he said and handed them back. "I gather the signatures are yours."

"As far as I can tell. I've no idea when she got me to sign."

The waiter came and they ordered sandwiches and beer. When he left, Wicknor asked, "What do they want from you—money?"

"Rail filed papers to invalidate Lucius's will."

Wicknor sat back, even more surprised. "On what grounds?"

"That he was deranged by what happened to him. Senile. It was only his final attempt to destroy his long-suffering wife."

Wicknor grunted. "That whore! So she wants the cabin too."

"They've offered to sell it to me if I give in."

"Christ!" Wicknor shook his head in disgust. "How much?"

"Fifty-five thousand."

Again Wicknor shook his head. "What's it worth—thirty?"

"Forty at the outside."

"So instead of inheriting forty thousand dollars, you've got to pay fifty-five thousand. That makes ninety-five thousand. Add the seventy she stole from your account and she's into you a hundred and sixty-five thousand dollars. What'd you ever do to her?"

"Nothing."

"Lucky for you," Wicknor said. "Imagine if you had."

"People like Vivian don't need a reason."

Wicknor nodded. "I see it every day. Take the divorce case I'm working on today. The wife left the husband for someone else. She's rich. He's middle-aged and has a middle-level job. Isn't likely ever to make much more than he does now. So she's suing him for divorce on the ground of adultery and demanding alimony. Not a lot— just enough to ruin his life. And she may get it."

"Which of them is your client?"

Puzzled, then amused, Wicknor said, "The guy, fortunately."

"If she had come to you first?" Hasher asked.

Wicknor shrugged. "You know the answer to that: 'I'm a lawyer.' "

Hasher nodded. Thank God he wasn't any longer. "Is it usually the women who behave that way?"

"Usually. Of course they usually have reason to be vindictive. It's usually the man who leaves the woman, he's footloose and fancy free, he has more money, he's got a better chance of getting another mate. It's enough to make anyone vindictive."

"But in the case you told me about none of that was true and she's still vindictive. Is that usually the way?"

Wicknor nodded.

"Why?"

"Who knows? Do you?"

"I suppose they feel they're victims," Hasher answered, thinking of Margaret.

"Maybe," Wicknor said. "But that has nothing to do with Vivian. She's nobody's victim. Every man who passes her on the street is hers."

Hasher nodded. Even Herbie Lime.

"Of course women like her always find the most vicious kind of lawyers to represent them," Wicknor went on. "Like Rail." He looked across the table with disgust.

"There's only one thing to do with a guy like Rail."

"What?"

"Kill him," Wicknor said with a laugh. "Our system provides no other means of protecting us against the Rails of this world."

Their sandwiches and beer came and both men ate and drank for a few minutes without talking. At last Wicknor asked, "What do you want from me?"

"First, a bill for the time we discuss this."

"Forget it."

"I insist."

Wicknor finished his beer and ordered another. "You mean so I can't be forced to testify about seeing those transfer papers? Lawyer-client privilege?"

Hasher nodded.

"Forget it. I never saw any papers. We never had this conversation." He took a huge bite of his sandwich.

Hasher recounted his appeal to the District Attorney, months earlier, that Vivian Slocum be prosecuted for perjury and Marvin Rail for suborning perjury.

Wicknor listened with amusement. "What'd he say?"

"That he had enough to do prosecuting real criminals."

Wicknor nodded. "Of course."

"Did you ever consider going to the Bar Association?" Hasher asked. "I mean to file a complaint against Rail?"

"Yeah. I not only considered it, I talked to a man I know on the grievance committee about it. A waste of time. The association exists solely to preserve the status quo."

"The ultimate corruption."

Wicknor's beer came and he washed down the last of his sandwich with it, then leaned back and lit a cigar. "I'd rather not think about what's ultimate in our line of work."

Hasher waited for a few minutes. "What would you do in my place?" he asked at last.

"Give in," Wicknor said unhesitantly. "If you don't, she'll destroy you too. She may anyway—just for the pleasure of it."

*   *   *

The subway platform at Lexington Avenue and 51st Street was unusually crowded for a Sunday and Hasher made his way through the throng toward the rear of the platform in the hope that it would be less jammed there. It wasn't and when the local train finally roared in, he saw that it was jammed too. Few passengers got off and many got on and he had to force his way into the last car and squeeze through the crowd to a spot a few feet from the door. He grunted as more people came in behind him, thrusting him against a fat woman, who glared at him as if the crowd didn't exist and he was there only to molest her.

The doors slid closed, banged open, and closed again. Suddenly Hasher froze. He sniffed once, then quickly several more times. The odor of cloves was unmistakable. He turned and saw the back of a man who had just edged through the crowd behind him, jostling Hasher as he passed. He was wearing a tan raincoat and a brown hat.

"Oh, my God," Hasher murmured. It was the rapist, it was the man who had followed him that morning. Then Hasher remembered the strange odor he had smelled in the hall below the trapdoor at the cottage. It was the same—cloves.

CHAPTER

12

When Hasher got back home forty minutes later—after getting off the subway at the next stop, taking a taxi down Lexington to Grand Central, running through the terminal and taking another taxi on Vanderbilt Avenue back up Park Avenue, then walking across 73rd Street to make sure he wasn't being followed—he suddenly realized that these precautions had been idiotic. The man already knew where he lived. Hasher swore viciously and stuck his key into the lock. He paused. The man had either got hold of a key to the apartment or could easily pick the lock; otherwise he could not have been there when Margaret had come home two days earlier.

Hasher closed the door behind him and leaned against it, weak with fear. He thought of the gun, hidden at the cottage, and swore again. If only he had brought it back. The man could simply have taken the subway uptown and walked to the apartment. But the doorman was on duty, Hasher remembered; it wouldn't be so easy; maybe the man had got in once but not twice.

Scarcely reassured by this thought, Hasher ran into the living room and grabbed the fireplace poker. He searched the apartment, just as he had searched the cottage— flinging open doors, looking into closets, peering under the bed, yanking back the shower curtain—with the same dread certainty that he was about to die. Finally, trembling but sure that no one was there, he went to the living room and collapsed on the sofa.

It was clear to him that he couldn't go on living in fear like this. If only he knew why Rail and Vivian had hired the man. To taunt him with their power? To find out what he was up to, whether he had sent the detective to plant the tap in Vivian's place? Or to scare him into paying up? He groaned and told himself to give in, as Wicknor had advised. It was the only way to get some peace. But Hasher knew that even his surrender wouldn't stop them. They had driven the old man to his death but that hadn't satisfied them, they had merely aimed the vendetta at Hasher. They had destroyed the law firm and driven him out of practice and now were blackmailing him. Giving up, letting her have the cabin or buying it from her at her own price wouldn't affect their being able, at any time, to turn him in to the D.A. for the theft from the Poulson estate. He could never escape.

The telephone rang and he jumped at the sound, then relaxed, sure that it was only Margaret. He answered. The line clicked and went dead. With an oath, Hasher slammed the receiver down. What a hopeless fool he was! The man was playing with him, laughing at him. Such a simple way to find out whether he had gone back home when he fled from the subway. He'd had a gun, Margaret had thought, or a knife. No, not a knife, not someone like him. He wasn't Lyndon James. He wasn't an amateur.

Hasher took out his address book and found the two numbers Lime had given him. The first reached an answering machine. The second was answered by Lime in person.

"Friend or foe?"

"Hasher."

"Speak to me."

"Are you in your car?"

"I am."

"Free?"

"As the proverbial bird—unless my wife calls."

Annoyed by the flippancy, Hasher tried to think of

what to say that wouldn't be revealing in case his phone was tapped. But he saw that there was no way out. If he left the building to go meet Lime, he would probably be followed; if Lime picked him up at the door, it would be the same. Either way, the man would know that he had an ally. While Lime wasn't much in that line, he was all Hasher had.

"Shit!" he muttered.

"What?"

"Come up to my place as soon as you can."

"That's what I thought you said."

"And unobtrusively."

"Right-o." Lime hung up.

Ten minutes later the doorman buzzed from the lobby to announce a "Mr. Herbert." Hasher told him to send the visitor up but when his doorbell rang, he still asked who it was.

"Herbie."

Hasher opened the door to find Lime wearing a houndstooth deerstalker's cap and a thick gray moustache. A curved pipe hung from his toothy grin.

"I said *unobtrusively!*" Hasher said, trying not to smile at the absurd figure.

Lime strolled in and removed the pipe. "Basil Rathbone I'm not but no one would expect a private dick to get himself up like this." He put the cap in his coat pocket and tore off the moustache, then sauntered into the living room.

Hasher had to admit that anyone who had seen Lime coming in would never recognize Lime going out.

He took off his raincoat and sat down in Hasher's easy chair. Hasher stood by the fireplace and said, "I've been followed."

Lime put a forefinger to his lips, got up, and motioned Hasher to follow him. They went into the kitchen and Lime turned on the faucet. He smiled. "If you're tapped, you're probably bugged too—through the phone," he said in a low voice. "Simplest thing in the world. Now go on. The running water will kill their reception."

Moving closer to the detective, Hasher quickly recounted in a low voice how he had spotted a man who seemed to be following him that morning when he went to his office and then, after lunch, how the man dressed the same way who smelled of cloves was on the subway.

Lime jerked his head back and stared at him. "Cloves?"

Realizing that he hadn't told Lime that part of Margret's experience, Hasher said, "She smelled cloves just before she was knocked out."

"You saw his face on the subway?"

"His back was to me."

"Cloves? You're sure?"

Hasher went to the nearby spice rack and took down a tin. He opened it and sniffed, then nodded. "Positive. Why?"

"Sounds like a guy who used to be around town. Quite a famous guy. But I thought he was still in the slammer."

Hasher paled. "What for?"

"Rape and murder," Lime said. "Buggered a little boy and broke his neck—while he was doing it, they said."

"The same—"

"What?" Lime asked, watching him closely.

Hasher shook his head. "Nothing." He went to the refrigerator and took out some ice. "Drink?"

"No thanks."

Hasher put a couple of cubes in a glass. As he returned the tray to the freezer, he paused, wondering if he should show Lime the copy of the old man's diary and the other evidence, which he had put back into the book bag and wrapped in foil and hidden in the rear of the freezing compartment. Why not? he thought and took out a couple of plastic containers and put them on a counter. He removed several small foil-wrapped packages and reached behind to the rear of the compartment. The bag wasn't there. He must have put it on the other side. Quickly he began taking out the contents of the freezer and tossing the stuff into the sink.

Lime stepped back. "I don't believe it!"

Frantically Hasher emptied the freezer and turned, wild-eyed, to Lime, "It's gone!"

"You hid something in there."

Hasher nodded. The freezer door swung closed and he slumped against the refrigerator.

"Important of course," Lime said.

"The blackmail evidence."

"I don't believe it," Lime said again. "Every dumb housewife tries that trick. It works only if the thief is even dumber. Not many are. One of the first places they look."

Hasher stared at him helplessly. "You must think I'm an idiot."

"It crossed my mind."

Hasher was about to fire him on the spot when Lime cocked his head and looked at him appraisingly. "I thought *you* were the one being blackmailed," he said.

"That's right."

"But the evidence is—*was*—in there?" He pointed at the freezer. "Rather careless of the blackmailer, wasn't it, letting you keep the evidence against you?" He grinned.

"That's enough!" Hasher said, too angry to bother explaining.

"Wrong," Lime said, still grinning. "*More* than enough. I don't mind being lied to. Everybody lies to me. Everybody lies to everybody. If they didn't, the fucking world would collapse. But a patsy I don't like being. Thanks anyway." He turned and walked into the living room and picked up his coat.

Hasher hesitated, wanting to let him go but knowing that he couldn't, then followed. When Lime got to the front door, Hasher said, "The evidence in the freezer was evidence from another source, showing they were blackmailing me." He wondered now, when he saw the expression on Lime's face, why he had bothered after all. Lime had his money, that was all he cared about—besides an excuse to cut out.

Lime ignored him and awkwardly got into his coat. "I'll send back two of the three grand you gave me," he said. "The other I earned."

"Earn the rest," Hasher said.

Lime looked at him and thrust out his jaw. "No thanks." He turned to the door.

"Keep the money and do the job I hired you for," Hasher said, not caring how anxious he sounded. "Not on Rail and Mrs. Slocum but this guy who's following me." The thought of the killer was enough to make him desperate. "I can't do it alone. If this guy's who you think he is—"

"Go to the cops," Lime said. He opened the door.

Hasher moved forward and closed it. Facing the detective, he said, pleadingly now. "Look, you can keep the two thousand if you do two more things."

"Such as?"

"Let me go out first. You follow and see if anyone's tailing me. If they are, follow them and find out who it is." Hasher waited. "What's the guy's name—the one you mentioned?"

"Spinner," Lime said. "Virgil Spinner."

"Okay, if it's him, then give me a written report, a rundown on his past. And where he lives now." He stopped.

Limes waited and when Hasher didn't go on, he asked, "That's all?"

Hasher nodded.

"Two grand?"

"Yeah."

"You don't want this place swept for taps and bugs?"

Hasher realized that the water in the kitchen was still running. "If they've heard this much, they've heard all they need," he said.

Lime thought for a minute, screwing his mouth up, his head to one side. At last he looked at Hasher. "Get your coat or whatever you were wearing before. I'll leave now and wait somewhere. Don't look for me. That would tip him off. Just walk. If he's there, I'll pick him up. Give me five minutes, then leave."

A minute after Lime left the telephone rang again.

Hasher hesitated, then answered nervously. It was Margaret and when she heard his tone, she asked, "What's wrong?"

"Nothing," he said curtly and was instantly ashamed of himself. She needed him desperately now, he knew, and felt anguish and remorse welling up in himself. He couldn't go on failing her this way. At the same time, though, he was anxious about her sensing every inflection in his voice, every sign of the tension within him. If it went on this way, sooner or later she would realize that it was more than his grief and anger over what had happened to Lucius. The pressure would be too great. If she was around when Hasher was talking to someone else— Sheriff Worthy, say—she would be sure to sense that he was lying.

"You sound strained," Margaret said.

"The exact word," he replied, as lightly as he could manage. "I went to clear out my office. A strain."

"I wondered where you were when I called earlier."

Suddenly irritated again—if he had to explain every move, it would be hopeless—Hasher forced himself to remember her agony. "Are you better?" he asked.

"A little." She paused. "I was thinking. . . ."

He waited impatiently.

"Maybe I'll stay here for a few days. The rest of the week."

He was relieved and again ashamed. "If you think it would help," he said lamely. He had to get off the phone. After what had happened, Lime might give up if Hasher was busy for too long. "I've got to go out now," Hasher said. "An appointment with Ed Wicknor. I'm late."

"Will you call later?"

"Yes of course." Now he was wild to hang up. "I love you," he said quickly.

There was silence on the other end. "I'm worried about you," Margaret said finally. "About us."

"We'll talk about it later," he said through clenched teeth. "I've *got* to go!"

"Then go." She hung up.

Hasher swore and slammed down the receiver.

Once outside, he hesitated, wishing he had asked Lime where he should go, what he should do. But he knew that he couldn't stand there aimlessly, so he turned to his left and started toward Third Avenue, half a block away. A car door closed behind him and he stiffened but walked on, trying to appear normal—a man on his way somewhere. Where? he asked himself and in answer turned left at the corner and headed downtown. It was all that he could do not to look back. After a few blocks, he crossed the avenue and continued on south. At every corner he had to force himself not to turn and glance back the way he had come.

Finally, a dozen blocks down Third, he found his destination: an Irish neighborhood bar that he had never been in before. It was like all such places: dimly lit to conceal its shabbiness and its woebegone patrons, who might have been subjects for Daumier. There were two slatternly women at the end, near the door, at the leg of the L-shaped bar, and four men, sitting a seat apart, down the rest of the bar. The women were talking drunkenly, the men were silent. Hasher took a stool at the far end.

He hated places like this: the seedy despair, the open hostility to strangers. No one looked at him, including the bartender, until finally Hasher had to rap on the bar with a coin for his attention. The man turned and said, "Okay, okay, keep your shirt on." Under other circumstances, Hasher would have walked out but he knew he had to stay for a few minutes at least, to give Lime a chance. The bartender walked down the bar and gave him a nasty look. Hasher ordered a glass of beer and was charged a dollar and a half for it. Outraged, he paid in silence, knowing that if he said anything, the man would tell him to get out. He looked like a nasty drunk.

So did the patrons. The one closest to him, a red-faced fat man three stools away, turned to the man nearest him and said abruptly, "You ever eat burled chicken?"

The other man looked at him in bewildered silence for a minute and shook his head. "Not so's I recall."

"I went to a place the other night with the wife. They gave me something called 'chicken dyvan' on the menu. It was burled. They didn't tell me that when I ordered. Seven bucks!"

"How was it?" the companion asked.

"Lousy! Burled chicken on broccoli with some kind of fucking white gravy. Fucking swindlers." He fell into a moody silence.

A man in a black-leather jacket, dark trousers, and a black Greek fisherman's cap came in, glanced down the bar and took a stool next to the women. Hasher watched to see if he was a regular customer but no one greeted him and the bartender avoided him as assiduously as he had Hasher. It wasn't the same man, Hasher decided—partly because his clothes were so different and partly because it seemed unlikely that anyone tailing him would come inside and show himself openly.

Hasher saw a telephone on the wall and got up; it would seem more natural if it looked as if he had come there to make a call and had a beer as an excuse. He put in a dime and dialed his own number and let it ring several times. When he hung up, the dime didn't come back. He sat down again and waited until the bartender turned, then waved at him.

The man walked down the bar. "Another?"

"No. I lost a dime in the phone."

The bartender shook his head and clucked. "Don't tell me things like that, mister," he said. "I'm sensitive. I might bust out bawling." He grinned nastily.

Hasher picked up his change from the bar and left. He was too angry now to be afraid and stalked up the street, looking straight ahead and not caring whether he was being followed. When he got to his building, he gave the doorman a brusque nod, instead of his usual friendly greeting, and went inside. The doorman ran after him.

"This was dropped off for you right after you went out," he said, handing him a brown envelope.

As Hasher took it, he saw that it was the book bag that had been stolen from the freezer. It had been resealed with Scotch tape but it felt empty. "Who?" Hasher said, panicked. "What did he look like?"

The doorman looked at him in alarm. "I hardly noticed. Just a guy." He hesitated and added, "Wearing a raincoat, I think, and a hat."

"A brown hat?" Hasher felt the fear return.

"Yeah—that's it, a brown hat."

"You were right," Lime said over the phone half an hour later. "You were followed to that bar and back."

Hasher held his breath, then let it out slowly, trying not to sound the way he felt. "Did he see you?"

"I don't think so."

"Was it the man you thought?"

"Hard to tell. It's been fifteen years. He was eighteen or nineteen when he went up. Besides, I never saw him in the flesh back then, only in newspaper shots. A lot of them but it's not the same."

"Where are you now?"

"Back in my car, outside your place."

Then the man had got away. Hasher swore silently. "How was he dressed?"

"Depends on when you're talking about," Lime answered. "When you came out, he was in a tan raincoat."

"And a brown hat?"

"Yeah."

"And then?"

"He ran to your building and gave the doorman a package, then crossed the street and tossed his coat and hat into a parked car. When he followed you, he had on a black jacket. Just before he went into the bar, he put on a black cap."

"I saw him," Hasher said with a gasp.

"I thought you might," Lime replied drily. "You saw him close up then."

Hasher's heart sank; he hadn't even glanced at the man on his way out of the bar. "Not really," he said. "The light was bad."

"Okay, so you come out of that place and a few seconds later he did too. He took the cap off again and when you went into your building, he went to the car and got out a raincoat and a brown hat."

"But you lost him."

"You could say that," Lime answered easily. "He went back to Third and waited until a lone cab came by and jumped in. Nothing I could do. In a town this size you need half a dozen men to do a tail properly. I'm only one."

Hasher was ready to dispute the number but let it pass. "And the car he used?"

"Stolen. I checked with the P.D. bureau by phone."

Ever since Hasher had got on the elevator to come back to his apartment, he had wondered why the man had returned the book bag. Now he told Lime about it.

"Empty?" Lime asked.

"Yeah. Why would he bother, do you suppose?"

"I would suppose he wanted you to know he had it," Lime said. "Remember, it was only because I was there that you happened to look for it and find that it was gone."

"But why would he want that?"

"He's your tail, not mine," Lime said. Hasher could almost see his teeth over the phone as Lime added, "If it's Virgil Spinner, better you than me."

"I had the goods, now he has them," Hasher said. "So it's pay up or else. They must all be having a good laugh right now."

Lime paused, then said, "You know, you're beginning to sound like me."

"I'm beginning to feel like you."

"I wouldn't recommend it." He chuckled at the thought and went on. "Now, I'll take a look at your place this week and see if I can pick him up and tail him home.

Unlikely but possible. The rundown on him you'll have in a day or two. If it's Spinner, there's only one thing to do."

Hasher waited.

"Go to the cops."

CHAPTER

13

"The older we get, the more we become like ourselves,"
Lucius Slocum had said to Hasher one day when the
lawsuit was going badly. Now Hasher thought of the
seams in his own character that were widening into cracks;
soon they would be crevices and in time. . . . The fury in
him that Margaret had spoken about so fearfully, had it
been unleashed by his killing Lyndon James? he wondered again. The answer was there at once for he knew
that he would have willingly killed Moss too, instead of
only breaking his jaw, if the circumstances had been as
dark and secret.

My God, Hasher said to himself, what am I becoming?
But he knew the answer to that question as well: he was
becoming like himself. He might have been back in
Vietnam; this world was that jungle. Virgil Spinner, if the
man was Virgil Spinner, was a killer. Rail and Vivian were
killers. Hasher stared back into himself, remembering the
savagery he had indulged in so heroically in that other
jungle. He had no choice now either.

Morosely absorbed by his thoughts, his will splintered
by fear and uncertainty, Hasher didn't leave the apartment for the next four days. He slept occasionally and
fitfully at odd hours; he ate only when he was famished
and then it was cold food, mainly sandwiches sent up
from the delicatessen at the corner; he drank far too
much whisky; he didn't shave and scarcely washed; and

he paced endlessly as he struggled to figure out what was happening and to decide what to do next. In the end all he knew was what he had known at the beginning and now he was more fearful than ever of going outside. He was sure that the man would be there, waiting.

As the hours and days slowly passed, Hasher began to dread the oncoming twilight and darkness for the first time in almost thirty years. To obliterate his awareness of the time of day, he lowered the shades and closed the curtains and turned on most of the lights. But this only deepened his fear until it was nearly the terror of his childhood. It had begun soon after his parents and Mary Slocum were killed in an auto accident when he was ten. The old man took young Thomas in to live with him for the first few months, so they might console each other, he told the boy, whose own blind grief left no room for anyone else's. Finally he went to live with his mother's unmarried sister but even then he spent much of his time with the old man at his cabin on the lake.

Thomas's fear of the dark then—at the worst of times, a screaming horror when he awoke from a nightmare, chilled with sweat and torn by longing for his mother—grew worse for months but slowly began to subside as the old man gave him the care and security he needed. As darkness fell, the man and the boy sat in the unlighted living room of the cabin, Thomas clenching his hands in fear, perspiration running down his back and sending cold tremors up it as he tried to hold onto himself. Then, when the darkness was full, the old man rose and silently took him by the hand and they went outside and walked together up the wooded and darkly ominous drive to the quiet back road. Once there, the old man took away his hand and they walked side by side into the black night. At last, after many months, Thomas was able, barely, to take the walk alone. Although the first time he was frightened almost beyond endurance, he forced himself on, each step into the darkness a torment, each night sound a terror. Finally his fear seeped away and within a year he had recovered. As young as he was, he knew what he owed Lucius Slocum.

Even the dark jungles of Vietnam hadn't brought back those childish fears. But now Hasher felt them again. He knew that the only way to dispel them was by action. But what kind of action? he asked himself again and again. "Where? When? How?" he asked aloud as he paced restlessly. He tried to suppress the answer that pounded at his mind: When, where, how didn't matter. He had to destroy them before they destroyed him. All three of them. He clutched his head as this awareness finally broke through. He couldn't do it, he told himself, even while he knew that he must.

Hasher telephoned Margaret twice a day and forced himself to sound calm, even cheerful. She seemed better after a couple of days and hinted that she was ready to come home. Panicked, he told her that he was scarcely at the apartment but was out most of the time, including evenings, talking to people about a new kind of career. The fear of being there alone put her off and she delayed her return. When she asked what kinds of things his friends were suggesting, Hasher said that nothing had jelled yet. He wanted only to have her with him and his longing and need for her almost drove him to tears. But he knew that he could not act if she were there. Even more, he could not subject her to the danger he was in now.

Late Thursday afternoon, the fourth day Hasher had been alone, the doorman rang up to announce the delivery of an envelope for him. Hasher had left word that if anyone inquired about him, he was not in, and now the doorman stared at him in surprise as he appeared in the lobby wearing rumpled brown corduroy pants and a dirty tan flannel shirt and battered slippers; he hadn't shaved since Sunday and his naturally heavy beard was filling out.

"Flu?" the doorman asked sympathetically.

Puzzled at first, Hasher understood and nodded. "Yeah —terrible."

He took the envelope with a trembling hand and saw only his name printed in block letters, with no return address, and knew that it was the report Lime had promised. Back in the apartment, he chained the door and went into the living room and sat in his easy chair. He opened the envelope and found a batch of old newspaper clippings, a small white envelope, and several typed sheets of paper.

The clippings were sixteen years old, yellowed and crumbling, and he could hardly make out the figures in the photographs. The headline on the top article said, "Youth Arrested in Rape-Killing Suspected of Mass Murders." All that Hasher could tell from the faded picture was that the suspect seemed slight and rather short compared to the policemen flanking him. Below was a caption: "Virgil Spinner, 19, in the custody of State Police officers, after booking on charges of sodomy and murder in the death of Bobby Winton, 10, last year."

The accompanying article reported that Spinner, described as "a drifter," had been accused of raping and killing the Winton boy, whose body had been found a year before in a woods near the summer camp he attended in the Catskill Mountains. Spinner, who worked in the camp kitchen, had a long arrest record, dating from the age of fourteen, when he ran away from his home in New Hampshire. Law-enforcement authorities in New York had learned of his whereabouts a few days before his arrest and were investigating the possibility that he had committed similar crimes elsewhere in the state. And police in Massachusetts, Connecticut, and Rhode Island had requested further details about the Winton murder to determine whether the suspect might be responsible for other such crimes in their jurisdictions.

The next article gave a brief description of the trial. The state's case against Spinner sounded overwhelming to Hasher and he wondered why the defense counsel hadn't pleaded insanity. Halfway through the account, though, he found the answer: The defense was led by a famous Boston criminal lawyer who prided himself on getting his clients off, without then having them locked up in asylums. But he was one of the highest-paid lawyers in the country and Hasher wondered where this drifter had got the money to pay him.

Moving on to the final paragraph of the story, Hasher gasped as he found the answer to that question too:

The only character witness to testify on Virgil Spinner's behalf was Mr. Lucius Slocum, a prominent attorney from New York City, at whose summer home the defendant was arrested last summer. Mr. Slocum stated that he had known Spinner for more than a year, having hired him to serve as a counselor in a school-plus-camp project that Mr. Slocum had set up as an experiment for wayward boys at his home at Lake Mercy, New York. The witness, under cross-examination, testified that he had not known about the defendant's criminal record when he appointed him as a counselor at the camp.

"It wouldn't have mattered a bit," Mr. Slocum stated. "After all, the experiment was to help wayward boys, and who is better qualified to do that than a wayward boy who has himself been helped?"

After the day's court session concluded, Mr. Slocum told reporters that he was convinced of Virgil Spinner's innocence. "I know this boy," he said.

"Oh my God!" Hasher cried and fell back in his chair. He *knew* this boy! Just as he knew Lyndon Johnson James! He would never, never admit the beast in humankind. He wouldn't even listen to talk of genetics, of character defects, of the natural disasters that environment could afflict on frail humanity, even of insanity. It could all be mended by care and attention and understanding and love.

Cursing the old man for the blind folly that now threatened to destroy him too, Hasher got up and resumed pacing. Bits and pieces came back to him now. Everyone had been oddly silent about the school-camp project when he got back from Vietnam. Lucius had written him there, asking permission to use his cottage for a year, at a handsome rent. The details of the project were sparse: eight boys, an elderly couple and a young counselor to supervise the boys, and the old man himself on weekends. By the time Hasher got home, it was all over. There had been some damage to his cottage, which had been scrupulously repaired, but the damage to Lucius Slocum's pride and beliefs had passed unmentioned. All that was said was that one of the boys had got into some kind of trouble near the end of the year and local of-cials had asked that the project not be renewed for the next year. Since the town's support was essential—the boys attended public school there and had to be accepted by the community if the experiment was to have a chance —the old man had reluctantly dropped it.

"The locals were nervous about it from the start," he had told Hasher later, in explaining the failure. "It didn't take much to close us down."

"Not much!" Hasher said aloud now. He grabbed the clippings and turned to the last one. Virgil Spinner had been sentenced to fifty years in prison.

Lime's typewritten notes contained even more alarming information:

> You may keep these clippings. I had them because I was retained, after Spinner's indictment, by a man whose kid had been murdered in a similar manner. The client was sure, I was half-sure, the cops didn't care because he'd been indicted, so the case was dropped. It was never solved.
>
> Virgil Spinner was paroled from Attica not quite four months ago, after serving 15 years and a few weeks. He was not a model prisoner. A loner, except when he needed someone's ass, which was about once a day. As you may have heard, homosexuality is not unknown in our "correctional" institutions. But Spinner seems to have set some kind of a record. An ex-con who does some odd-jobs for me and who was there for a few

years when Spinner was told me that what he lacked in size (it was too short to massage the prostate properly, the fellow complained) he made up for in energy and was known among his fellow inmates as "the Jackhammer." It also seems that he had the disagreeable habit of holding his partner by the throat while buggering him, which did not, considering his conviction, give much comfort to his partners, or much assurance of ultimate reform.

When released on parole, Spinner went directly to Poughkeepsie, where a job had been arranged for him in a printing plant (his "training" at Attica). He lasted for six weeks and then disappeared. His parole officer said he should never have been let out in the first place. There is a four-state alarm out for him. He is believed, as the saying goes, "to be armed and dangerous." I'll say!

Now to explain why I thought the man who followed you must be Spinner. It was the smell of cloves about him. If the smell was strong enough for you to catch, ditto your lady before he conked her, it couldn't have been from just clove mints or gum. Not that potent. Spinner chewed cloves—*whole* cloves—throughout his trial. He became known in the tabloids as "the clove boy" and there were a lot of desperate jokes about "cloven hooves" and such.

He always carried a small cloth bagful of them (the kind used for tobacco by those who roll their own) and he chewed the things incessantly. I checked this with the ex-con and he said it was the same in the slammer. Some other inmate once stole his supply and Spinner went wild until he could replace it. No one seems to know why he's addicted to the spice, but my informant said maybe it was because his breath smelled like an open sewer.

P.S. In your place, I'd notify the police. If he continues to follow you, they could nab him easily. Good luck.

Hasher put down the notes and picked up the plain white envelope. Inside were ten $100 bills and an itemized account. Hasher was surprised and impressed. Maybe he would use Herbie again later on.

As Hasher walked into the precinct house late that afternoon, he was sure it would prove to be a mistake. But it seemed even a greater mistake not to try. If it was Spinner, he was dangerous. If it wasn't Spinner, they could at least question whoever it was and maybe find out what he was up to and possibly scare him off. Still, Hasher was nervous—and knew that he had reason to be. Cops seemed to dislike and mistrust everyone except other cops, and sometimes even them. Facts were all they trusted, he thought and remembered the line from the old "Dragnet" series: "Just the facts, ma'am." Facts could be put through the bureaucratic machine, registered, disseminated, added up to demonstrate the difficulty of their task—even if, as usual, nothing came of it. But what he had to report—a harrowing fact to him—wouldn't be a fact at all to them.

A middle-aged woman standing in front of the high desk was telling the sergeant on duty that her purse had been snatched only minutes before and only a block away. "All my credit cards," she said, "and nearly two hundred dollars in cash."

The sergeant looked at her wearily. "Numbers of the cards, denominations of the bills," he said.

"The card numbers are at home," she said, her voice wavering as it rose. "Nine twenty-dollar bills, I think, and some singles."

"You *think?*" He stared at the ceiling and said, as if reciting, "Go home and get the numbers. We can't find something we can't identify."

"You won't find it anyway," she cried. "You won't even try. I've been waiting twenty minutes and this is the treatment I get."

"Look lady," the sergeant said in a low ugly voice as he leaned forward and glared at her, "you want to report a crime, report it. You want to talk about the police force like that, go someplace else."

The woman turned away, muttering an epithet under her breath, and walked out.

As Hasher stepped up to the high desk, the sergeant rose and left through a door behind him. Five minutes later he came back and busied himself with some papers, ignoring Hasher. He waited, angry at the treatment and dreading its end.

At last, after several more minutes had passed, the sergeant looked up at him. "Yeah?" he said.

"I understand you're looking for a man—"

"Your name, address, occupation," the officer snapped.

Hasher responded evenly, only hesitating a moment before saying that he was a lawyer.

When he did, the policeman grimaced slightly. "Okay, what's the complaint?" He turned away as if there was nothing in the world Hasher could say that would interest him.

"I understand you're looking for a man—" he began again.

"What man?" the sergeant asked and turned to the officer at a switchboard nearby. "Are we looking for a man, Bill?" The operator grinned over his shoulder. "A lot of men, we're looking for a lot of them," the sergeant said to Hasher. "Which one you got in mind?"

Hasher was afraid he was going to lose his temper. He had changed into a pair of flannel trousers and a tweed jacket but he hadn't shaved and felt scruffy; the feeling hindered him from being himself and he knew as he glared across the high counter that the policeman thought he was drunk.

"His name is Virgil Spinner," Hasher said, trying to sound calm. "He spent fifteen years in prison for the rape and murder of a child—a ten-year-old boy. He was paroled about four months ago. He jumped parole. There's a four-state alarm out for him."

Looking unimpressed by this recital of facts, the officer leafed through some papers. "It'll be in the lieutenant's office," he said, as if to himself. Then he looked at Hasher. "So a guy jumped parole. You know how many items like that we got on the book?" He paused for emphasis, though it was clear he expected no answer, and went on, "The fucking parole boards shouldn't let none—*none*—of them out. You read the papers?"

Hasher nodded.

"Then you know what happens. Let them out, let them out! The fucking bleeding hearts! They're worse, these guys, when they come out than when they went in."

Hasher smiled. "Maybe the solution is not to put them away then."

The sergeant looked at him with disgust. "So what d'you want—" He paused to look down at the paper in front of him. "Mr. Hasher?"

"Spinner is said to be extremely dangerous. I think I know where he is."

"So why didn't you say so? Where?"

"He's been following me."

The officer stared at him in surprise, then craned around to look behind Hasher. "You must have shook him," he said, grinning.

The man on the switchboard laughed. "Jesus!" he said.

At once Hasher realized that there would be no way of explaining without saying too much. If he said too little, he would sound crazy and it was clear that was what the sergeant thought he was. He waited silently.

The policeman wrote something down and said, "Okay, I got the name of the guy. If we find out anything, we'll let you know."

It was hopeless, Hasher knew, but he made one final try. "You said the lieutenant would have the information. Could I see him?"

"He's not here," the sergeant said, too quickly.

"I'll wait."

The man shrugged and turned away.

Hasher took one of half a dozen chairs across the seedy room and no more than a minute later a lieutenant and a captain came in and stood talking in the center of the room. He waited for their conversation to end but when it went on at length he finally got up and went to stand near them. At the first pause, he said, "Excuse me, Lieutenant."

The lieutenant turned to him impatiently. "I'm busy," he said.

"So am I," Hasher replied.

"Then come back when you're not."

"He's being followed by a paroled murderer," the sergeant called out. "Should we have the station house surrounded?"

Hasher turned and walked out, his face crimson as he heard the laughter behind him.

CHAPTER

14

The night doorman, a fat taciturn old German, awoke with a jolt, his eyes wide and unfocused as he gripped the arms of the small chair that the night man was allowed to use. "Oh, it's you, Mr. Hasher," he said gutturally, sounding relieved, as if every minute in that job he expected the worst. He looked at his watch. It was just after 5:00 A.M. "You rise early today," he said and got up to unlock the door.

Hasher thought of the Thurber parable that ended, "Early to rise and early to bed makes a man healthy, wealthy, and dead." It could happen today, he thought, and told himself that it was only his weariness. This was the fifth day, Friday, that he had been alone and again that night he hadn't slept more than two or three hours.

"Would you leave a message for the day man?" he asked. The doorman grunted his assent and Hasher went on, "If Miss Green calls, would you tell her that I had to go out of town on business and I'll be back tomorrow?"

The doorman rubbed a huge hand across his puffy face. "Okay." He opened the door.

"Miss Green," Hasher said, certain that the man would be asleep again within moments.

Hasher saw no one on foot in the three blocks to the garage and only two cars, both taxis, passed him going in the opposite direction. He waited impatiently for his car, gave the attendant a dollar, and drove off. As far as he could tell, no one followed him either in the city or on the highway as he headed north to Lake Mercy. For the first hour, it was still dark but then the sky lightened slowly to the color of pewter; Hasher waited for it to brighten still more but it stayed as it was and then began to rain.

He swore and leaned forward over the wheel and switched on the wipers. Within minutes the rain was so hard that he could scarcely see. A neon sign ahead caught his eye and he slowed down, uncertain if it was Rose's Diner. It was and he pulled in sharply and parked as close to the front door as he could manage. As he got out, he saw that the car beside his had a gutted deer, its long red tongue hanging out of one side of its mouth, tied to the roof rack.

Inside, it was bright and comfortable with the smell of food cooking and the sound of the gas heater at the end of the room hissing out its warmth. There were only three other customers, men dressed in hunting clothes who were seated in the end booth. Hasher slid into a booth two away from them, with his back their way, and looked for Rose. She was there, behind the counter, but if she saw him she didn't let on. Perhaps it was his beard, he thought. He desperately wanted coffee but he knew he couldn't, or shouldn't, hurry her, so he waited.

In a minute she came over to the booth. "I wondered if that was you under all that hair."

"Hello, Rose," he said, smiling. He waited for her to smile back at him but she didn't: she rarely smiled at all anymore. The ordinary disappointments of life had hit her harder than most people. A dozen years ago, she had been a handsome, spirited, witty woman with fine black hair and a wide lush mouth. Now she looked much older than her age; her hair was gray and pulled back in a pony tail, her trim body settled into square dullness, her lips thin and turned down at the corners. Looking at her now, Hasher could scarcely believe the change. Her husband, five years younger than she, had run off with an even younger waitress and Rose had never got over it.

"The usual?" she asked, holding her pad and pencil ready.

Her hands hadn't changed at all, he thought, and felt them on his body again. He nodded. "Especially the orange juice and coffee," he said with a smile.

A few months after her husband left her, Hasher had been there one late afternoon, just before she closed the diner for the day, and they had chatted amiably, lazily, sitting over coffee with the door locked. It was hard to believe now how engaging, even enticing she had been, he thought as he watched her walk away. And if she understood his reference to orange juice and coffee, she gave no sign of it. The place served fresh orange juice and superb coffee but what he had meant was a line of hers from back then, that afternoon. Rose had invited him into her little apartment, behind the restaurant, to see something. Once there, she turned and said, simply, "Fuck me, Tom." He had, with great fondness and pleasure. Afterward Rose had smiled warmly at him and said, "Three things never fail—fresh orange juice, the first cup of coffee of the day, and a friendly fuck."

The encounter had never been repeated. A few weeks later Hasher had suggested it but Rose had said, "No, Tom. It was nice but I wouldn't want to get interested in you. I hurt enough as it is."

Now she brought the orange juice and coffee and he drank both quickly. When she served his food, she picked up the empty glass and cup without a word and went to get him more coffee. A minute later she put it down on his table and straightened up slowly, as if her back hurt. The men behind him laughed at something. Rose didn't look at them but stared out the rain-streaked window. He followed her glance and saw the deer.

"That's all men really want to do, isn't it?" she said wearily. "Kill things, that's all they want."

Hasher looked at her worn face, then thought of how he had killed Lyndon Johnson James, how Rail had killed the old man, how Spinner had killed a small boy and was waiting to kill him. "Some of them do," he said.

"*All* of them." She turned away and left him.

The outer door opened and a man came in. He was wearing a tan raincoat and a brown hat. Hasher stared at him in sudden fear, trying to match the face with the faded photographs in the clippings that Lime had sent him. The man's age seemed about right but Hasher couldn't be sure even of that because the hat and coat collar obscured part of his face. The man glanced down the narrow room quickly toward him and then sat at the counter and ordered coffee.

Rose brought Hasher a third cup of coffee, which he didn't really want, and cleared the table. He nodded toward the figure at the counter and asked in a low voice, "You know him?"

She looked over her shoulder briefly and shook her head. "Should I?"

Hasher shrugged to avoid answering and picked up his coffee. It was too hot and he put it down. Rose left and as he watched her he thought of Margaret and longed to be with her. When he got to the cottage, he would call her. For all he knew, she might be on her way back to the apartment from the Island.

Glancing covertly at the man at the counter, Hasher caught his eyes in the mirror behind it and quickly looked away. He hadn't realized that he could see the face, and be seen, in the mirror. He looked quickly at the image several times until he had the man's face fixed in his mind: pale and narrow with a sharp nose, prominent cheekbones, a wide thin mouth, a small round chin. Wishing that he could see the color of his hair, Hasher looked into the mirror again and the man stared directly into his eyes. A moment later the man slid off the stool and stood up and slipped his right hand into his coat pocket. Hasher froze. But the man only took out some change, put it on the counter, and turned. He paused long enough to stare again, briefly but directly, at Hasher, and then left.

Hasher waited a few minutes until he saw the car, which had apparently been parked out of sight around the side of the buildings, pull slowly out; it was a dark color, difficult to identify in the heavy rain, and had a New York license that he couldn't read from that distance. The car paused at the exit and pulled onto the highway and headed north.

When Rose gave Hasher his change, her fingertips brushed his hand. He trembled. She looked at him appraisingly for a moment and asked, "What's wrong?"

"Nothing," he said quickly, avoiding her eyes.

"That man?"

Now Hasher looked at her. Christ, if I could only tell her, he thought. But he knew he couldn't.

"If you need help. . . ." she began, then trailed off.

He forced a smile and said, jokingly he hoped, "I'm beyond all help."

"I know the feeling." Now, for the first time, she smiled and Hasher saw a trace of the old Rose.

When he had driven a mile or so north, he passed a dark-colored car with a New York license plate parked on the shoulder; a figure was in the driver's seat but he couldn't tell whether it was a man or a woman. Seized by a shudder of premonition, he locked the doors and speeded up. The car pulled onto the road and kept at an even speed three or four hundred yards behind. Hasher increased his speed and the car kept at the same distance. He slowed down and it slowed down too.

"Oh my God!" he murmured. It was Spinner.

Hasher had little more than an hour's drive ahead of him. The rain had let up and now was only a steady drizzle, just enough to require the wipers. Their soft whooshing rhythm lulled him nearly to sleep several times. Periodically he switched them off to break the soporific cadence, then switched them on again. The back of his neck and the tops of his shoulders ached painfully. He tried to relax and massage the muscles, first with one hand and then the other but that only made the pain worse. From time to time a car would pull into the gap between him and the car behind, wait for a stretch of clear road, and roar past, spewing dirty water onto his windshield.

Ten minutes passed, fifteen, twenty, half an hour; the dark car was still there behind him. Hasher cursed. Now he did not dare go to the cottage.

When he was fifteen minutes away from it, he suddenly made a turn onto a road going to the east, in the opposite direction from Lake Mercy, then turned onto a major highway and sped north. He looked in the rearview mirror. The car wasn't there. He drove on, checking the mirror every few seconds. One car, then another appeared in the distance behind him, closed the gap, and passed. But neither resembled the car that had been following and now the road to the rear was clear as far as he could see.

Hasher let out a long sighing breath, drew in deeply, and relaxed. Ten miles farther on, he turned off the main highway onto a spur road and within a couple of miles was back on the narrow back highway he had been traveling before. He slowed down as he approached the weathered wood sign saying "Lake Mercy 1½ miles" but drove on past the side road and headed for town.

It was a little before eight o'clock when he pulled into the parking lot of the Sheriff's Office and stopped. Waiting for a minute or two, he watched the street but saw no car resembling the one that had been behind him. He got out and went inside.

He had to wait a few minutes before seeing the Sheriff and when he went into the office Worthy waved him to the chair beside his desk and stubbed out a cigarette.

"We seem to be seeing a lot of each other these days, Thomas," he said. His tone was noncommittal.

After the policemen at the precinct house in the city the night before, Hasher was grateful for even that. He nodded. "I came to ask you about a man—Virgil Spinner."

Worthy stared at him without speaking for a few seconds. "I had expected something to happen," he said. "This must be it." He smiled thinly and went on, "Funny how we talked about Lyndon James that day but never mentioned Spinner. Of course he was in prison—or I thought he was still in prison. You must have known him."

Not wanting to say that he hadn't ever heard of him until a few hours before, Hasher merely said, "I was in Vietnam at the time."

"Oh, of course," Worthy said, as if he had known it when he asked the question. "What about him?"

"You know he was paroled about four months ago," Hasher said.

Worthy nodded.

"You know he jumped parole."

Again Worthy nodded.

"I think I saw him a few days ago."

Worthy sat forward a little. "Where?"

"On the street in New York. Last Sunday afternoon."

"But you had never seen him before, I thought." Worthy lit a cigarette and inhaled deeply.

"As far as I know, I hadn't. But I saw pictures of him."

Worthy thought for a minute, examining the business end of his cigarette, then said, "As long as he's in the city and not here."

Hasher wanted to tell him about the man at Rose's and the car that had seemed to be following him but refrained: he could never explain it without explaining everything.

"This is the last place he'd come," the Sheriff added. "A small town like this, everybody knowing who he is and what he did—or what they sent him away for. He'd done a good deal more, I'd say. He wouldn't be here an hour before I'd be told of it."

"I'd like to make sure about the man I saw in the city," Hasher said. "Do you have a more recent photograph of Spinner? I've seen only the ones from the time of his trial."

Worthy smiled and opened a manila folder. He took out a few small photographs and handed them to Hasher. "Arrived in yesterday's mail. Since he was arrested here, they figured he might come back. Maybe to get even."

"For what?" Hasher asked, surprised.

The Sheriff shrugged. "Who knows? With a guy like that it could be for anything. He's a killer. Not a heat-of-the-moment killer but a real killer. We're pretty sure he murdered at least four other boys."

Hasher shuddered.

"And the grandparents of one of them."

Hasher looked at the top photograph and found himself staring into the eyes of the man at Rose's. It was the face in the mirror, he was certain. Trying to restrain himself, his fear and excitement, he nodded to Worthy. "It's him."

"You're sure?" Worthy took a drag on his cigarette. "Look at the profile shots."

Hasher put down the top photo. As he studied the left profile, he was suddenly less certain. The nose was shorter and the chin fuller than he remembered. He looked at the right profile and his uncertainty grew stronger.

Worthy caught his doubt and said, "As a lawyer, you know how unreliable eyewitness identification is. If the suspect wore a moustache, any man with a moustache is him. Same with glasses. I once had a case where a guy almost went up for life because he wore a tweed hat. Must be millions of tweed hats around. But the woman who identified him swore he was the man. When we caught the real guy, there was no resemblance at all. Except the hats."

Hasher nodded. "And if anything lies, it's the camera," he said. He turned back to the full-face photograph and studied it for several minutes. Finally he looked across the desk at Worthy. "It seems to be the same man," he said, "but I'm not positive."

All that he knew for sure now was that he was exhausted. The strain of the past days, the lack of sleep, too little food and too much liquor had told on him. He wanted to leave but was afraid that if he stood up he would faint. Slumping back in the chair, he fought against his lightheadedness and nausea.

"Put your head between your knees," Worthy ordered abruptly.

Embarrassed that his condition was so obvious, Hasher did as he was told. The Sheriff put out his cigarette and opened a window and in a few minutes Hasher felt better. He sat back slowly and smiled weakly. "Sorry," he said. "Guess I'm coming down with something."

Worthy watched him without speaking. At last he said, "I hear you quit your law firm."

Hasher was stunned by the speed of rumor and the distance it could travel.

"Because of Mr. Slocum?" the Sheriff asked. "If I'm not being nosey."

He was but Hasher didn't want to say so. "That and other problems," he replied. "I'm fed up with the law."

Worthy squinted at him. "Fed up how?"

Realizing that his words could have sounded as if he meant that he was fed up with law itself, rather than the practice of law, Hasher smiled. "It's a rotten business, Bill."

"What isn't?" Again Worthy fell silent, then asked, "Did you come all the way up here to see those pictures of Spinner?"

Alarmed, Hasher shook his head. "No, I forgot some papers at the cottage. But I remembered seeing that fellow and thought I'd drop by to check with you. I knew you're usually here early." Feeling that he was explaining too much, he stopped.

"I wouldn't leave any valuables in that cottage."

"Anything more on that prowler your men saw?"

"Nope." Worthy watched him for a moment, then asked, "You feeling better?"

"Yeah." Hasher slowly got to his feet. "Okay now."

"You staying at the lake or going back to the city?" the Sheriff asked. He reached for a cigarette but stopped himself.

"I don't know." Hasher looked at him, waiting. "It's lonely out there this time of year."

"By the looks of you, I'd say get some sleep, before

you turn around and drive back. You could try shaving too."

Hasher smiled and turned to go but stopped. How had Worthy known that he had just driven up from the city? But he was too weary and confused to care. "See you, Bill," he said. "If I stay over, I'll let you know, so no one gets nervous about seeing lights in my place." He went to the door.

"Do that." Worthy lit a cigarette. "By the way, Vivian Slocum's in town."

Hasher paused, his mind reeling, and turned back slowly. "Oh?"

"Staying at the inn. With some guy."

"Marvin Rail?" Hasher gripped the doorknob.

"So I hear," Worthy answered. He blew a series of smoke rings, then poked a forefinger through one of them. "Separate rooms, though."

"I bet." Hasher hesitated before saying, "Do you know why they're here? Isn't the cabin sealed?" He cursed himself silently for revealing that he knew it had been. Again he felt lightheaded.

"They were out there yesterday," the Sheriff answered. "I figured you might like to know, so you don't bump into them." He paused for a moment and went on. "I understand Lucius left the place to you and she's fighting the will. Right?"

Hasher nodded. He had told Worthy that much himself.

"Best all around if the two of you don't meet, I'd say."

"You mean not in your jurisdiction at least," Hasher said.

Worthy grinned. "Somthing like that."

"Nobody in the world I want to meet less."

Worthy grinned again.

Except Virgil Spinner, Hasher thought.

CHAPTER
15

A deep winter chill had pervaded the cottage. It was damp inside and bleakly unwelcoming in the gray light of the autumn morning. Standing inside the back door to the kitchen, Hasher shivered, wanting only to get the gun and leave. But he knew that Worthy was right: he had to have some sleep before driving back. Still, he was afraid to stay. Despite the Sheriff's assurance that Spinner wouldn't dare show up there, Hasher was sure that he was somewhere not far away. He must have come to confer with Rail and Vivian—or he had followed Hasher.

Muttering an oath, he locked the door behind him and searched the house again. Everything seemed as he had left it. He pulled the curtains in the living room closed, turned on a few lights, lit the gas heater and put it on high, spread the electric blanket and a comforter on the bed in the main bedroom, and went to the kitchen to put on the kettle. He made an extra-strong hot toddy in a mug and took it to the living room. As he sat near the heater, sipping the drink and sensing its warm power spread through him, he began to feel better. Within fifteen minutes he was almost relaxed. A few minutes later he barely had strength left to take off his clothes and get into bed.

Distorted replicas of events and people over the past few weeks spun around him as he moaned and flung himself about, now and then crying out a name or a warning or a plea. Yet he slept on, his mind transforming hideous reality into merely frightening images and thereby keeping him asleep enough to repair some of the ravages on his exhausted body. Even so, he seemed to sleep only reluctantly and at times he gave a shuddering cry and strained to rise, as if trying to awaken himself. But then, again and again, he would fall back and lie silently unmoving.

A vision of Lyndon Johnson James's dead face, with reeds waving eerily in the dark water around it, brought Hasher awake with a muffled scream. He had forgotten to turn the electric blanket down and was shaking with the artificial fever it had induced. His face and neck and chest were dripping with sweat and he dried himself with the top of the sheet. Turning, he looked at the electric clock beside the bed: 12:10.

There was a sharp report outside, then another. He sat up. Gunshots! And not far away. A third went off and he thought he heard the dying whine of a spent bullet.

Hasher jumped out of bed, slipped on his pants and shirt, and ran into the living room. He yanked open the heavy curtains over the porch windows and saw that it was daytime. The lake, dimmed by a low mist hanging just above the water, was pebbled by a light rain. There was no one in sight.

Had he dreamed the gunshots? he wondered but knew that he hadn't; he had heard the last one when he was fully awake. Uneasily he let the curtains fall, even though he couldn't have been a target in the darkened room. He hurried back to the bedroom and put on his socks and shoes and jacket. He had moved a step toward the closet to get his gun when he heard footsteps pounding up the wood stairs to the front porch and across the porch to the house.

There was a furious hammering on the door. "Anyone there?" a man shouted. "Let me in! I gotta call the police!"

Wondering if it was a trick, if the man was Spinner trying to lure him into the open, Hasher walked quietly into the living room and stood uncertainly, waiting.

"Hello?" the man cried. "Hasher!"

"Who is it?" Hasher called.

"Pete Linzer! For God's sake, open up!"

Hasher recognized the voice now: Linzer, who owned the Ford agency and had sold him his last car. Going to the door, Hasher opened it and a heavyset man dressed in a red-and-black checked hunting outfit tumbled in. He was carrying a rifle.

"What's happened?" Hasher asked. "Leave the gun outside."

"What kept you?" Linzer cried, his face almost as red as his jacket. "Christ! I knew you were here—saw your car in back when I went by on my way down the lake." He stood the gun, stock down, on the floor and leaned the barrel against the wall beside the door.

"I was asleep," Hasher mumbled.

"You didn't hear the shots?"

"I thought I heard something but wasn't sure."

"Christ!" Linzer shouted. "One of them went 'plunk' into a tree right past my head."

He saw the telephone in the corner and hurried over to it. Standing with his back to Hasher, he dialed, waited a few seconds, and said, "This is Pete Linzer. Give me the Sheriff. It's urgent." A minute later he said, "Bill, I'm out at Hasher's place on Lake Mercy. . . . What? . . . No, he's okay. But it's not so okay outside. I came here about an hour ago. Parked my car on the road and walked down Hasher's drive and around past the cottage into the woods. . . . Keep your fucking shirt on! I was stalking that buck everybody claims to have seen. To make it short, I got halfway down the west bank of the lake when I look across and there, on the other side, was the buck. Biggest fucking deer I ever saw. It was a little misty and a light drizzle. But it was the buck, no doubt about it. The size of a fucking moose!"

He paused to listen, then hurried on, "Okay, okay, I'm about to get to that. What happened is I shot at it and it shot back!"

Hasher stared in astonishment at Linzer's back and

when he heard a shout of laughter from the receiver, he grinned.

"Goddamnit, I'm telling it straight!" Linzer roared. He turned, saw Hasher's smile, and turned back. "Not a drop! I never mix booze and guns—*never!*" He listened for a moment, said, "Yeah, do that," and slammed down the receiver.

Facing Hasher, he put his left hand, palm down, against his chest and raised his right arm. "I swear it," he said. "A fucking deer shot at me."

Hasher stifled the laugh rising in him. "Seems only fair."

"Yeah, funny," Linzer said sourly. "You got binoculars?"

With a nod, Hasher took a pair out of the telephone stand and handed them to Linzer, who went out onto the front porch. Hasher followed, nervously staying behind the big man. Linzer put the glasses to his eyes, focused them, and scanned the east bank, halfway down toward the old man's cabin.

"See anything?" Hasher asked, shivering in the cold.

"Not now. You didn't expect it to wait around, did you?"

"You can't tell," Hasher said, "what an armed deer might do."

"Funny," Linzer said again in the same tone. He handed him the glasses and pointed down the shoreline. "Over there, just past that big white rock."

Hasher nearly gasped. Quickly taking the glasses, he refocused them and found the great rock. The scene swam before his eyes and again he thought he was going to faint. Breathing deeply, he waited until he had recovered, then asked, "What did it look like?"

"Like a fucking deer!" Linzer shouted. Then, more quietly, he added, "It was standing there, just beside the rock, tall as a man. I thought it was looking right at me but I guess it wasn't because then it knelt down to take a drink from the lake. I fired—twice."

Tall as a man, Hasher thought, a man in a tan raincoat

and a brown hat. He lowered the glasses, shivering, and said, "Let's go inside. I'm freezing." Whoever it was might still be there.

Hasher's hands were trembling so that he began laying a fire to calm himself. A man in a tan raincoat—the man at the diner, Spinner?—bending down by the edge of the lake to look at something, maybe something in the water by the rock. Oh my God, Hasher said to himself. He had found it. The rope. Or worse, the body had worked its way out of the cavern. . . .

"Say, the shot could have come from somewhere else and not the deer at all," Linzer said and smiled.

Dazed, Hasher lit the fire and got up. "What?"

Linzer repeated the statement.

Hasher nodded, seeing that it would be best to encourage him in that idea, rather than have him—and the Sheriff—realize what had happened and where. "Of course," he said, "that's it."

"A stray shot. A coincidence." Now Linzer relaxed. "How about a drink? I'm through hunting for the day. After that, maybe for good."

Grateful for the suggestion, Hasher went to the kitchen. But how would Spinner, or whoever it was, know about the rock? Hasher asked himself. He turned and called back through the doorway, "You want it hot or cold?"

Linzer appeared a few feet away. "Cold, for Chrisake. I'm suffocating." He tore his hunting coat off and tossed it on a chair. "Isn't it hot in here? Maybe it's my longjohns."

Hasher gave him his drink and took his own along as he went to turn the heater down; he had forgotten that it was on full and now, for the first time, felt the heat in the room. "I had a chill when I came in," he said.

"*You* had a chill! You ever had anybody take a shot at you? Plunk! Right in a tree beside my head." Hasher didn't answer and Linzer looked at him for a moment, then said, "Oh yeah, I forgot you were in Vietnam. Must be kid stuff to you."

"Being shot at is never kid stuff," Hasher said. He took

a long drink to steady himself. The man at the rock must have fired back to give himself time to take cover. Hasher glanced at Linzer and was sorry that he had missed his buck; it would have solved a lot.

By the time the Sheriff and Timmons, his huge deputy, arrived, Hasher was more apprehensive than ever. Worthy was bound to examine the site of the shot. If Hasher had left something by the rock. . . .

Linzer excitedly described what had happened, as Worthy listened somberly and Timmons stood behind him, trying not to laugh. It was clear that they had been kidding about the story on the ride out to the lake.

As Linzer finished, saying that maybe the shot had come from some other place than the spot where the deer was, Worthy squinted at him through his cigarette smoke and asked, "Did the buck go down on one knee or fire from a standing position?"

Timmons crumpled against the wall, screaming with laughter. Linzer, his face suffused with anger, grabbed his coat and stomped out onto the porch. "Okay, smartass, you coming or not?" he called back. "No need to be afraid. I'll take care of you." He came back to the door and got his rifle.

"It might be safer all around if you left that here," the Sheriff said.

Timmons emitted another hoot of laughter and Worthy shoved him through the door to the porch and turned to Hasher. "You joining the posse for the killer deer?"

Hasher got a jacket and when he joined Worthy on the porch, he saw that the others were already a hundred feet off, on the rocky shore.

"What if Pete hit him?" Hasher asked.

"Then we'll have venison for Sunday dinner."

Hasher was tired of the joke. "Look, Bill, if there's a wounded man out there—"

Worthy shook his head in disdain. "Linzer couldn't hit this house from the inside."

"All the worse. If he gets excited, he could hit one of us."

The Sheriff considered this for a moment and called to the others to wait. Linzer ignored the summons until the deputy shouted at him and he turned back suddenly and sat down on a rock. Worthy went ahead and as Hasher made his way, more slowly, he heard them arguing. When he joined them, he saw Linzer furiously yank the magazine out of his rifle and shove it into a coat pocket.

This time Worthy led the way, with Hasher immediately behind him, Timmons a few yards back, and Linzer in the rear. Desperately trying to think of a way to get out in front so that he would be the first to reach the site of the great rock, Hasher called to Worthy and asked, "Shouldn't we fan out, in case the guy was hit and crawled away somewhere?"

Worthy stopped and turned. "He wasn't hit. When I got Pete's call, I checked with the patrol car in this sector. It reported a car parked earlier over there"—he paused to gesture back through the woods toward the road—"so I told them to recheck. It was gone. Must've been his."

"What kind of a car?" Hasher asked, trying not to sound too concerned.

"Chevrolet. New. Dark green. New York plates. They got the number. The office is checking it out." Worthy turned and clambered over a pile of rocks and rotting tree trunks.

Hasher didn't know one car from another and when the man at Rose's drove out, and later when Hasher passed the car parked by the side of the highway, he hadn't been able to tell what color it was; but he remembered that it had New York plates.

A few steps farther on, he saw the rock. The Sheriff was on the near side of it, checking the ground, probably for a shell casing, Hasher thought. He hurried on, around the great outcropping, trying not to think of the corpse inside it, to the other side, out of Worthy's view.

"Anything over there?" Worthy called.

"Not so far," Hasher answered. He scrambled down to the edge of shore and fell to his hands and knees. He peered into the black water, his face only a foot away from it. Reeds dimly visible below. He thought he saw something white and bent closer. Blood pounded in his temples as he made out a faint white curl among the reeds. The rope!

Hearing the sound of Worthy climbing around the back of the rock, Hasher got up quickly and grabbed two handfuls of dry grass. As the Sheriff slid down the steep hill, Hasher pretended to dry off his hands with the grass, then casually tossed it into the water to conceal what he had seen. "Nothing at all," he said, his voice sounding hollow to him.

"Except this," Worthy said, getting on one knee and reaching down among the small stones. He held up a brass shell casing.

Thank God! Hasher thought. That would distract him. And even if he were to look into the water, he would be unlikely to see the rope—unless he got down close to the surface and knew what he was looking for.

Timmons and Linzer came around the rock and slid down beside them. They looked at Worthy and he held out the shell.

"Looks like your buck was packing a revolver," Worthy said. "This is from a handgun."

Timmons grinned and Linzer glared at both policemen.

Hasher, standing a few feet away, bent over and picked up something on top of a flat rock.

"What is it?" Worthy asked.

"Just a twig," Hasher said and tossed the clove into the lake.

When they got back to the cottage, Hasher made coffee for the four of them while the Sheriff called his office to see if there was any report on the green Chevrolet that had been parked by the lake. As Hasher stood near the stove, waiting for the kettle to boil, he wondered why he had thrown away the only evidence of Virgil Spinner's presence. The act had been reflexive and at that moment he had been sure that it was the only thing to do. Now he was less sure but felt that he had probably been right.

The last thing he wanted to do, Spinner or no Spinner, was attract Sheriff Worthy's attention to that rock.

Steam rose out of the kettle's spout and he turned off the stove and made the coffee. As he waited for the water to run through the old-fashioned drip pot, Worthy came into the kitchen.

"The car was stolen," he said and lit a cigarette. "In New York City."

That settled it, Hasher thought; it was Spinner. He turned to Worthy, who was staring abstractedly out of the window at the dark, nearly bare trees. "Any ideas?" Hasher asked.

"Only one."

Hasher waited.

"Virgil Spinner is back."

"But why? You said he wouldn't dare."

"Maybe I was wrong," Worthy said, looking out of the window still. "My thinking was based on the wrong premise."

"What?"

"That he's sane."

Hasher repressed a shudder and handed him a mug of coffee, then took some into the living room for the others.

"Who's he think it was?" Linzer asked him.

Hasher shrugged. He didn't even want to consider it. And, above all, he didn't want to start a conversation that would lead to speculation about why Spinner had come back, what was he doing in the woods armed with a handgun, why was he in that particular spot, and why had he risked shooting at Linzer, who had him in the sights of his high-powered rifle? Hasher was certain that Spinner had thought that it was Hasher who had fired at him. There was no doubt in his mind that the man had come there to kill him.

At least his failure would provide a breathing spell, Hasher thought; he wouldn't take another chance like that for awhile. How long? he wondered.

When the others left, the Sheriff asked him if he was staying for long. Hasher shook his head; he'd had enough of mysterious prowlers and gunplay and would leave as soon as he could gather a few things together.

Worthy nodded. "Let me know before you go."

After Worthy had gone, Hasher went to the bedroom closet to get the gun and leave too. He wrapped it and a small box of extra shells in a wool scarf and put the bundle into the creel, then replaced the floorboard door and shoved the boots and shoes back on top of it. He slung the creel over his shoulder and went to unplug the electric blanket and turn off the gas heater.

As anxious as he was to get away from the place—in a way he hoped he would never see it again—he forced himself to consider his next steps. He had fled too often in panic, he knew as he sensed something contrary to his desire to leave tugging at the back of his mind. To give himself a little more time, Hasher put down the creel, now his only baggage, and washed out the coffee mugs and reheated what was left in the pot. He took a mugful and went to sit in his chair by the fireplace.

When the idea began seeping into his consciousness, he rejected it at once. He *couldn't* stay there. However much sense that course might make, he admitted that he was too afraid. But they were all here, he told himself—Vivian, Rail, Spinner. . . . Unless he was prepared to go on running, being hunted. They were sure that they had him now, defenseless . . . but if he could turn that around. . . .

He shook his head. How? It was hopeless.

Still, he hesitated. If he ran again now, when could he stop running? In the city he had even less of a chance. He could never be sure who might be in the crowd, around the next corner. Spinner had got into his apartment easily. . . . Sooner or later. . . .

Hasher swore and looked at the creel. He was probably as safe here as anywhere, he told himself. No one could get in once the doors were double-locked from the inside. He had the gun. With the curtains drawn, no one would know for sure whether he was inside the cottage or, if he was, which room he was in. He thought of the man behind him on the subway, the man at Rose's, the man at the rock. Sooner or later he was going to come for Hasher. Why not here? A prowler killed by mistake.

Hasher stopped, asking himself again, as he had ever since Linzer told his story, why Spinner had been by the rock. What did he know? What could he know? He was the key to everything—especially Hasher's fear. Once Spinner was out of the way. . . . If he could be lured here. . . .

Needing more time before he decided whether to stay or go, Hasher suddenly felt famished. He got up to see what there was in the kitchen. He would eat and think things over. But when he saw the supplies in the cupboard —virtually survival rations in case they got snowed in— he closed the door, revolted at the idea of canned soup or beans or Spam. He realized then that he hadn't had a decent meal in a week. The thought of a steak made him weak with hunger.

The Busy Bee was the only place within miles fit to eat in. He would stop there—it was roughly on the way back to the city—and make up his mind over lunch. Picking up the creel, he left, examining the woods around the rear of the cottage carefully. He locked the door, found a scrap of paper in his pocket, tore off a corner, and stuck it in the hinged side of the storm door as he closed it. The front door was double-locked, so if anyone tried to get in, or *got* in, he would know when he got back, he thought. Then he knew that he was going to stay.

On a back road about five miles from the Busy Bee— once the main highway running north and south in that part of the state—Hasher saw a car pulled off onto the shoulder. A man dressed in a tan duck-hunter's outfit was taking something out of the trunk and as Hasher drew abreast, he saw it was a shotgun and that the hunter was Marvin Rail. Rail didn't look at the passing car and neither did Vivian Slocum, who was sitting in the driver's seat. A hundred feet or so past the parked car was a rough rutted path, an old logging road down to Goose Pond, a quarter of a mile away. The pond, shallow and marshy, was rarely visited, except by wildfowl in migration.

Hasher wondered, as he drove on, whether old Matthew Barnham, who owned the pond and several hundred acres around it, had opened the place up to hunters. In the past it had always been posted. But maybe Rail had bought shooting rights from him for a few days. Hasher looked in the mirror and saw Rail bending over by the window on the driver's side. It would be like him to buy the right to shoot sitting ducks.

This year the deer and duck seasons overlapped, Hasher realized. The deer population must have grown too large, so the season had been lengthened to let hunters decimate the herds and save next year's crops from them. Maybe, he thought with a smile, he should give Linzer a call and tell him that the big buck had been seen at Goose Pond. One glimpse of Rail's fawn-colored hunting outfit and Linzer would blaze away.

"Not Linzer—me," Hasher murmured. Then he was stunned by how calmly and easily the thought of murder came to him now. He felt no anguish over the desire to kill, no remorse even as he imagined the deed already done. Only a tightening in his throat—a mark of fear in him, fear of the consequences, not of the act itself. Maybe it was what Ed Wicknor had said about killing Rail, he thought. Or maybe it was because he had already killed James.

He wondered what Rail's and Vivian's plans were right now. Surely she hadn't gone with him to sit in the cold waiting to fire at a bird. She must have been in the car only to drop Rail off. Then Rail would be alone for at least a couple of hours. And they hadn't seen Hasher as he drove by. Maybe he should go and stalk the man, make a dry practice run. He couldn't shoot Rail with a revolver anyway. It would take a crack shot like Spinner to pull that off. The shot would have to be from a good distance if it were to look like an accident on the part of some hunter who had then run off when he discovered that he had killed a man instead of a deer. Besides, the slug from a handgun would be a sure giveaway that it wasn't a hunting accident.

At the most, a dry run, Hasher thought, but then he rejected that idea too. It was far too haphazard. He had been lucky with James but this time he would have to stalk his quarry with care. As it stood, he had no plan at all. When he parked at the Busy Bee, he got out and locked the creel in the trunk.

Relax, he told himself as he walked toward the restaurant, relax. Then think it through. The cheerful hubbub inside made him feel better immediately. "Busy, I see," he said to the hostess.

"As bees," she replied pertly and led him to a small side table in the crowded barroom.

Ordinarily he would have asked to sit elsewhere but today he wanted the noise and conviviality. He had been alone too long. He ordered a Scotch and sat back to watch the patrons—milling about, shouting, laughing, talking animatedly—and wondered if he would ever be like that again. Probably not, he thought, then doubted that as he repeated to himself the only truth: This too shall pass. He asked for another drink and when the waitress brought it he ordered his meal: a large and very rare steak and hashed-brown potatoes, with half a bottle of red wine.

He ate like a wolf and washed his food down with gulps of wine as if he were on fire inside. At last he finished and sat back and belched comfortably. He felt better than he had in weeks. A little lightheaded from the drinks maybe, but fine. All he lacked now was a brandy and a good cigar.

He turned to look at the waitress, her back to him, a few tables away. When he turned back, he saw Vivian sitting in the chair across from him at his table. She was sipping a martini and watching him, amused by his stunned look.

"How nice finding you here," she said, as if nothing in the world had ever been wrong between them. "I couldn't imagine what I was going to do with my afternoon."

Hasher shoved back his chair and started to get up.

"I have a proposal to make to you—actually two proposals," she went on and smiled. "One decent and one indecent."

"I bet you have," he said and thought how beautiful she was.

"Sit down and I'll tell you." She raised her glass, as if in toast, and took a sip.

He sat down without speaking.

"I've been thinking about your offer for my cabin," she said, giving no sign that anyone might have disputed her ownership for a second. "It seems a shame for us to quarrel—now that everything else is over. We used to be friends. Weren't we?"

He didn't answer.

"I've decided to accept your offer of fifty thousand," she went on, a little smile on her lips.

"Fine," Hasher said, "except my offer was forty thousand."

"Oh!" She put the tips of two fingers to her mouth and looked surprised, although he was sure that she wasn't. This was her idea of negotiating. "But I asked seventy. Forty's much too low."

Hasher shook his head and grinned at her audacity. "Forty."

She smiled engagingly. "Well, let's not talk about it just now then. It's only that Marvin's been at me to settle it. He wants to go to the District Attorney or the bar association about that—"

"Culpability?"

She nodded. "He said lawyers like you should be punished."

Hasher laughed and got up. "Go right ahead."

"Don't you want to hear my other proposal?" she asked, her great brown eyes wide as she stared up at him.

"The decent one?"

"I just made the decent one," she said, smiling again.

"Do sit down, Thomas. It's the only way to hear what I want to say."

He looked at her for a moment in silence, then sat down, unable to resist his curiosity.

Vivian leaned forward a little, her elbows on the table, her hands loosely clasped below her chin, her eyes moist, her lips open slightly. "You've always wanted to make love to me," she said simply. "I'd like that—a lot."

He started to rise again but she reached out and stopped him. "It's true, isn't it?"

He shook his head.

"What's to stop us?" she demanded in a low voice.

Hasher felt almost lightheaded with relief as he said, "Hatred."

"Don't hate me, Thomas, and don't make me hate you."

Remembering what Wicknor had said, Hasher waited, wondering if he should lead her on to get her alone somewhere. And then? He knew he couldn't do that, not to a woman, however much she deserved it.

"Please," she said softly.

Why not trap her? he thought. Surely she deserved it more than James had. If she only knew about that. . . .

"When?" he asked.

Vivian's fingers trembled slightly as she picked up her drink. "Now." Her eyes glistened. "I'll follow you to your cottage."

Hasher shook his head. "Margaret's there."

He was sure that Vivian knew he was lying. How? he asked himself, then understood at once. Spinner had told her Hasher was alone. If he agreed to her proposal, she would go to the ladies room and call Spinner and he would be waiting for them. Hasher was almost tempted to test his theory by agreeing to go to the cottage with her. But he knew that he had to have time to get ready for Spinner.

"You won't be sorry, Thomas, I promise," Vivian said. Suddenly she laughed and the sound was a sexual melody.

Jesus, he thought, she's good at this. "When?" he asked again, stalling now.

"I'll be back in the city Sunday," she answered. "I'll be home all evening. Alone."

He looked away. Not alone certainly. Spinner would be there. But at least the two days gave Hasher time to plan. He nodded and said, "Okay."

"You promise?" She was smiling, sure that she had him now.

He nodded again and forced a smile.

"Don't think about Lucius," she said quickly. "You were always wrong about him."

She was trying to make it easier for him to betray his dead friend, he realized and cursed her under his breath. It was to be the final humiliation.

Vivian leaned over to one side and reached into her handbag, hanging by its shoulder strap from the back of her chair. She took out a record book that looked like the diary. Then Spinner had already gone to the cabin to retrieve it. Hasher waited.

"Do you like fairy tales?" she asked lightly and opened the book.

Hasher didn't reply.

"Fairy tales in both senses of both words," she said. "Lucius was very fond of them—in both senses. He even wrote one himself."

Now they had both the original and the copy, Hasher thought and swore at himself for not taking this one from the cabin before Spinner got it. They had *all* the evidence. If there had been any hope of redressing the wrong done the old man through publicity, that was gone now. Hasher knew he had no choice—once again it had been made for him.

"Would you like to read it?" she asked and held out the diary.

He could be audacious too, he decided as he stood up. "I've read it."

Vivian's eyes widened slightly. "That explains a lot," she said. "I'll explain the rest, the truth, on Sunday."

Hasher cursed himself again. She had trapped him into admitting that he had read the diary and now they would know that *they* had no choice but to get rid of him. He would have to move fast.

"Sunday then," he said.

Vivian smiled her most sensual moist smile. "You might shave before you come," she said.

CHAPTER
16

Hasher's hand shook so that he had trouble getting the key into the ignition. They were ready to take him, naked and defenseless. And there were three of them—that evil woman, the vicious lawyer, and a mad killer. Hasher clutched the steering wheel as he wondered if he should go to the Sheriff. That idea vanished in an oath as he realized there was nothing he could tell Worthy. The evidence was in their hands. James, who might have been frightened into a confession, was dead. What had Hasher to report to Worthy—that Vivian tried to seduce him?

He backed out of his parking space and pulled out onto the highway and headed north, back toward the lake. As Hasher approached the old logging road, he slowed down and looked up the rutted path. There was no sign of anyone. He wondered how long Rail would stay there. A couple of hours at least. Would Vivian join him soon? Hasher dismissed the idea at once. She had gone to the Busy Bee for company and she would find it easily. He had noticed a couple of men there watching her. Some of them would know her, some would know about her. It wouldn't take her long. There were plenty of men who would give a year of their lives for a few hours with Vivian Slocum.

That must have been how she had got the old man. Back then, he would have been vigorous still. Lonely too—celibate for all those years after his wife died, and now reborn with desire. Hasher remembered the pale drawn face of the old man in the courtroom as Lyndon Johnson James gave his obscene testimony, and then saw the police photograph again, with the black hole in the white hair. And there was Rail too, his puffy vulgar face triumphant as he destroyed his helpless victim.

Now Hasher recalled that he had promised himself that day in court to destroy Marvin Rail, and realized that the promise had not been the usual outburst of passing rage; it was fixed, deeper than ever; it had to be satisfied. After all, Lyndon James had been the least guilty of the three and to stop with his death would be almost to exonerate the other two.

Three, he thought, surprised that he had forgotten Spinner.

When Hasher reached the cottage, he took the creel out of the trunk and let himself into the house. The piece of paper fell out of the door as he opened it. Then no one had been there. Even so, he took out the gun as he headed back to the trapdoor up to the attic.

A khaki uniform, with the silver bars of a lieutenant on the collar and a ribbon denoting the Bronze Star above the pocket of the shirt, was on top in the old steamer trunk where he had stored all his Army clothes. He dug down, through shirts, underwear, an unadorned wool uniform in a plastic bag, extra cotton trousers, socks, until he came to the camouflaged combat fatigues and, at the bottom, a pair of well-shined boots with a rolled-up round-brimmed fatigue cap sticking out of one of them. He took out the fatigues and boots and closed the trunk.

As he moved away, back toward the ladder, something crunched underfoot. Hasher bent down and picked up and smelled the crushed fragments of a clove. Confirmed in his suspicion that Spinner had been the prowler that Worthy's men had shot at that day, Hasher shivered slightly. He told himself that it was the damp cold of the attic for he wasn't frightened now; emboldened by the drinks he'd had or by his determination to fight it out here, on this line, he was even calm.

He undressed in the bedroom, donned a suit of long underwear, and got into the fatigues and boots. He put the clothes he had taken off into a shopping bag, so he would have them ready for a quick change, and slipped the gun back into the creel and the creel into the top of the bag. At the rear door, he paused, then put down the bag and went to the spice shelf and took down the tin of cloves. He poured a few into one hand and stuck them in a pocket of his fatigues.

The parking lot at the near end of the shopping center, around two sides of the huge A&P, was crowded. Hasher drove on to the opposite end, where there was plenty of room, and backed into a space at the outermost line of cars, only a dozen or so feet from the woods that enclosed that side of the center. The nearest car on his left was parked three spaces away and the one on the right was two spaces away. He stayed in the car for a minute or two, studying the scene in front of him. No one was closer than a hundred yards: two people with their backs toward him headed for the center.

He slid out of the seat, keeping his head lowered, closed the door, and walked to the back of the car and took the creel out of the trunk. He looked over the top of the car and saw a woman with a child and two bags of groceries fumbling at the locked door of her car three rows ahead and off to the right.

He turned quickly and walked back into the woods. A man in a raincoat and rain hat on his way to take a pee, he hoped, if anyone noticed him. Now he wished he had thought to bring the compass he had used as a boy when he explored the woods. But he didn't know even where it was any longer. He also wished that he had measured the distance from the logging road to the shopping center on his speedometer when he came back from lunch. He had no idea how far it was—half a mile or more, he guessed, as he headed on through the woods, trying to keep to a straight line. He had been known for his sense of direction among his men in Vietnam and could only hope that he still had it.

After a hundred steps, he stopped and took off his raincoat, folded it into a small bundle, and stuck it under a fallen tree trunk out of sight. He opened the creel and removed the gun and slipped it into the top of his trousers, under the loose fatigue jacket. He put the creel in with the coat, then broke off a few small branches nearby to mark the site. He studied the ground around him and saw that it was only damp from the light drizzle that had filtered through the trees. The earth was covered thickly with dead leaves. There would be no footprints.

"Okay, let's go," he said in a half-whisper, as if speaking to his platoon.

He marked his trail every twenty feet or so with a broken branch, peering ahead more and more intently so that he would know when he got close to the pond and had to stop making any sounds. A moment later he muttered an oath as he realized that Rail must have a dog with him; he could't shoot birds over water without a retriever. Hearing a shot, Hasher decided to go on anyway—at least he could reconnoiter and find the enemy, as he had in Vietnam. How many times? he asked himself. He had no idea. How many men had he killed? he wondered, as he had so often since he got home. He had no idea of that either.

There was another shot, closer now. Hasher crouched down and took out his gun. The sound had been too loud to be anything but a shotgun. Creeping forward to avoid branches underfoot, he felt his heart beating faster and the gun cold in his hand. At last he made out an opening ahead through the bare trees and saw the reeds along the bank of Goose Pond. He stopped and put a forefinger in his mouth and tested the air; as he expected, there was no movement, no breeze in the woods. At least the dog wouldn't scent him. And if it did and came into the woods after him, he would shoot it and get away. It was only a game now; he was just stalking a man as practice. Later on. . . . He thought of Spinner.

Slowly Hasher got down on his knees, then stretched out on his stomach and began crawling forward, using his elbows and knees as he had learned in the Army, without making a sound. It was a lot harder work at forty than it had been at twenty-five and after a few yards he got up and went on in a low crouch. Better, he told himself; he would be ready if the dog attacked. But that was unlikely for Rail could be anywhere around the sizable pond—or even on it if old Barnham had rented him a boat along with his shooting rights.

Suddenly Hasher was at the edge of the woods. He got down on one knee to reduce his size and visibility, hoping that his camouflaged clothers would conceal him for the time he needed to spot his quarry. He stifled a gasp as he saw Rail, seated on a wood box with his back to the woods, not twenty feet away. In front of him was a V-shaped duck blind made out of a wood frame with reeds thatched over it. There was no dog in sight. Hasher eased back into the woods a little way and stood up to look out over the pond in case the dog had swum out to retrieve a dead bird after one of the shots. All he could see were half a dozen black dots a hundred feet or so out on the pond. They were ducks. A moment later he realized that there was no dog. Rail didn't care about taking his kill home then; all he wanted was to kill. A duck, an old man, Hasher himself—it was all the same. Except that he had to hire someone else to take care of Hasher.

He saw that the ducks were moving slowly in the direction of the blind. There must be decoys out in front of it, he thought. He waited. Even now he had no plan. . . . Maybe an accident . . . Rail stumbling . . . the shotgun going off. . . . When he fired was the time to move, while he was still deafened by the shot.

The ducks were close enough now for Hasher to see by the males' iridescent green necks and black heads that they were mallards. Rail was getting ready; he had the gun up and had risen a little off the box in a half-crouch. Hasher silently moved forward to the edge of the woods. He stopped and tried to make out if the shotgun had a single or a double barrel but couldn't tell. Probably double, he thought; Rail was the kind of man who would take every advantage he could get. Anyway, it had to be empty before Hasher could make his move.

He studied the ground in front, between him and the box, and saw that it was rock and gravel for the most part, with here and there some tufts of rough grass. No footprints would be left there. But Rail was sitting at the muddy edge of the pond and Hasher knew that would be the danger spot. Ordinary footprints would be one thing; strange footprints on top of Rail's would be quite another. Worthy would spot that in an instant.

Hasher took a deep breath and let it out slowly, to calm himself. But he was surprised at how calm he was. The rage within had turned him cold, without remorse over what he was about to do. As he stared at Rail's hunched shoulders and the back of his thick neck, Hasher knew that his hatred was deeper and older than hatred for a man who had destroyed his friend. Rail stood for all that Hasher most despised: the liar, the dealer, the conniver, the fixer, the blackmailer, the corrupter who believed that everyone else was corrupt. He had made his living, fed his children, paid his mortgage, entertained his guests, and supported the woman, his wife, whom he must have thought he loved at one time, all from the bits and pieces of malevolence he found around him. That was his life—putting them together into an evil big enough to ruin someone for pay. He fulfilled himself by catering to the worst in people.

Hasher's finger tightened on the trigger but he stopped himself in time. Not that way, not in the back, he thought. That was Rail's way. It had to be face to face. Hasher wanted that most of all, to see the moment of terror in Rail's eyes, the realization that he was about to pay.

The birds were no more than eighty feet from the blind when Rail rose and put the gun to his shoulder. There was a babble of warning sounds from the ducks as the lead one began flapping its wings and paddling away to rise in flight. The others followed and soon they were a few feet off the water. Hasher quietly took a step forward out of the trees, then another.

Rail fired and a bird fluttered out of the flock and fell. Rail yelped jubilantly and Hasher took several more steps. And, as Rail fired again and another duck flopped into the water, Hasher ran the last few steps and jammed the muzzle of his pistol into the back of Rail's neck.

"What the—"

He tried to turn his head but Hasher grabbed his jacket collar with his free hand and jerked him backward and struck him with the butt of the pistol as he fell. Rail grunted from the blow, just behind one ear, and slumped onto his back on the gravel, the shotgun lying on his right side, his cap on the stones behind his head.

Stunned and breathing heavily, Hasher bent down over him. He knew that he had only a few minutes before Rail regained consciousness, for the blow had been a short one and would not leave him out for long. Rail was wearing shooting gloves and Hasher pulled them off, put them on his own hands, and picked up the shotgun. He flicked the thumb latch, and the gun popped open and ejected the shells; he felt in one of the unconscious man's pockets and took out two fresh shells and inserted them in the gun. He slammed it shut and pointed it down at Rail's head.

But he couldn't do it. And a moment later he realized how fortunate it was for him that he couldn't: a shot from his position, with Rail on his back, couldn't be viewed as an accident later. Hasher stepped back a pace. He would have to wait until Rail came to. . . . Order him to his feet, make him bend over, like a man who had stumbled. . . . Hasher wondered if he could do it that way.

Thinking he saw a flicker in one of Rail's eyelids, Hasher crouched beside him. He stared at the slack puffy face, waiting for a movement, and marveled at how ordinary this man seemed. Now the vicious predator was only an overweight man asleep. Impatiently Hasher shook his shoulder. There was no response.

When Rail hadn't moved several minutes later, Hasher took off one of the gloves and lifted the man's wrist to test his pulse. He felt nothing. Dropping the hand, he placed two fingers alongside Rail's throat at the carotid artery. Again he felt nothing.

Slowly Hasher put the glove back on and got to his feet and stood staring at the body. He had killed again, as unintentionally—and intentionally—as before. The rat of his soul, he thought numbly, feeling almost nothing. Rail had deserved to die and he had died. A moment later, though, Hasher felt a sense of regret—that this foul creature had not been made to suffer . . . at least a few seconds of terror at the certainty that he was going to die.

Finally a sense of urgency overcame Hasher as he realized what an autopsy would show now. . . . He stared around distractedly and saw an angular rock with a jagged corner lying a few yards away. It was worth a try, he decided. Anything was worth a try now.

He put the shotgun on the ground and knelt down; he grasped the body under its arms and lugged it to an almost upright position. Then he lifted it until its feet were just off the ground, Rail's chin on his shoulder, his cheek against Hasher's. Moving slowly, he carried the body a yard or so toward the rock and stopped. He carefully lowered the form so that the head was just above the rock and then slammed it down on the sharp corner just behind the ear where he had sapped the man with the gun.

Letting the body fall now, he ran back and got the shotgun and cap. He placed the gun just out of Rail's outstretched reach and the cap a few inches away from the rock. The corner of it was smeared with blood, he saw and turned away. He took off the gloves and put them down neatly on top of the box.

He surveyed the scene and tried to imagine Worthy doing the same. They would find the spent shells and the dead birds floating in the pond. Rail had reloaded and got up to walk back toward the woods, maybe to pee. He had stumbled and fallen. His head . . . Hasher cursed. Fallen backwards? It was possible of course. The man could have twisted as he fell and landed on his back, his head crashing into the rock. Unlikely but possible. If the police had nothing else to go on, they would have to settle for that.

Hasher looked around to make sure that they would have nothing else. Then he stopped, wondering if they should have something else, something specific. At last, he nodded and took out the cloves he had stuck in his pocket at the cottage. He looked around carefully and chose a large almost flat rock and put a single clove in a narrow crack on top of the rock so that it wouldn't roll off or wash off if it rained again. As he stood up, he could hardly see the dark-brown spice. But Worthy or one of his men would find it. And Worthy would remember Spinner's weird habit. Fifteen years was a long time but one didn't forget something like that.

Looking around once more, Hasher stared for a moment at Rail's body, then turned and walked back into the woods.

CHAPTER
17

It seemed to him a paradox that the more people he killed, the less remorse he felt. And yet it was true for he felt almost nothing about Rail's death. Less even than about James's. In that case it had been self-defense and only the grisly task of hiding the body still affected him. It was his own near death when he almost became trapped in the cavern in the rock that now haunted him most. And his memory, even in his sleep, of the dead boy's eyes did not so much accuse him of murder as remind him of his own certain death someday. Whether it was by Spinner's hand tomorrow or in bed forty years from now was all the same. He would be dead and nothing he had done or had not done before that moment would matter.

This awareness had given him the mock bravery he had assumed in Vietnam. And yet he had survived all of his own audacious and foolhardy acts there, as if fate were amused by his defiance. Perhaps he had been allowed to live as a punishment. For what? he wondered and tried to dismiss these thoughts. But the answer came, from that primordial recess of the mind that is every human's curse: For being born.

Hasher shivered involuntarily—from his wet fatigues, he told himself uncertainly—and swung into the driveway to the cottage. Something in the light and shadow of the place reminded him again of Vietnam and he remembered the first life he had taken: a boy of no more than sixteen who had burst out of an unseen hole and come at him with a machete raised over his head, his mouth distorted in a war cry. . . . Hasher thought of James flinging himself across the old man's study at him. Hasher had also fired point-blank from no more than six feet at the Viet Cong boy, who had died with a look of stunned disbelief on his face. Then Hasher had vomited, just as he had later when he found James's teeth, and had been racked by a feverish ague for days. But that had passed, he had killed others— how many? he wondered again— and he had almost gotten used to it. That was the paradox: the worse he had been, the better he felt. Was that how Spinner felt each time?

Well, *he* was used to it now, Hasher thought as he pulled up by the cottage. He looked at his watch and saw that only twenty-five minutes had passed since he left Goose Pond.

Hasher changed into the clothes he had worn to the Busy Bee, put the fatigues and long underwear into the washing machine for a short wash, and tried to decide what to do with his boots, the only certain evidence of the crime. Even if he had left no tracks near the body, he was fairly sure that there would be some within the woods. Everything depended on the extent of the Sheriff's investigation. And that of course depended on any suspicions he might have of foul play.

Given Rail's vicious reputation as a lawyer, probably a good many of his victims wanted him dead. But who besides Hasher had both motive and opportunity? Spinner? Not if Vivian told the Sheriff that he had been working for Rail—unless Worthy concluded that the two men had fallen out over something. When he found the clove at the scene. . . .

"Jesus Christ!" Hasher cried and leaped for the door of the washer. He had forgotten the other cloves in the pocket of the fatigues! His hands trembling, he found them still in the pocket, carefully removed them, and restarted the machine. What else had he forgotten?

Vivian was certain to tell the Sheriff that Hasher had been at the Busy Bee not long before Rail's death and not far from the scene of it. If she told him about the $70,000 missing from the Poulson estate and Rail's intention to report it to the D.A., and if Worthy recalled Hasher's rage at what had happened to the old man. . . . He felt weak and leaned against the counter for support. That made enough motive to convince any jury.

Hasher stared down at the boots standing on a newspaper on the floor and swore at himself for having acted so hastily after all he had drunk. He had meant only to stalk the man, he told himself, to get the feel of it before deciding whether he should fight them here, on this ground, or in the maze of the city. But he suspected that wasn't true, that he had gone out to kill Rail.

A moment later Hasher realized that if the Sheriff didn't arrest him, he would be wholly in Vivian's hands. She could keep her knowledge of his motives, and his opportunity, to herself and use this to take away the cabin. And probably more. Cash.

"Shit!" he said and kicked the boots across the room.

Feeling panic rise in him again, he tried to calm down. He picked up the boots and went to the bedroom closet, cleared off the floor, and opened the trapdoor. He jammed the boots in around the steel box. He would have to find a pair like them at an Army & Navy store, he told himself, and get rid of these.

He swore ferociously as he realized that he had forgotten the gun. Running to the living room, he grabbed the creel from the chair where he had left it and returned to the closet. When he finished there, he went back to the kitchen and cursed again as he saw the wet cloves on the counter. Hopeless! he muttered to himself, hopeless! He took the can of cloves off the spice shelf and stared at it, wondering whether police-laboratory technicians would be able to trace the clove he had left on the rock at Goose Pond to this tin. A moment later he realized that the question was irrelevant; he had to get rid of the whole lot.

Hurrying through the house and out to the end of the dock, he knelt down and filled the tin with water. He put the lid on and pressed it down. Standing up, he hesitated for a moment, then threw the tin as far as he could out into the lake. It would sink into the muck, he thought, hoping that he was right. Suddenly he remembered the boy's teeth, which he had missed when he cleaned the ashes out of the fireplace and emptied them here. He peered down into the water a few feet away from the end of the dock, wondering if they too had sunk into the muck. He shivered and went back inside.

He would buy another tin of cloves to replace that one, he decided as he returned to the kitchen. With a violent oath, he realized that he hadn't even noticed what brand they were. But Margaret would; she was particular about what she bought and how much she paid. If Worthy happened to ask her. . . .

Hasher paced back and forth through the cottage, trying to stem the panic that his mistakes had aroused. He wanted to flee again, go back to the city, go anywhere, and had almost made up his mind to leave when he realized that that would be exactly what he would be expected to do if he was guilty. When Rail's body was found—Hasher looked at his watch and saw that it wasn't quite 4:00— Worthy would be certain to want to talk to him. But he had said that he was leaving right after Worthy and the others left.

Hasher grabbed his head and squeezed his temples. He would never make it—never!

Startled by the ring of the telephone, he ran into the living room and grabbed the receiver on the second ring. The line went dead.

Spinner! Checking to find out where Hasher was. He groaned and slumped down in his easy chair. That was what he had wanted: to lure Spinner here. Well, he would have his wish. At least he was ready. He got up and went back to the bedroom closet and dug out the gun. He thought of Rail, then James. For the first time he wondered if the corpse of the boy had begun to decompose. Perhaps the icy water would preserve it through the winter. Then, in the spring. . . . He shuddered and closed the flooring and got up. Idly, almost uncaring, he examined the butt of the gun to see if there was any sign on it of the blow to Rail's head.

The telephone rang again. It wouldn't be Spinner this time; he had found out what he wanted to know. Hasher hurried back to the living room and answered. It was Margaret.

He barely stopped himself from hanging up. She was the last person in the world he could deal with now. The others he could lie to, insult, evade, joke with. But he couldn't face her even over a telephone. He had failed her too grievously, even forgotten her, and he knew that every nuance in the tone of his voice revealed something more to her that he didn't want known.

"Where are you?" he asked and stuck the gun into the telephone stand.

"Back at the apartment."

His throat constricted; she was in the one place she was most afraid to be alone in and would try to force him to come home. "Why so soon?" he asked. "I thought you were staying till Monday." It came out all wrong: he had as good as told her that he didn't want her around.

She was silent for a minute. "When are you coming back?" she asked. "Can you come tonight?"

"If you need me, of course," he said quickly. He would find some excuse later for not being able to. And yet, why not? he asked himself the next instant. He could tell Worthy that he had decided to leave as he had said, had gone to the Busy Bee to get something to eat on his way home, had changed his mind, and had come back here, only to find that Margaret had returned to their apartment and wanted him there. He would explain about the rape and Worthy would accept it. "I'll leave in a little while," Hasher told her. He thought of Vivian's invitation and wondered if Rail's body had been found yet.

"Why did you go up there?" Margaret asked.

Suddenly infuriated at her prying, at her not being satisfied with his promise to return, Hasher didn't answer.

"For the love of God, he's dead!" she cried.

Stunned, thinking she meant Rail, that his body had

been found already and that Worthy, assuming Hasher had gone back to the city, had called there, he asked, "Who?"

"*Lucius!*" she nearly screamed. "Who else?"

Desperately he fumbled for something to say but when he did, it was only to promise her that he would leave at once. There was no answer. She had hung up.

He made a drink, took one taste, and poured the stuff down the drain. The wash cycle wasn't completed but he decided that a little soap in the fatigues wouldn't matter and put them in the dryer along with the underwear. He put the kettle on to boil and made coffee and took it to the other room. Standing by the front window and looking out over the lake and down to the log cabin at the other end, he wondered if he could go on. He remembered the photograph of the old man dead at his desk and turned to look at the telephone stand, where he had put the gun in a small drawer. He shook his head. Not his way. He had killed two men with that gun but he would not be the third.

He sipped the hot coffee and realized that he had a hangover. He had to stop drinking. The least misstep. Deceit wasn't a tangled web, it was a minefield.

He wanted a fire but feared to let his presence there be known, until he remembered that Spinner already knew he was there. He saw that dusk was gathering and looked again at his watch: 4:32. Surely they must have found Rail by now. When Vivian went to pick him up at the end of the logging road and he didn't appear, she would go to look for him or get help. Either way. . . .

The telephone rang. "They've found him," Hasher said aloud.

"I thought you were going back to town," Sheriff Worthy said.

"I was. But I only got as far as the Busy Bee. Stopped for lunch but had a little too much to drink, so I came back here to sleep it off." Hasher was pleased; he sounded just right. "Why?"

"There's been an accident."

"Now I couldn't have forgotten *that!*" Hasher said lightly. "But I'll go out and check my fenders if you like." Enough, he warned himself; in a moment he would be suspiciously unconcerned. "What happened?"

"Are you still planning to leave?" Worthy asked.

"I just promised Margaret that I'd be back this evening. Why?"

Again Worthy didn't answer his question but said, "I wish you'd stick around, at least for a few hours."

"Why?" Hasher repeated.

"As I said, there's been an accident. You know Marvin Rail of course."

"Of course!" Hasher said at once. "If an accident has happened, I hope it's happened to him." Again he was pleased with himself; no guilty man would dare talk like that. But he cautioned himself against going any further.

"He's dead," Worthy said flatly.

Hasher allowed a suitable lapse of time for shock to pass before he said, "What happened?" He was back in the minefield.

"You know Goose Pond?"

"Jesus Christ, Bill, you and I used to play there!"

"Yeah. I forgot."

Hasher wondered if he actually had.

"Rail was there duck-hunting."

Hasher paused and decided to take the risk. "I hope he blew his head off."

There was a pause on the other end and Hasher wished he hadn't said that. "Not quite," Worthy said at last. "But for all the good it'll do him, he might as well have."

"Does Vivian know?" Hasher asked.

"She found him."

"I wondered what they were doing up here," Hasher said. "Did he shoot himself—I mean, accidentally?"

"No. He seems to have fallen. Hit his head on a rock."

Hasher heard the squashing cracking sound as the head slammed against the sharp corner of the rock. He was silent for a few moments, his mind racing, as he decided whether to tell Worthy about seeing Vivian. He knew at once that he had to. "I ran into Vivian at the Busy Bee," Hasher said. "About one-thirty, maybe two. She had the gall to come over and sit with me." He stopped, wondering if he should tell about the pass she had made, and decided not to.

"You and a couple of others," Worthy said curtly.

So she had gone on. Hasher smiled again. It couldn't be better. Alibi or not, her word wouldn't be worth much against his own. He put a hand to the back of his neck and found that it was damp.

"I'll be out that way in an hour or two," Worthy went on. "If you don't mind sticking around, I'd appreciate it."

"Of course," Hasher said.

After he hung up, he called Margaret and told her what had happened. She didn't seem surprised and she didn't seem to care that he wouldn't be back that night.

Even with time to reflect—as he paced around the cottage, or stood lost in thought, or stared glumly into the fire from his easy chair—Hasher felt no remorse about Rail. And if one who lived by the sword was doomed to perish by it, so be it; sometimes there was no choice, he told himself, for, as Wicknor had said, society provided no legitimate means of controlling evil men like Rail. Anyway, Hasher had no room for remorse or guilt or redemption. His mind was taken up with his fears about what Worthy's arrival might bring. But in the end the questions that flashed and tumbled and collided in Hasher's mind left him more befuddled, and more afraid, than he had been at the start. He could only wait.

He waited for nearly two hours and when he heard the sound of a car outside, he was almost relieved. At least he would soon know. He got up and went to the kitchen and looked out the window of the back door. A tall figure was moving toward the cottage; behind it was the dark form of a car with its parking lights on. He opened the door.

"Evening, Thomas," the Sheriff said. "Sorry to inconvenience you like this."

"No trouble." Hasher stepped back to let him in. "Anything new?" he asked, and told himself to shut up and let Worthy do the talking.

Worthy didn't answer. He walked through the kitchen to the living room and stood by the fire to warm himself.

"A drink?" Hasher asked. "Or are you still on duty?"

Worthy turned to look at him for a moment or two before answering and Hasher wondered if he was studying him or thinking about something else. "I guess I'm off now," he said finally, "as long as I've got a driver." He turned back to the fire.

When Hasher walked into the kitchen, he nearly cried out as he saw the dryer in the corner and realized that he had forgotten to take out the fatigues and return them to the trunk in the attic. Trembling, he made drinks for the two of them, gulped his own down and refilled it, then went back to the other room. Afraid that his hand would shake if he gave the glass directly to Worthy, Hasher put it on the mantelpiece beside him and sat down. "Cheers," he said, raising his glass. His hand was steady.

Worthy took his drink and sipped it slowly and nodded. "The first drink of the day is the best one."

Hasher thought of Rose's description of the three things that never failed one in life.

"You know Vivian Slocum better than most people," Worthy said, his back to Hasher. Then he turned from the fire and faced him. "You think she's capable of murder?"

"Isn't everyone supposed to be?" Hasher asked, too quickly.

"So they say." The Sheriff waited for his answer.

"I think she's capable of anything," Hasher said at last. He wanted to say more but stopped himself. If the flame of suspicion had been lit in Worthy's mind, let it burn there unaided. "You said it was an accident, I thought."

"I said it *seemed* to be. Has all the appearances of one." Worthy took a drink and fell silent.

Hasher waited, then said, "Why would Vivian want him dead? I thought they were lovers."

"Best reason in the world sometimes."

Feeling foolish, as if he had never thought of the passion of love turning into the passion of hate, Hasher determined again to keep quiet and let the other man do the talking.

"You had reason," Worthy said, watching him.

"To what?" Hasher asked and knew that it had come now, far sooner than he had expected.

"To want him dead."

"There must have been legions of us who felt like that," Hasher said, amazed at his calmness. "Rail is the worst prick I've ever known."

"Was," Worthy corrected him.

"Surely you don't suspect me. I didn't even know where he was this afternoon." His indignation sounded false to him and he stopped.

Worthy lit a cigarette and threw the match in the fireplace. "I don't suspect anyone."

"Not anyone, just everyone."

Worthy grinned. "You could say that. It's my job."

"Well, it's not mine. I don't even see why Vivian would want him out of the way—at least not *that* badly."

"Maybe she was tired of him," Worthy replied.

"Then tell him to run along and peddle his papers— that's her style. Why kill him?"

"Or have him killed?" Worthy asked suddenly, his eyes fixed on Hasher now.

"But why?"

"Maybe he had something on her too, like he did on Mr. Slocum, and she couldn't just drop him."

Hasher shrugged. Then he thought of the clove he had left beside the body and wondered if that was the answer, if Worthy had found it and suspected that Vivian had hired Spinner to kill Rail.

But a moment later Hasher discovered that wasn't it at all when Worthy went on, "I hear you were awful cozy with Vivian this afternoon at the Busy Bee."

Someone had overheard them, Hasher realized. More angry than frightened at the idea of his being Vivian's accomplice, he smiled at Worthy and said, "She made a pass at me, if that's what you mean."

"That's part of it," Worthy said and took a long drag on his cigarette. "The other part is that you accepted." He smiled. "Not that I'd blame you for a moment."

Hasher felt his face redden. "Your eavesdropper had it wrong."

"My eavesdropper is Vivian Slocum." Worthy tossed his cigarette into the fireplace. "I couldn't imagine why she told me."

For a moment, Hasher couldn't either, until he realized that Vivian had an alibi and was only trying to make trouble for him, to pay him back for his contempt toward her that afternoon, in case he couldn't account for his time. "She made a pass at me and I played along," he said calmly. "I wanted to find out what she was up to— I mean, with Lucius's will and the cabin." He stopped and glared at Worthy, then let his indignation burst out. "Jesus Christ, Bill, do you mean to say you think I ran into her, she made a pass, so I rushed out and knocked off her lover? That's absurd!"

Worthy grinned at him. "It surely sounds it."

Bristling at being toyed with this way, Hasher got up abruptly and went out to make another drink, without asking Worthy if he wanted one too. He slopped the whisky over the glass onto the counter and stifled a curse. Now he was desperate with wondering if she had told Worthy about the money missing from the Poulson estate. He knew that he had to find out. Once that had been revealed, he would be the prime suspect—if the Sheriff concluded that Rail's death hadn't been accidental.

"What else did my favorite perjuror have to say?" Hasher asked, none too casually, as he came back into the room. "Sorry, you want another?" he added, pointing to Worthy's glass.

Worthy shook his head. "This will do me now. One more when I get home, then bed." He yawned. "That was about all she said, as far as I recall." He yawned again. "Anyway, I wouldn't give a rat's ass for what Vivian Slocum says."

Hasher looked at him in surprise, waiting.

Worthy yawned a third time and looked at his watch. "I saw her out in the woods once, three years ago, maybe four. It was summer. She and that black kid—James. Naked as babes. But a lot less innocent. Like a couple of wild dogs. Jesus Christ!" He passed a hand over his eyes wearily, then looked at Hasher. "Did Mr. Slocum know?"

Hasher nodded.

"I always wondered."

"He knew everything. Even had proof."

"Like him not to use it," Worthy said. He shook his head slowly and repeated, "Jesus Christ." Then he smiled and turned to Hasher. "I know two things. One, I never saw anything as beautiful as that woman naked. And, two, I'd take her up on that offer if I were you, Thomas." He drained his glass. "I've got to go."

Hasher followed him out to the kitchen. "Where's Vivian now? Still at the inn?"

"She wanted to go home. Considering that Rail's wife was on her way up here, I thought it was just as well." He looked at the half-filled glass of whisky in Hasher's hand and said, "I guess you're staying over, huh?"

"Until morning."

Worthy nodded and put down his glass. "Sleep well," he said and turned to the door. He opened it, paused, and turned back. "If you happen to see anything of that fellow Virgil Spinner, let me know. Soon as you can."

"I thought you said he wouldn't dare show up here."

"I was wrong."

Then they had found the clove.

CHAPTER
18

He was lying on his back, his parched mouth open, his lips dry and cracked. He had been awakened by his own snoring and now he moaned softly and turned on one side, wanting only to go back to sleep, even if the dreams came again. He opened his eyes a slit and tried to make out if it was light yet but the heavy curtains kept the window as dark as the rest of the room. He closed his eyes and begged for sleep.

An instant later he was wholly awake. He eased one arm up under the pillow beside the one he lay on and slowly felt for the gun. It was gone.

He lay still, his body stiff with terror. Someone else was there in the room, he knew. And he knew that it could only be Virgil Spinner. It was over, Hasher thought and clamped his jaw to keep himself from screaming.

Then he smelled cloves.

Slowly, groaning a little like a man asleep, he rolled over to face the other way. He squinted in the darkness but could see nothing. Soon it would be like that forever, he thought and wondered why the man hadn't killed him while he slept. He must want more than simply his death. Hasher saw Margaret now and trembled in the dark. Was that it? And then a bullet?

He mustn't let it be as easy as that. He slid one leg over to the side of the bed, feeling with his foot around the mattress edge and downward a little. Then he moved the other leg in the same way. He had nothing to lose, he told himself, and tensed his body. Moving his hands upward slowly under the covers, he got them in position, palms down under his chest. He felt the damp of his pajama top against the backs of his hands and realized that he was soaked in the sweat of his fear. The toes of his right foot touched the floor. He braced himself and raised the trunk of his body slowly upward, ready to spring, to fling himself across the room with a shriek, no matter what he struck or how.

A light went on.

Hasher collapsed back onto the bed and buried his face in the pillow.

"A person could get hurt that way," a voice said.

Slowly Hasher turned his head and saw what he expected: a man in a tan raincoat and a brown hat—the man at Rose's. He was standing beside the door, near the lightswitch. In his hand was a revolver and Hasher was sure that it was his. It was the face in the police photograph: the high cheekbones and long nose and small round chin. He smiled thinly and gestured with the gun for Hasher to get up.

"What do you want?"

"Right now, I want you to get up," the man said. His voice was soft, almost womanly. "With your hands above your head." He waved the gun. "A guy nervous enough to have this under his pillow could have a whole arsenal tucked away in there. Up!"

Slowly Hasher rose and got out of bed and stood with his hands laced on top of his head. The man motioned to him to move forward, then stopped him after he had taken two steps. All Hasher could think of was that he must not let on that he knew who the man was. Spinner frisked him in front for a weapon. He moved around behind Hasher and ran a hand around under his arms and down his sides, then up between his legs.

Suddenly Hasher felt his pajama bottoms being yanked down and a hand caressing his buttocks. "What the—" he cried and began to turn. Then the cold muzzle of the gun was eased between his cheeks. Stricken with terror, Hasher begged, "Please . . . please" brokenly. A moment later he flew sprawling face down, his pajamas around his ankles, as Spinner shoved him in the middle of his back. Hasher rolled over quickly and stared at him. The man stared back—at his genitals—then aimed the gun at them. "Oh, my God . . . please . . . please," Hasher mumbled and put his hands over his crotch.

Spinner chuckled softly. "Not my type," he said. "Too old, too heavy. No spring and bounce in an ass like that."

Hasher had never felt such gratitude.

"Get up and get dressed." He bent over and picked up Hasher's shoes. "All except these. You're too handy with your feet."

Dumbfounded, Hasher stared at him. What did he mean? He couldn't possibly know about the fight with Lyndon James. Hasher began dressing slowly to give himself time to think ahead. But he could only think behind, of the past, and wonder if Spinner had seen him hide the body. Why else had he been at the great rock the afternoon before? It could have been coincidence of course . . . but handy with his feet? He knew.

Hasher put on his shorts and trousers. The back of the clock was to him and he asked, "What time is it?" The question was so absurdly commonplace under the circumstances that he didn't expect an answer; maybe a laugh.

"Four A.M.," Spinner said.

Hasher put on his shirt and sat on the side of the wicker chair where his clothes had been and started to put on his socks. His tongue felt like a wad of dry wool and he desperately wanted a drink of water but was afraid to ask. He tried to work up some saliva, without success. He had to be able to talk. The bathroom . . . he would ask if he could go to the bathroom.

He finished putting on his socks and stood up. "Can I go to the bathroom?"

Spinner smiled bleakly without opening his lips. "Sure," he said.

Hasher put on his sweater and went to the door. Spinner followed closely and they walked the few steps down the half-dark hallway to the bathroom.

"Nothing cute," Spinner warned.

Hasher turned on the light and saw that Spinner had come in behind him and was standing by the basin. He was going to watch. Hasher thought he wouldn't be able to manage it that way but he did, quickly, then went to the basin and washed in the icy well water and splashed his face repeatedly. He calmly brushed his teeth and rinsed his mouth and gulped down the cold water until Spinner finally turned off the tap.

"We don't have all night," he said.

Hasher dried his face and hands and turned to him. "What do you want with me?" he asked, dreading the answer.

Spinner emitted a curt little laugh and now Hasher saw his small teeth, stained brown from cloves. "I got something to show you," Spinner said. Again he smiled the same bleakly hopeless smile.

He jerked his head toward the door and Hasher left, asking, "Where?"

The living room, Spinner told him and switched on the hall light. He turned on a table lamp near the fireplace and motioned Hasher to his own easy chair. When he had obeyed, Spinner took the chair facing his at an angle and swung it more directly toward him, then sat down with the gun aimed at his chest.

"We got a few things to straighten out first," Spinner said.

Before what? Hasher wondered and fear rose in him again. "How did you get in here?" he asked, stalling. "The doors were locked from the inside."

Spinner shrugged, as if the question wasn't worth discussing. "Glass cutter," he said shortly. "Rear bedroom. You were snoring like a wart hog."

"Who are you?" Hasher asked.

"You got a lot of questions—considering that I got the gun," Spinner said. "Pointless questions, dumb questions."

Hasher waited.

"My turn," Spinner went on. He raised the barrel of the gun a few inches so that it was aimed at Hasher's face, and said, "You killed Rail."

"For God's sake, put that down!" Hasher said and the gun was lowered until it was only pointed at his stomach. Now he had to respond but had no idea of what to say. He was surprised—not by Spinner's conclusion but by his admission that he knew who Marvin Rail was. "The Sheriff said it was an accident. He fell and hit his head."

"Yeah? Gee, I must've got it all wrong."

Hasher ignored the sarcasm. Rail had hired Spinner to get rid of Hasher but now Rail was dead and there would be no pay. Then Spinner had come here to get the money due him—for *not* killing Hasher. He took comfort from the thought, but only a little. It was all conjecture; there was still Vivian, who would want revenge now too.

Spinner reached into a pocket and took out something and popped it into his mouth. In a few moments Hasher smelled cloves.

"What's that smell?" he asked, feeling foolish.

Spinner shook his head wearily. "The only thing dumber than being dumb is playing dumb."

With a sudden feeling that he was at a precipice, Hasher pulled back as he remembered the single clove he had left near Rail's body. If Spinner knew that. . . .

"They think I did it," Spinner said.

"Did what?" This time Hasher was not playing dumb.

But Spinner gave him a warning look of exasperation. "Killed Rail," he said.

Trying not to show his relief as he realized that the police were now his allies, a moment later Hasher tried not to show his fear of what this man would do instantly if he knew what had put them on his trail.

"Why would you kill Rail?" Hasher asked, thinking of how perfect it all was: the hit man being wrongly accused of murdering the man who had hired him to kill someone else. "Who are you anyway?" Hasher leaned forward intently to make the question seem convincing.

Spinner rose and placed the muzzle of the gun against

Hasher's forehead. "As you well know, my name is Virgil Spinner, I spent fifteen years in the slammer for murder, and I'd as soon blow out your brains as listen to any more of this shit. Sooner!"

Hasher pulled his head slowly away from the gun and stared up at the man in terror, knowing that it could happen at any moment.

"That guy who followed me when I was following you," Spinner went on, still aiming at his forehead, "who was he—a cop?"

"Private," Hasher said weakly and silently cursed Lime for his incompetence; he couldn't have followed Helen Keller without her knowing it.

"I could tell he recognized me."

My God, Hasher thought, had Lime gone up and measured the fellow's face with calipers?

"Why?" Spinner demanded.

Confused, Hasher asked, "Why did he recognize you?"

"Why did he follow me?"

"For Christ's sake!" Hasher cried. "I was scared!"

Spinner grinned at him. "Not as scared as you are now."

"Why were *you* following *me?*" Hasher asked. "Why are you here? What do you want?"

Spinner motioned with the gun. "Get up. We're going."

Hasher didn't move. "Where?"

"Anyone ever tell you you're a nosey son of a bitch?" He gestured impatiently with the gun again. "Up!"

Hasher rose and Spinner backed away a step, to be out of reach.

"Don't," he said.

Hasher hadn't been even contemplating that. Instead he had been thinking that now might be his last chance to play the big card—or what he thought was the big card, the only one he had. "Lucius Slocum was your friend," he said quietly. "He testified on your behalf."

Two round red spots appeared on Spinner's cheekbones.

"He was my friend too," Hasher went on. "My best friend."

"I thought you were a lawyer," Spinner said.

Puzzled, Hasher stared at him and waited for an explanation.

"Us being friends of the same person doesn't make *us* friends."

Surprised, Hasher could only say, "But it shouldn't make us enemies."

"Why not?"

More surprised, Hasher waited again.

"Takes almost nothing to make enemies," Spinner said. "Where I come from a bad look will do—enough to make a man kill."

It hadn't worked, Hasher realized. The old man must have let Spinner down in some way, or maybe even betrayed him in *his* mind. So Spinner had gone to Rail and Vivian when he got out of prison. Suddenly Hasher was struck by an idea: Maybe Spinner had killed the old man for them.

Spinner handed him his shoes, waited until he had put them on and laced them, then pointed toward the kitchen. "Let's go."

"Where?"

Spinner hesitated, as if contemplating whether he should answer. Then he grinned and said, "To see Vivian Slocum."

The night was unusually dark. The black bulk of the car was just visible a dozen paces from the rear door and the black woods on either side seemed more a threat than a sanctuary. He would never make it that far, Hasher knew as he remembered the shot across the lake that had missed Pete Linzer the day before so narrowly—an incredible piece of marksmanship with a handgun. Now it would be only a few yards at best and even in the dark. . . . Maybe he would get a chance in the car.

At the passenger door, Spinner put the gun in Hasher's neck and told him to get in slowly and slide over behind the wheel. Hasher obeyed, feeling the cold muzzle against the side of his throat. Spinner transferred the gun from his left hand to his right, shoved the barrel hard into Hasher's ribs, and reached around behind him with his free hand to snap the door lock down.

Hasher swore silently. Now it would take two motions for him to get out. But that was a risk that he wasn't going to have to worry about, he discovered when Spinner took a coil of wire out of a pocket, placed a loop of it over his prisoner's head and around his neck, where he tightened it until it was only a little looser than Hasher's collar, ran the rest of the wire down under his jacket, and wound the end around the steering post just below the wheel.

There was no hope now, Hasher knew. He looked at Spinner and said, "If I have to stop suddenly, I'll be decapitated."

"Don't stop suddenly." Spinner took off his hat and for the first time Hasher saw his dark thin hair, plastered down, and recalled the photograph Worthy had shown him. Spinner pulled something light-colored and fluffy-looking out of his other coat pocket and put it on his head. Hasher stared at the blond wig in astonishment. Spinner reached into an inside pocket and took out a small gold tube. He opened it and began applying lipstick to his mouth. Finally he took out a bright red-and-yellow silk scarf, tied it around his throat, and buttoned his raincoat up to the top.

He turned to Hasher and said, "Okay, sweetie?"

Hasher had never seen anyone look so ludicrous. But a moment later he realized that the crude disguise would probably work—as long as they remained in the car in the dark; even a policeman's stopping them and flashing a light through an open window wouldn't give Spinner away, Hasher thought. He woud turn on that soft womanly voice of his and in the dark it would do.

"No lights until we're out on the road," Spinner ordered. "Let's go."

Hasher started the engine and eased the car forward

slowly toward the barely visible drive out through the woods. The disguise would work at night, he thought as he peered through the darkness ahead, but it wouldn't fool anyone in the daylight. He was about to ask Spinner where he had hidden out the past day when he realized the answer: the old man's cabin. As a counselor at the camp-school project years before, Spinner would know about the door in the roof. He had gone to get the diary for Vivian and Rail and realized that it was the perfect hiding place when they heard Hasher was at the lake and told Spinner to stick around in case he was needed.

He had been needed all right, Hasher thought grimly as he reached the road. Suddenly he remembered that Vivian had gone back to the city but in the hope that Spinner didn't know it, Hasher turned to the left, toward town and the inn.

"Right!" Spinner ordered. "And turn on the lights."

Hasher obeyed. Spinner knew. The headlights displayed the loneliness of the barren trees in the autumn night. He remembered the nights so long ago when the old man had made him walk along this road in the dark to conquer his fears. He nearly shivered at the remembrance. Then he felt nausea rising in him as he saw the truth: Vivian hadn't gone back to the city. She was waiting for them on some deserted road in woods like these miles away. That was where it would happen.

Hasher hadn't thought it possible that he could be more afraid than he had been when he awoke in the dark bedroom and knew that someone was there. But he was. He glanced at Spinner in his grotesque get-up and wondered if he could be bought off. Rail was gone, Vivian night be scared now of going on. . . . It was worth trying.

Hasher waited until they had driven several miles in silence, then asked, "What've you been living on since you got out?" He had spoken too abruptly, too loudly, he thought and cursed his clumsiness.

Spinner didn't answer for a minute but finally said, "No problem." A moment later he turned and said, in a falsetto voice, "So nice of you to care."

Startled, Hasher remembered that Spinner had worked for some weeks at a printing plant in Poughkeepsie before violating parole. He didn't seem like a holdup man, surely not a burglar—despite his fierce demeanor, there was something frail about him just below the surface. He must have gone to Rail after he left Poughkeepsie, Hasher thought, and realized suddenly that no, he would have gone to see the old man first. He had been turned down then. Maybe that was the motive; as he had said, it didn't take much to make an enemy in his world. Hasher thought of the photograph of the old man dead at his desk, the dark hole in his white head, and shivered.

"Scared?" Spinner asked.

"Yes." Hasher didn't look at him.

"You should be." There was a silence, then Spinner went on, "Just do what I tell you and you'll be all right. Try something and you won't be."

Hasher thought of the ambush at Qu'an Tu. He and his sergeant had been the only survivors of his platoon. He had never thought that he would get out of that one either. He ground his teeth at the silliness of the comparison: he hadn't been captured then.

Abruptly he turned to Spinner. "How much are they paying you?"

Spinner looked at him, smiling. "Who?"

"How much?"

"Forget it."

"What makes you think you'll get paid when it's over?"

"I said, 'Forget it.'" He sounded angry now.

"You think I killed Rail?" Hasher asked after a minute.

"I know you did. They think *I* did."

"Who?"

"Worthy." Spinner leaned forward and peered through the windshield. "Turn right at Collins Service Station."

It was the shortcut to the Taconic State Parkway. Maybe they were actually going back to the city after all, Hasher thought. He was about to ask why Worthy believed that Spinner had killed Rail when Spinner turned on the radio and adjusted the dial until he found an all-news station.

Hasher scarcely heard the announcer's description of the weather and the events of the day. Something had reminded him of Margaret's allusion to the fury hidden in a dark place within him and as he glanced at the figure beside him he realized that there was little else inside this man. No one but he knew how many times he had killed already. No one, not even he, could measure the demonic rage that must possess him always. And Hasher knew that his own chance of surviving was very small. He wished that he had called Margaret. If only he could hear her voice once more. . . .

As he turned at the gas station and headed east on the narrower back road, he heard the announcer say, "Now more about the manhunt for Virgil Spinner, who is being sought in the mysterious death of Marvin Rail, a prominent attorney from New York City, whose body was found yesterday at a hunting site on Goose Pond. Police say that Spinner is reported to be in Poughkeepsie, where a gas-station attendant identified him after he stopped last night to refuel his car. Poughkeepsie law-enforcement officials have alerted the entire police force, and state police have set up roadblocks around the city. An arrest is expected imminently. Spinner, who was convicted of the sexual murder of a ten-year-old boy and spent fifteen years in Attica Prison, is said to be armed and is extremely dangerous. Any information on this man should be telephone to the following number—"

Spinner turned the radio off. "Assholes! They couldn't find their own footprints in the snow."

If only Worthy had set up roadblocks in this area, Hasher thought as the last of his hopes collapsed. They were hunting for a man alone forty miles away and here he was, the wrong half of a couple. Hasher leaned back to ease the ache that had begun to settle into his shoulders. The wire tightened around his neck and brought him forward.

"Just relax," Spinner said, almost amiably. He reached

220 /

into a pocket, took out something, and held out his open hand. "Here, try these."

Hasher looked and saw half a dozen or so cloves on his palm. "No thanks."

Without a word, Spinner popped them into his own mouth and began chewing noisily.

"You knew they were after you from the radio?" Hasher asked.

"Yeah."

"In Lucius's cabin?"

Spinner looked at him sharply without answering at once. Finally he said, "You're smarter than I figured. Don't get too smart."

They rode on in silence for a few minutes until Hasher asked, "Why do you chew those things?" The car was redolent with the smell of the cloves and he opened his window slightly.

"The oldest known remedy for anxiety depression," Spinner answered, as if he were glad to be asked. "Used thousands and thousands of years. Without them, I go crazy."

Hasher hoped he had a plentiful supply.

CHAPTER
19

Spinner told him to head south on the Taconic and to keep their speed under 55. From the time they left Lake Mercy until they reached the parkway, they had not passed a car going in either direction. But now, even though it was only a little past 4:30, there were a few cars; Hasher passed two, and half dozen or so passed him. One of these was a state-police car and when Hasher saw its flashing rooflights in the rearview mirror, his hopes and then his fears soared. A few seconds later the car swept past, without a glance from its occupants toward Hasher or his passenger.

Spinner slipped the gun between his legs when he saw the car. "If we get stopped, it'd be a good idea for you to cooperate with me," he said mildly. "I got nothing against you—personally, I mean—but if you try to help them take me, you're dead. Them too."

"If there's nothing personal, let me go," Hasher said, knowing it was useless but wanting to get the man at least to talk.

"I got a job to do," Spinner said flatly.

"But he's dead."

"Doesn't matter."

Hasher knew what that meant: now Vivian was the boss.

They rode in silence for a long time. Finally, Hasher tried again. "I understand you're from New Hampshire," he said, feeling absurd. "But you don't have a Yankee accent."

Spinner gave him an amused look. "It's been more than twenty years."

"You've never been back?"

"I'd go back to Attica first."

Hasher hesitated a moment, then asked, "What was it like?" Again he felt foolish but again he knew that he had nothing to lose.

Spinner didn't speak for several minutes. "No better way to describe it than by the old phrase: 'serving time,'" he said at last. "Time is there everywhere, dripping, dripping, dripping—like it was an hourglass the size of a mountain and each grain of sand is a second. Dripping, dripping, dripping. All you think about, all you hear, all you believe in is time. 'Serving time,' like they say." He stopped.

Hasher was astonished at the vivid image. "Did you read a lot?" he asked, thinking that must be where Spinner had found it.

Spinner glanced at him with the same amused look. "For fifteen years," he said. "About all I did—except fuck when I could. I hardly knew how to read anything better than comic books when I got there. But I learned. Everything. I've been through college three times."

Pulp novels, Hasher thought, girlie magazines, maybe a few third-rate books.

"I've got a hundred and seventy I.Q.," Spinner said, without turning.

Flabbergasted for a moment, Hasher was sure it was a lie. Whatever else this man was, he was hardly a genius. "My God," he said, "that's high." He cursed himself; it was all too clear that he didn't believe a word of it.

"So they told me," Spinner said. "They told me I could do anything with an I.Q. like that. So what am I doing?" He grinned at Hasher.

They were silent again for a few miles, then Spinner said, "Homer, Aeschylus, Sophocles—that's where I started. After that, Plato, Aristotle and on and on for centuries. Jesus Christ Almighty!"

Hasher looked at him and saw his jaw clamped in anger, as if he was thinking about the fifteen years he had wasted. "What did you get out of it?" Hasher asked, wondering why he couldn't say anything that sounded natural.

Spinner's head jerked around as he faced him. "All *bullshit!*" he said through his teeth. "A bunch of desperate men trying to show that life has meaning. Bullshit!"

Hasher didn't speak. The self-made murderer's philosophy, he thought and yet knew that he shared it. Then he realized that of course he did; that was what he was too. "What was it like at Attica?" he asked again, for the sake of keeping the conversation going.

"You planning on going there?"

Startled, Hasher knew that this was exactly what he had been thinking without knowing it.

"Because of Rail? You ought to get the Medal of Honor for that."

Hasher stared at him in amazement: the man was full of the unexpected.

"I heard you almost got that in Vietnam," Spinner went on before he could say anything. "You really are an asshole—killing for them."

"Them?"

"Yeah—them who run everything. If you're going to kill, kill for yourself. Like you killed Rail."

Like I'll kill you, Hasher thought.

"And James," Spinner added.

Hasher didn't speak. The man seemed to know everything. Now one of them had to die. Looking at the glint of the gun in Spinner's lap, Hasher had a pretty good idea of which one it would be. "You're crazy," he said.

"At least I know it," Spinner replied calmly. "It's you nitwits on the outside who don't know your ass from a five-dollar bill who're really apeshit." He took out more cloves and popped them into his mouth.

Soon the car was filled again with the redolent odor. They drove on in silence.

"I used to have the same dream a lot in the slammer," Spinner said suddenly. "What do you call that—having the same dream over and over?"

"A recurrent dream," Hasher answered, feeling silly now.

"Yeah. Freud—another bullshit artist. It wasn't Oedipus who wanted to fuck his mother, it was old Siggy." He chuckled softly.

"Your recurrent dream," Hasher reminded him, trying not to sound too interested.

"Funny," Spinner said after a pause, "I haven't had it since I got out. Before, it was once a month, maybe more, year in and year out. I must've had that dream a hundred times. It got so I knew I was dreaming it when I was and I'd add to it, play with it. A glorious dream."

Hasher waited.

"You want to hear it?" Spinner asked, sounding almost hurt.

"Okay." Hasher took a slow deep breath.

Spinner's dream began with the creation of the earth—an explosion of matter out of the nothing of infinity, of a universe out of a black void without time, without space. "A neat fucking trick, that," he said with a grin and went on to describe his own imaginary version of Genesis. "Those patsies, Adam and Eve, never existed," he said. "Cain was the first human being, the father of the race." But few of the Biblical figures held much interest for him. What his dream centered on was the battle between Good and Evil, the fight between God and Satan, after which, the Old Testament relates, God, triumphant, cast Satan into the nethermost reaches of hell.

"Actually, Satan won," Spinner said matter-of-factly. "He threw God out of heaven. And then the first thing Satan did was to dictate *his* account through the Bible to make mankind believe that God had won. To give the human race false hope, to make them yearn for eternal reward for their pain on earth, to lead them to goodness."

Spinner laughed his soft womanly laugh. "I've seen them in my dream—the martyrs, the saints, the simple good people—writhing in hell. In heaven are only Satan, his devils, and the six most evil people who have ever lived. When the seventh gets there—probably the guy who pushes the button, I figure—the world will end."

"Oh my God," Hasher said softly. He could almost hear the Satanic laughter.

"Don't be an asshole," Spinner said. "There is no God, no Satan. Even we don't exist."

"And if we did?"

Spinner laughed again. "We'd be driving through the night headed nowhere."

The monstrous dream shattered the little hopes that had begun to spring up in Hasher as they talked—hopes that he might reach this man somehow, to touch his inner self, to remind him that they were both only lost and suffering human beings. But now Hasher saw that to succeed in such an attempt would be fatal. Inside this man there was only evil.

They drove on, silent, for nearly half an hour. Hasher's shoulders and neck ached painfully and his mouth was so dry that it hurt to move his tongue. He desperately wanted to ask if they could stop and get some coffee but knew that it would be useless.

"You know New Hampshire?" Spinner asked abruptly.

Bewildered, Hasher remembered that Spinner had grown up there. "A little," Hasher said, not wanting to reveal that he had gone to Dartmouth; that could be fatal too.

"A little is too much." Now there was a touch of the swamp Yankee in his voice. "The part you know wouldn't be the part I know. Back in the mountains off a dirt road. A shack with a cowshed on one side and a privy out back. No electricity, no running water, little heat, and less food. But hate—plenty of hate. We had enough we could have sold some. Except up there everyone's got enough of their own already."

He was quiet for a mile or two, then said, "I never had a chance."

Hasher's heart sank. This maniac, this pervert, this killer was going to appeal for sympathy. Then he would surely kill to stop the ears and tongue of the person who had heard him reveal himself. "A lot of people never had a chance," Hasher said quickly to stop him. It would be better to make him a little angry now rather than enraged later on.

Spinner ignored the challenge. "My old man was lower than a wormy dog's ass," he went on. "The personality of a polecat, the heart of a rattlesnake. He was twenty years older than Ma. He hated her but hated me even more. Always told me he wished I'd died at birth like all the other kids Ma bore him. I was sickly and he hated that too, because I couldn't help out like he wanted. He did a little farming, kept a cow and some chickens, hunted for extra food, and stole when he could."

There was no stopping him now, Hasher saw; he had to show some interest or make things worse. "Why did your mother marry him?"

Spinner gave him a look of contempt. "Why does anybody marry anybody? All they think about is the frying pan they're jumping out of. They were cousins and knew each other from the time they were kids. It happens."

That was it—inbreeding, Hasher thought and glanced at the bewigged lipsticked face in the dark. Six people, maybe more, had died because two cousins had mated. And he would be the seventh. He wondered if the number had anything to do with Spinner's dream.

"I doubt there was a boy in those mountains as horny as me," Spinner continued. "I got to manhood early—a little past ten. A good thing too. I nearly went crazy before that. I had a hard-on most of the time, day and night, but nothing to do with it. The first time the jism spurted out, I knew the wait had been worth it. Jesus Christ Almighty! Coming is the only thing that could ever make me believe in God. Who else could have thought of *that*?

I couldn't get enough. It made the whole stinking world suddenly worth living in."

He fell silent, as if relishing the memory of his early masturbatory days. Finally he went on, "The old man was away a lot. Had a woman somewhere, I always figured, though I can't imagine why when he couldn't make it with the one he had at home. Not since I was born, she told me. She was still young but you wouldn't have known it without her birth certificate. No teeth, hair like an old mule's, and dirty. I *hate* dirt!"

He stopped and looked at Hasher. "You like getting head?"

Here it was, Hasher thought and gripped the wheel. Not rape this time. A pass, an offer. Then a gunshot in the head. "It depends," he said, amazed at how matter-of-fact he sounded. "The right time, the right woman, the right place."

"Yeah," Spinner said and chuckled. "The first time it was early morning, at dawn, the summer I turned eleven. The old man had gone hunting—poaching actually—when she got in bed with me. Claimed she was cold. I said it was summer. She said it must be a chill. She crunched up to me to get warm. I got hard. The next thing I know she's got it in her mouth. Jesus Christ Almighty! And I thought jacking off was good!"

Hasher wasn't surprised. He knew that incest was notoriously common among mountain people and suspected that it was a lot more common than realized among everyone else. "Only that once?" he asked.

Spinner's lipsticked mouth opened wide as he laughed outright for the first time—a high trilling giggle that exploded into a kind of screech and subsided. "Once?" he cried. "Three, four times a day wherever and whenever we could. In the house when the old man was sleeping off a drunk. In the cowshed, in the woods."

Hasher waited for a few moments, then asked, "That was all? You never had real sex?"

Spinner snorted with contempt. "Real? Shit, what's real is what happens." He was silent briefly and went on,

"We did more after a little time. Turned out she liked it in the ass. Said the other way wouldn't be decent." He grinned. "As you say, 'the right time, the right woman, the right place.'" He laughed again.

Hasher waited before asking, "What happened?"

"We went on like that for close to three years before he caught us. I always knew he would."

Hasher turned and stared at him: Was he a patricide too?

"He said he was going hunting and wouldn't be home till dark. Well, he was home half an hour after he left. I was humping her. She was screaming for more—'Harder! Deeper!' she kept yelling. When he went for her, I got away. Stark fucking naked. For a day and a half running and hiding in the woods. Until I found some clothes on a line, left out all night—girl's clothes." He stopped and giggled. "Sort of like now."

"Your mother?"

"I went back, after he was gone, but nobody was real anxious to tell me what happened."

"But you found out?"

"Yeah, I found out." Spinner sounded suddenly angry.

Frightened again, Hasher said, "Sorry. I shouldn't have asked." Jesus Christ, he thought, it sounded like cocktail-party chatter.

"That's all right," Spinner said, almost cheerfully. "It won't matter."

The remark took Hasher's breath away.

Before he could speak, Spinner went on, "They found her with the barrel of his rifle jammed up her ass. The slug, a thirty-thirty, went all the way up through her and out her shoulder."

Hasher coughed violently and tasted vomit. Spinner waited, silent, not looking at him. When the coughing spell subsided, Hasher was seized by shame: He had suppressed all thought of this man committing that act upon Margaret. Was it because of his fear? Hasher wondered. But he knew that wasn't reason enough; he had failed her

/ 229

again. His longing for her—just to be alone and quiet together. . . . Too late, he thought bitterly, too late.

"Somebody came by two or three days later looking for my old man," Spinner said. "He was sitting in a rocking chair on the porch, his mind all gone. They put him in jail. He hung himself."

Was that the story that had touched the old man and persuaded him to befriend this creature when he was a youth? Hasher asked himself. Or his startling intelligence? It seemed impossible. But when Hasher thought of Lyndon Johnson James and Vivian, it no longer did. The old man had been destroyed by his own innocence.

"What?" Spinner asked, suddenly suspicious. He raised the gun an inch or two from his lap.

Wondering if he had spoken out loud without realizing it, Hashed said, "You were only thirteen?"

"Yeah. I've been on my own ever since," Spinner said, with a note of pride.

At the Hawthorne Circle, Spinner told him to take the Saw Mill River Parkway south. Hasher's spirits rose a little at the order for about fifteen miles further on, just below Tibetts Brook Park, was a toll booth. If he could manage a signal of some discreet kind—maybe make the guard see the wire around his neck by one means or another that wouldn't be visible to Spinner—the police would pick them up down the road. Or if that failed, there would be one final chance, at the last tollbooth, on the far side of the Harlem River just inside Manhattan.

He could grab the tolltaker's wrist to alert him and at the same moment smash the rigid side of his right hand against Spinner's throat to stun him momentarily, long enough at least to loosen the wire and get out. . . . Hasher scowled. Spinner would have the correct change for the automatic lane.. There would be no guard, scarcely a stop as Hasher tossed the coins into the receiver bin. But he could drop them unobtrusively onto the pavement, so the alarm would go off as they drove on through. Was there just a stop light at the tollbooth or a gate? he wondered, but couldn't remember.

Sometimes the police parked in the bays off to one side. . . . That would be enough. Even if Spinner was supposed to be in the Poughkeepsie area, the police around here must be on the alert. But he might still shoot Hasher and make a break for it. If there was no police car when they went through without paying the toll, a guard would take the license number. Hasher would get a summons after he was dead.

Hopeless, he told himself again, hopeless.

"I can hear your mind clicking," Spinner said and grinned at him. "Don't try it."

Any hopes Hasher had about getting help or making an escape at a tollbooth vanished when Spinner ordered him to turn onto the Cross County Parkway, a mile short of the tollbooth on the Saw Mill. Now Hasher knew their route—on the Cross County, where there were no tolls, and then south on the Thruway, a couple of miles below the last toll stop, and finally onto the Major Deegan Expressway, where there also were no tolls, and across the tollfree bridge into Manhattan at 138th Street. He swore under his breath and turned just in time to see Spinner give him one of his smiles and pop some more cloves into his mouth. It was as good as over.

To Hasher's disgust, he even made the traffic light at the entrance to the ordinarily jammed-up bridge. There were cars on every side of him now. But that only made him feel more frustrated for even if he could signal to someone, nobody would help him—not in New York. He looked at a digital clock on a nearby building: 5:48. It would be light in less than an hour . . . maybe then. But he knew that was a futile hope too. By that time they would be wherever they were going . . . Vivian's or someplace Spinner had picked out to get rid of him. Then leave the car back at the lake.

"Over to Fifth Avenue and straight down," Spinner ordered as they swung down the end of the bridge ramp into Manhattan. "Left on Eightieth."

Vivian's place. At least Spinner had told the truth about that.

"I wonder what it'd be like with Vivian," Spinner said casually. He grinned at Hasher. "That's some ass she's got—if you like women. I like them sometimes, just for old time's sake."

"Like mom's apple pie?" Hasher said.

Spinner gave him a murderous look. "She wouldn't be as good as that woman of yours," he said evenly. "Now *there's* an ass! Juicy even. Jesus Christ Almighty!"

Blood pounded in Hasher's temples and his throat constricted to stop the scream of rage.

"Too bad she was out cold," Spinner went on. "She might've enjoyed it as much as I did."

Hasher turned in inflamed fury. "One chance, just one," he choked out, "and I'll kill you!"

Spinner removed the wig and scarf and wiped the lipstick off his mouth. He looked at Hasher with the same thin bleak smile. "Sorry," he said, "but I've got other plans."

CHAPTER

20

It seemed absurd to be going to Vivian's if they intended to kill him, Hasher thought, wondering idly in his stupor of fear how they would dispose of his body. And it seemed even more absurd if they didn't intend to. He shivered slightly as it occurred to him that perhaps they meant to torture a confession out of him about his murdering James and Rail, then turn him over to the police. But, whatever they intended, here he was, in the vestibule of her house, with Spinner behind him, the gun in his hand inside his raincoat pocket.

"The bell," Spinner said impatiently for the second time.

Hasher looked back at him, as an excuse to peer through the windows of the tall vestibule doors to the sidewalk below. But it was still too early, only a little past six, and a Saturday. And even if somebody passed, what would he do—cry out? That would mean only an earlier death. Now he scarcely cared. Numbed with exhaustion and fear, he wanted it over with. He wanted to sleep.

Spinner swore ferociously and reached past him to press the doorbell—two long rings.

Half a minute passed, a minute, without a response.

"She's not home," Hasher said. But he knew she was; she would be waiting for them but couldn't have known the hour of their arrival. They had to exonerate themselves from responsibility for Rail's death—especially

Spinner, now that Worthy was after him. This was the only way to do it. The Sheriff must know, or at least suspect, that Rail had hired Spinner or was connected with him in some way and that would connect Vivian to the killer as well. . . .

Spinner swore again and jabbed the bell for one long ring.

Hasher glanced at him, almost disinterestedly; now he could only wait.

"Who in the name of God?" came a metallic screech over the intercom. "It's the middle of the night!"

Spinner took out the gun, jammed it into Hasher's side, and moved close to the mouthpiece of the intercom. "Police!" he shouted in a voice unlike his own.

Hasher's head went back in astonishment, his mind reeling as the fog blew away in an instant. A code signal? A joke? A surprise? That must be it—a surprise; Spinner had brought Hasher to her as a prize, a trophy, and didn't want her to know until the last moment.

"What do you want?" her tinny voice demanded suddenly.

In a calmer tone but still the artificial voice, Spinner answered, "Sheriff Worthy from upstate called to ask us to check and see that you're all right, ma'am. Are you?"

"Of course I am! What is this?"

"A man called Virgil Spinner is known to be here in the city," Spinner said. "The Sheriff thinks he may be headed your way."

"The man who killed Marvin Rail?" her voice screeched.

"Yes, ma'am. All we want is to see you're safe. If you like, we'll search the house to make double sure."

It had gone much too far to be a surprise, Hasher realized. And when he saw the man take out some cloves and begin chewing furiously, he knew that Spinner was facing a crisis too. A moment later Hasher was sure he had the answer: Spinner was going to use him to blackmail Vivian; he had the copy of the diary and the notes that the old man had hidden in the lining of the book bag; he had everything except the money he had been promised and now that Rail was dead only Vivian. . . .

There was the sound of a lock being turned and a bolt sliding and the door opened a few inches. Spinner was standing to one side, out of sight, and Vivian could see only Hasher.

"Thomas!" she gasped, her eyes wide. Suddenly she moved to shut the door but Spinner slammed against it with one shoulder and flung her backwards. She screamed and fell.

In the few seconds that elapsed, Hasher knew that he had to act and he clasped his hands together and swung them over his shoulder, ready to smash them down on the back of Spinner's neck. But the gunman saw it in time and whirled around thrusting the muzzle of the gun into his throat. Hasher groaned and fell back a step. It was over.

He stared at Vivian, lying on her back on the pale carpeting of the foyer, her mouth open to scream again, her face twisted in fear. But he saw that she was frozen in terror. Her eyes bulged, one hand clutched her throat. Her thick hair was down around her shoulders. She was wearing a rich red-and-blue embroidered silk dressing gown; it had fallen open to reveal one long exquisite leg and thigh.

Spinner motioned him inside and followed and closed the door. He too looked down at Vivian and Hasher saw, to his amazement, an expression of raw fury. Stunned, Hasher watched as Spinner stared at Vivian. Slowly her contorted mouth, still ready for a scream, closed, her eyes seemed normal; within seconds she had composed herself. Hasher marveled at her self-control: she was planning her next move. He waited.

Vivian looked at him now. "Is *he*—?" she began.

Hasher nodded. "Meet Virgil Spinner." At last he understood what had happened: Rail had hired the killer without telling her.

She sat up and arranged her gown and held out a hand. "Could one of you at least help me up?"

Hasher took a step forward but Spinner waved him back with the gun. "You spent most of your life on your back," he said to her. "Did they all help you up afterwards?"

A flicker of rage passed through her eyes and she started to speak but checked herself and got up unaided. She looked at Spinner without fear. "I heard about you years ago—from Lucius," she said calmly. "I believe his description was 'a hopeless pervert.' "

"That and a lot worse," Spinner said and slapped her hard across the face. "Turn around!"

Hasher wanted to slap her too before she got both of them killed on the spot. She wasn't afraid because she had always won and was sure she would now. But it was folly, he thought, absurd audacity. She had no idea of what this man was capable of.

Her cheek crimson from the blow, she stared at Spinner with hatred for a few moments before obeying. Spinner waved the gun at Hasher and he went and stood beside her. They were allies now, he thought, more bewildered than ever.

"Upstairs," Spinner ordered. "Slow and easy, side by side. One move from either of you and you're both dead."

As they walked up the steps, Vivian's hand brushed against Hasher's once. He wondered if it had been a signal but it didn't happen again. At the landing, they stopped.

"Into the living room," Spinner said, as if he knew the apartment well.

An antique brass chandelier in the hallway at the top of the stairs was on and its light spilled into the handsomely proportioned and elegantly furnished sitting room. Once the two were in the center of it, another light went on behind them. At a glance, Hasher saw that all traces of the old man who had paid for this—his collection of *art nouveau* pieces, his matching Tiffany lamps, his Picasso drawings—were gone. Another quarter of a million stolen, Hasher thought.

"Okay, turn around," Spinner ordered.

When they turned, still beside each other, Hasher saw that Spinner was standing by the fireplace. One arm was still out at a slight angle, left there as if forgotten after he turned on a green-shaded table lamp. Hasher recognized the lamp; it was a duplicate of the one on the desk in the study at the old man's cabin; if it was still here, he thought, it couldn't be worth much.

Spinner noticed his look and glanced down at the lamp and nodded slightly, as if he remembered too.

"Why did you kill Marvin?" Vivian asked Spinner suddenly.

He smiled wtihout answering.

"You didn't even know him, did you?" she went on.

Hasher moved away from her, to make it more difficult for Spinner to shoot both of them. He got only a step away when the killer stopped him with a stab of the gun into the air. "Rail hired him," Hasher said quickly.

"Marvin hired this man to kill *him?*" she asked with contempt. "Nonsense!"

"No, to kill me," Hasher said, wondering why he bothered; it couldn't matter now. Spinner knew the truth and Spinner had the gun.

Vivian turned back to Spinner. "But why?" When he still didn't answer, she faced Hasher. "Why would Marvin want to kill you? He had nothing to fear from *you.*" She lowered her eyes momentarily, then looked up into his directly. "We laughed about your wretched anger." She hesitated and added, "Your impotence."

Hasher felt the color rise into his cheeks and heard Spinner's soft laughter.

"You want to show her different, Hasher?" he asked.

Hasher looked at him and saw his wan brown smile.

"*He* killed Rail," Spinner said.

She looked at them in turn, then shook her head. "Not Thomas," she said to Spinner. "He hasn't got the guts."

Hasher felt as if he were the one who had been slapped.

"Maybe in Vietnam," she went on, "but not here, not in cold blood."

"He killed Rail all right," Spinner said. "And I've got a strong suspicion you're next."

Vivian stared at Hasher in alarm for a moment and shrugged contemptuously. Turning back to Spinner, she said, "And I suppose you're going to watch."

He grinned. "Something like that." He took off his hat and raincoat and tossed them on the sofa.

"Is he going to fuck me first, like he promised yesterday?" she demanded defiantly, her eyes blazing.

Spinner glared at Hasher, who listened, dumbfounded.

"Do you want to watch that too?" she cried to Spinner.

His grin twisted into a grimace. "Before or after you're dead?"

The color left her face and she swayed slightly.

"He killed that nigger too," Spinner told her.

Vivian stared at him, waiting expectantly.

"Lyndon Johnson James," Spinner said. He reached into his jacket pocket and, stepping over to the long coffee table near him, put down two tapered scorched-looking objects on a white ashtray.

Hasher stared at them and closed his eyes, murmuring, "Oh my God."

She looked at him, then at Spinner, and asked, as if she couldn't have been less interested, "And what may those be?"

"Those are Lyndon Johnson James's teeth," Spinner said matter-of-factly.

Vivian blanched again and put a hand on the sofa for support.

"Hasher kicked them out of the nigger's mouth, then shot him," Spinner said. "With this." He held out the revolver.

She stared from the teeth to the gun to Hasher's face, then shook her head. "I don't believe it. How can you prove those are Lynnie's?" She colored slightly at the intimate sound of the nickname.

"I don't have to," Spinner said. "I saw it happen. Through the cabin window." He glanced at Hasher and said, "Careless of you leaving those in your fireplace."

Then the teeth hadn't been in the pail of ashes he had dumped into the lake, Hasher realized as he remembered wondering at the time why he hadn't heard even the tiny splashing sounds they should have made.

"Anyway, I don't have to prove anything," Spinner told her. "I've got all the cards. The fact is, I've got everything—except money. How much?"

"For what?" she asked, watching him nervously.

He jerked his head toward Hasher. "To kill him."

At least he had been right, Hasher thought helplessly. Except he hadn't expected that he would have to listen to the bargaining over the price of his death. He caught the triumphant look in her eyes: she had won; her kind always won. He looked away.

"How much do you want?" she asked.

A trembling smile crossed Hasher's lips. It was over at last.

"Twenty-five thousand," Spinner said.

Vivian gasped. "So much?"

"You seem to forget," Spinner said. "He's going to kill you if he lives. It's your own life you're buying."

"All right," she said at once. "Of course I don't have that kind of money here."

"I didn't expect you to. There's something else."

She frowned. "What?"

"The diary you took from the cabin."

Surprised now, she asked, "How did you know?"

"I read it," Spinner said calmly. "As a matter of fact, I was there in the back room when Rail came in through the roof and got it."

Vivian nodded. "In the desk." She pointed to a French provincial table that served as a desk.

Spinner backed over to it, opened the center drawer, and felt around inside, holding the gun on them with the other hand, until he found the red record book. He took it out, opened it, and leafed through it. Nodding, he put it on the desk and walked over to Vivian. He smiled at her, revealing his small brown teeth. She eased back a step.

"Kill him—now!" she cried, pointing at Hasher.

"Not just yet," Spinner said calmly. "Not till I've got the money."

"But it's Saturday, the bank's closed," she said. "I can't get it until Monday."

"Then we'll just have to wait," Spinner said. He surveyed the room. "Seems comfortable enough." He grinned at her horrified expression.

The reprieve gave Hasher new hope—until Spinner went to his coat and took out the coil of wire he had bound Hasher with in the car. Spinner ordered him to lie on the floor on his side and bound his wrists together, then tied them to his ankles, so that he couldn't move an inch without cutting off the circulation in both his hands and his feet. He twisted his head to look up when Spinner finished and saw Vivian, amused, watching him.

"Whore!" he shouted.

She stepped forward and spat on his face.

Spinner watched her, smiling, his eyes glittering. When she turned to see his reaction, he nodded approvingly. She kicked Hasher in the groin with her slippered foot.

He cried out and Spinner laughed.

Vivian's eyes were bright, glistening eagerly as she turned back to the killer.

"Take off your robe," he said, still smiling. His mouth was open slightly and the tip of his tongue ran back and forth along his lips. His eyes were like lights. "Off!"

Vivian stared at him in surprise. She shook her head, then frowned and shrugged and slipped off the robe. It fell to her feet. She was naked.

Even through his tears of pain Hasher could see that she was as extravagantly beautiful as his dream of her. He closed his eyes.

"Turn around—slowly," Spinner ordered.

"Put down the gun," she said. "You've got what you want. What you don't have, I'll give you."

He grinned and put the gun on an end table beside the sofa, a couple of feet from where he stood. "Okay?"

Vivian nodded and smiled slowly, lasciviously. She

turned and stepped out of the robe crumpled at her feet, until her back was to him. She kicked off her slippers.

"Jesus Christ Almighty!" Spinner murmured. "Look at *that*, Hasher!"

He opened his eyes and saw her extraordinarily white body. It seemed to him as cold, as lifeless as a statue—and as perfect.

Vivian stood unmoving until a shiver rippled up from the small of her back to her shoulders and she clasped her arms around her breasts.

"Be a dear and touch your toes," Spinner said.

Surprised at the tone of his voice and the words he used, Hasher looked up and saw the gloating crazed face of a medieval satyr. Vivian slowly lowered her arms and bent over.

Hasher thought about Margaret and groaned.

Spinner looked at him. "Hungry? You want some?"

"Fuck you!"

Spinner laughed and Vivian slowly straightened up and turned around and held out her arms to him. Her mouth was open, her nipples erected. Something—this madman, the danger, her nakedness, the man on the floor about to die—excited her beyond control.

"Fuck me!" she cried. "I'll do anything you like!"

"Okay," Spinner said.

Vivian laughed with delight.

Hasher closed his eyes again.

When he heard her cry out, he looked up and saw her lying face down on the sofa with Spinner, naked too, on her back as he thrust himself into her ass. She screamed in pain, then moaned and begged, "Slowly, slowly—please slowly!" Hasher turned his face down into the rug and closed his eyes. But he couldn't stop the sounds, especially the slapping noise as Spinner's pelvis and hips rose and fell on her buttocks.

And then the words, the cries and moaning pleas: "Deeper!" she cried. "Deeper—please, please, oh my God! Yes!" And Spinner's heavy short gasping breath as he shouted, "You like it?" and she cried, "Yes! Yes! Oh my God, faster, faster!" Suddenly she cried out, "Ohhhhhhhhh! Ohhhhhhhhh! Here it is! Ohhh, yes, yes, yes!" Then she shrieked in ecstasy and there was a sharp cracking noise and Spinner cried out too, a long dying, "Ahhhhh!" and finally silence.

Hasher looked up and saw Vivian grinning at him. He looked at Spinner, lying on top of her, his face turned away. After a minute, he raised himself off her back and Hasher looked away from the slack cock and the thin white legs back to Vivian. Her expression was the same. Hasher cursed her taunting grin. As Spinner got off the couch, Vivian's head fell at an odd angle but the grimace was the same taut grin, full of hatred, and her eyes were wide, staring at him.

Hasher gagged, tasting vomit, as he realized that she was dead. The smile was a rictus smile. The cracking noise he had heard had been her neck breaking as Spinner jerked her head back a moment after she came. He had finished inside her after she died. Hasher passed out.

CHAPTER
21

The first snow of the year had fallen during the night and it covered the unkempt matted grass and softened the angular tombstones and sparkled in the dark bushes. At the entrance to the graveyard, Hasher hesitated, reluctant to mar the forlorn peace of the place with his footprints. It had been nearly six weeks since the old man's burial and Hasher had meant to come here earlier but hadn't been able to muster the courage. There was still one question to be asked; perhaps he would find the answer now by the grave.

He started forward, thinking that it would be his last visit here, but stopped and stared pensively over to one corner where his parents were buried. He was ashamed that he hadn't been there in many years. It always seemed pointless: he scarcely remembered his father and of his mother he could recall only her long fine blonde hair piled on top of her head in a bun, her pale blue eyes, and her kindly smile. He saw no reason to look down at her grave and imagine her bones.

The last visit but one, he told himself and moved slowly on toward the old man's grave, in the far corner. The Hasher plot had room for one more. He had not meant to use it but now that Margaret was gone. . . . He ached with longing for her and yet knew that she had been right to leave him. . . . A wall between them, she had said, a wall that she had not built and could not tear down. He glanced back toward his family's plot. It would be as good a place as any. He could only hope that his wait wouldn't be too long.

That was all most people did—wait to die—he thought as he looked around at the nearby graves. They spent their lives waiting. They didn't venture on any great quests or have any great thoughts. There were no soaring dreams for them. They only waited.

Remembering Spinner's dream, Hasher shook his head slowly in wonder because now it didn't seem at all fantastic. He stopped at the foot of the Slocums' grave and looked at the snow-edged letters chiseled in the simple double tombstone. Under Mary Slocum's name and the dates of her life were the words: "A woman who lived and loved." Under the name Lucius Avery Slocum was only his birthdate. Hasher told himself to have the date of death added. Then he laughed briefly, angrily, as he thought of an epitaph:

> We live in darkness
> Lighted only
> By deceit

When Hasher had regained consciousness, he had found that the wire binding his wrists and ankles together had been removed. Vivian's body was covered with a blanket, leaving only a tumble of brown hair visible at one end and her bare white feet at the other. Hasher moved his head slowly so that he could see the rest of the room without making any noise. He saw Spinner sitting, fully clothed, at the desk writing something. Surprised, but hardly grateful, that Spinner hadn't killed him while he was unconscious, Hasher lay still, trying to figure out what to do, wondering if the man had waited in order to watch his conscious terror before he died.

"Welcome back to this happy world," Spinner said, not looking up from his writing.

Hasher was silent for a time but knew that any attempt

to escape, any attack would be futile. "Why?" he asked finally.

"You mean Vivian?"

"Yes." Hasher sat up.

Spinner turned to him. "Because I knew you couldn't do it."

It was true, Hasher knew, he couldn't have. James had been one thing—self-defense; Rail had been another—almost an accident. But to kill a woman coldly like that. . . . Then, suddenly, Hasher heard the answer again— "Because I knew you couldn't do it"—and stared at Spinner in astonishment. "Why did it have to be done?"

Spinner shrugged. "I promised."

My God, Hasher thought, there had been no bottom to that pit that was Marvin Rail. A moment later the room swam before his eyes and he thought he was going to faint again as he understood at last. He buried his face in his hands and waited for the dizziness to pass. When he looked up again, tears were streaming down his cheeks.

"Lucius?" he asked.

Spinner nodded. "He paid me thirty thousand dollars—ten apiece. I guess I owe you twenty for James and Rail but it's all gone. Less than two hundred left. Boys—the right kind of boys—cost a lot these days."

Hasher stared at him in horror.

"He was the only person in the world who was ever decent to me," Spinner said. "He gave me all those books, one every month when he came to visit me in prison. He made me study them, asked me questions." Spinner paused. "I would have killed them for nothing but he insisted on paying. Said he must be responsible."

Hasher thought that he had gone insane, that he would turn and see Vivian get up and smile at him, that it was all a mad joke.

"He wanted you to do it," Spinner went on, "but he thought you didn't—"

"Have the guts."

Spinner smiled. "It turned out he was wrong. Anyway, he had already sent you that package with the copy of his diary and the notes and letters, so he called me up to the cabin and asked me to do the job. That's why I had to break into your place and steal the evidence."

Spinner stopped for a moment, then said, "Sorry about what I did to your woman but I had to make you think that's what I was there for. I needed time." He smiled. "The old man even told me that you hid stuff in the freezer."

Hasher stood up and saw his gun on the desk.

Spinner shook his head. "Don't try it," he said. "It won't last much longer."

Hasher's mind was reeling. He had killed, twice, for no reason. "Why didn't you do what you promised him?"

Spinner smiled his old bleak smile. "I was following James with exactly that in mind the night you killed him. You were pretty good." He smiled, encouragingly now.

Sickened, Hasher turned away.

"Except you clearly didn't have a plan—just acted. That's not smart. From that moment, I had everything planned. I followed you to scare you into thinking Rail was after you, so you'd take him out too. Why not have it happen like the old man wanted? I thought. And it did. Up to a point anyway. I planned it all."

Hasher looked at him in amazement. The man was utterly mad.

"It worked, didn't it?" Spinner demanded, as if he knew what Hasher was thinking. "The minute I heard Rail was dead, I knew what happened. And I knew what to do next." He gestured toward the body on the sofa. "It worked just the way I planned it." He paused and looked at the piece of paper before him on the desk. "Now it's almost over."

"If Lucius called you to the cabin after he mailed the evidence to me, you must have been there just before he died," Hasher said.

"Before and while," Spinner said, not looking up.

"Oh my God," Hasher murmured. "You killed him."

"He asked me to. He couldn't do it himself." Spinner took an envelope out of an inside pocket and opened it.

He removed two pieces of paper and placed them on top of the diary.

Hasher moved closer to the desk to see what they were.

Spinner picked up the gun. "Here's how it happened," he said and placed the muzzle slowly against his own temple. "He had nothing to live for, less than nothing. He knew it and I knew it. But he couldn't pull the trigger. He asked me to help." Spinner looked up at Hasher. "Give me your hand."

Hasher put his hand over Spinner's, with his forefinger over Spinner's trigger finger.

"That's right," Spinner said. "That's how it happened."

When the gun fired, Hasher didn't know if he had pressed the trigger. But it didn't matter, he knew; nothing mattered now or ever would again.

He looked down at the desk beside Spinner's body and saw that the pieces of paper on the diary were the blackmail letter from James and Vivian's note to him. Hasher stared at the red hole in Spinner's temple and saw that there had been almost no bleeding. A drop or two had fallen on the paper he had been writing on. Hasher bent down to read it:

I killed Marvin Rail and Vivian Slocum to pay them back for what they did to Lucius Slocum. He was innocent and never did the things they said about him. Vivian Slocum stole the money from his law firm, which she confessed before she died. This diary and notes prove everything.

I swear this before Almighty God.

Virgil Spinner

Now Hasher turned away from the grave, the one remaining question—*Why?*—unanswered. He knew that it would always be like that. It was just as well. The truth was probably something like Spinner's dream.

Snow was falling again and as he looked back toward the old man's grave, he saw that his footprints were filling up. Soon there would be no sign of his presence here. But that didn't matter either—whether he had lived or not. Now there was nothing more for him but to wait with the others.

Hasher shivered and turned up his coat collar. He would stop for coffee at Rose's.

About the Author

Richard Harris was for many years a staff writer for *The New Yorker* and the author of many well-received works of nonfiction, including *The Real Voice, A Sacred Trust, The Fear of Crime, Justice, Decision,* and *Freedom Spent.* His first novel, *Enemies,* was published in 1979 and is available in a Ballantine edition. He lives in New York, where he is presently writing a work of nonfiction and another novel.